# Advance Praise for *Our Sister*

"I read *Our Sister Who Will Not Die* in one sitting, as if diving into dark waters. After each story, I resurfaced with a gasp, certain only that I must dive again, reach deeper. A dazzling darkness beckons at the heart of these stories. The people Bernard writes into existence have unsettled me deeply. I care about them with an intensity that stuns me."

—Miroslav Penkov, author of *East of the West*

"All real lives are full of dark instincts, lost chances, moments in which everything hangs in the balance, or tips sideways. We're struck by chance, how one thing becomes another over a lifetime. *Our Sister Who Will Not Die* is all about these moments and connections: moments of grief but also loose threads that reconnect in a profound way. A truly great story collection."

—Scott Blackwood, author of *See How Small*

"This ambitious, daring story collection takes the reader to strange and unsettling places. Bernard explores, with great skill and unfailing compassion, subjects which many other writers would simply find too daunting to take on."

—Ian McGuire, author of *The Abstainer*

"If Mary Gaitskill's *Bad Behavior* and Ottessa Moshfegh's *Homesick for Another World* had a lovechild, it would be *Our Sister Who Will Not Die*. Wild and subversive in the very best ways, these stories had me by the throat."

—Nick White, author of *How to Survive a Summer*

# OUR SISTER WHO WILL NOT DIE

*THE JOURNAL* NON/FICTION PRIZE

# OUR SISTER
# WHO WILL NOT DIE

## STORIES

*Rebecca Bernard*

MAD CREEK BOOKS, AN IMPRINT OF
THE OHIO STATE UNIVERSITY PRESS
COLUMBUS

Published by Mad Creek Books, an imprint of The Ohio State University Press.

Library of Congress Cataloging-in-Publication Data
Names: Bernard, Rebecca, 1984– author.
Title: Our sister who will not die : stories / Rebecca Bernard.
Description: Columbus : Mad Creek Books, an imprint of The Ohio State
    University Press, [2022] | Summary: "Short fiction exploring the complexity
    behind brutal human behaviors such as murder, grieving, and addiction"—
    Provided by publisher.
Identifiers: LCCN 2022016646 | ISBN 9780814258408 (paperback) | ISBN
    0814258409 (paperback) | ISBN 9780814282250 (ebook) | ISBN 0814282253
    (ebook)
Subjects: LCSH: Short stories, American—21st century.
Classification: LCC PS3602.E75948 O97 2022 | DDC 813/.6—dc23/
    eng/20220415
LC record available at https://lccn.loc.gov/2022016646

Cover design by Alexa Love
Text design by Juliet Williams
Type set in Baskerville

*For my parents, Betty, Peter, and Susan*

# Contents

# In the Family

Three days before her son's funeral, Maxine hears a rumor from her next-door neighbor that two or three of the mothers from the neighborhood have decided they might not attend. These women, struck by grief, by pettiness and intrigue, by righteous anger, will not, cannot bring themselves to come, and she, his mother, must not put stock in them, their judgment. And this is fine, this she can handle, but not the destruction of her flowers. Because someone, some cruel person, has wrought havoc on her garden. The tulips in the front yard, the pansies in the flower boxes, the daffodils along the driveway, and the zinnias from the pots on the front porch—all have been uprooted, torn apart, petals scattered to kingdom come, and for what? Maxine Jackson is laid bare. She was already laid bare.

When her husband Frank died, three years earlier, the neighbors of Dew Meadows came in full force. They brought casseroles, condolences, ferns, offerings of neighborly concern and empathy. They pet her sleeve and rubbed her son Zachery's head. The men offered to repair the missing fence post that Frank had planned to fix before dying suddenly of a heart attack. The women, black bosomed and perfumed, complimented her tea cake at the wake, sent meals, and dropped off care packages of detergent and toilet paper.

And, granted, back then, Maxine was a different kind of woman. A widow. All veil and worth in the eyes of the so-called suburban holy, the pure of hedge and carport. The mothers whose sex was true and chaste. The ones who did not make mistakes, who did not trespass. Who had not felt the frailty of loss, of where it might bring you.

And yet, thinks Maxine, gripping her glass of wine, worrying the armrest of her chair—when a child dies, see how the blame must surface.

Alone now, except for Georgie, the family cat, Maxine sits in the green velvet chair by the living room's bay window and views her flowerless lawn, her flowerless porch. Breathing shallowly, she sips her glass of wine, concentrates on the armrest's wooden knobs. On the ground by her feet she notices one of Zachery's soccer cleats. She picks up the shoe and breathes in deeply, the smell of sweat, of teenage boy, of longing and loss, then tosses the shoe to the floor and wraps the thin, cotton robe tighter around her shoulders.

Zach will be buried in two days. No, not buried, cremated. Like Frank, he will be burned and released into the world. And the death, an accident—it was an accident—will live on in her, the mother. Five nights ago, the policeman rapped on the door. His eyes weren't downcast, they were direct. *The kids they go to the quarry. They drink, they drink too much. And sometimes, they don't make it home. I'm so sorry.* Maxine sucks in her breath and the gasp of her suffering is like a meal to be eaten now, tomorrow, forever. She presses the soft green velvet with her fingers. The only thing to do, keep breathing.

\*

Maxine and Frank had been the kind of in-love that even after seventeen years of dating and marriage, they could not seem to get enough of one another. It didn't matter what they did, they were happy-happy. Afternoons perusing sweaters at the Gap, evenings at Outback Steakhouse feeding each other bites of rare, over-priced sirloin, Saturday mornings at the community golf course holdings hands and Zach, their smiling child, riding along in the golf cart—a kind of easy, dumb bliss, too good to be true in its simplicity. When Frank mowed the lawn, trimmed the hedges, Maxine would come outside in cut-off shorts to offer him an iced tea, pass him the sweating glass, and watch him swallow the cool drink as moisture gathered between her narrow shoulder blades. Sometimes she wondered if her happiness was just too much to be believed, to be deserved.

But, of course, the death changed all that. It was a leveling device, something to make everyone even, even if it felt somewhat, or very, uneven at the time. So, Frank died and then it was just her and Zachery. Zach. Z. Her son, her baby, the only thing left, so it made sense they became closer. He was fourteen then, but still downy behind the ears, still sweet and meandering in his pubescence. He was a child, but not quite a child. He was a memory. A small glimpse of the love of her life who had left early, so early, but not Zach. He was still there. Still fresh. Still lithe. Still hers.

And so, in the wake of Frank's death, Maxine could recognize she had been something of a mess. It wasn't until after the first full month of mourning that she and Zach began venturing into public, and it had been her idea to make these necessary trips into a game. The Pity Party she called it. They'd dress all in black, drive the family's silver Subaru to the Kroger, and she'd pretend to be unmoored. Zach guiding her down the aisles, his hand on her lower back, stopping only occasionally to giggle at his mother's pretend stumblings, her quiet moaning, as they gathered bags of Sun Chips and organic chicken breasts, Hot Pockets for Zach and boxes of wine for Maxine. The strangeness of their display safely warded off the pushier neighbors with their endless condolences, the pity which at first felt honest, but later, Maxine thought, felt the tiniest bit smug.

The first weeks after Frank's death were something like that, a strange mix between loss and absurdity. How the dead person was like a crater, impossible to avoid, and yet she would somehow forget, find herself turning to speak to him, to ask Frank a question and realize once again he was dead. She was constantly between tears and hiccups of inappropriate laughter, and she and Zach both agreed that Frank would have thought they were acting crazy, but that he would have understood, and he would have loved them for it just the same.

It took about three weeks after the funeral for her and Zach to fall into a new post-Frank pattern. She'd pick him up from school, leaving her job at the plant nursery, and then he'd do his homework in the kitchen while she started on dinner. Though at the beginning, dinner was usually what they referred to as "guess the casserole."

"So, what do we think?" Maxine stood, staring inside the refrigerator at the neatly stacked Pyrex containers. The lids were all different colors, and Monica Allen, head of the neighborhood association, had told her that the moms had coordinated this to make returns that much easier, which turned out to be true.

From the kitchen table, Zachery raised his head from his geometry textbook and shrugged his shoulders. "Maybe one with not too much brown in it?"

Maxine nodded, then tapping her foot, bent farther into the fridge to select a green-lidded square. Opening the lid, she revealed a crust of browned cheese.

"What is it?" Zach called from the table.

Maxine gazed at the gelatinous square then over to her son. His hair was getting long on the sides, giving off the same overgrown look that had plagued Frank till the balding began. "You need a haircut."

"Yeah, but what kind is it?"

"Partially brown one. Maybe macaroni?" Maxine took a fork and poked beneath the crust. An ooze of tomato sauce broke through.

"I'm hungry. Whatever is fine, I guess."

Maxine nodded and turned on the oven, set the temperature to 350 degrees, and went over to the table where Zach sat, the table where they'd eaten countless meals together as a family over the last fourteen years.

She squeezed onto the bench beside Zach and leaned her weight against him. He pushed back slightly, so she pushed harder, making him lean to the side. Then she released all control and slumped against her son, knocking the pencil from his hands.

"Mom. You're so weird."

"Well, you're my kid. So, what does that make you?" Maxine sighed, her weight leaning against her son, and pictured Frank's face. He'd been a slight man. They were a slight family. Though Zachery was getting tall, would be taller than his father, it seemed likely.

She sat up, then pushed her shoulder into Zach again, stopping him from picking up his pencil. This time Zach pushed back against her with more force, so she started to tickle him, like she'd done when he was little, like she and Frank had done to Zach on any number of occasions. And she kept going, tickling his skinny middle, her hands moving fast, his elbows trying to knock her away, but she didn't stop, not until she saw he was crying, begging her to stop, his face red like a child's.

"Please, stop." She saw him then, his hands balled into fists and rubbing at his eyes, whether in tears or laughter it wasn't clear.

"Oh baby, I'm sorry." She put her hand on his forehead, and he let her. Then she pulled him into a hug, and he let her do this as well.

"Dad's just not here to protect me is all."

Maxine loosened her hold and pulled back slightly to see her son's face. His eyes were slightly red, but it looked like he was starting to smile. "Protect you?"

Zach nodded, "Or you." He reached for her, hands poised to tickle her sides, and she scooted off the bench, half laughing, half crying, until she got her footing on the cool kitchen tile, one hand bracing herself against the granite counter.

"Truce?"

Her son faced her. Standing now, his legs slightly apart in a wrestler's position. He looked older to her then, mature almost. He nodded, "Truce."

The oven beeped, and with an exaggerated motion, Maxine wiped her right hand across her forehead, whistled "phew." Donning oven mitts, she placed the casserole inside the oven and set a timer to check it in twenty minutes. She glanced back at her son who had resettled himself on the bench, found his pencil, and was back to work. His head was down, the shaggy hair on the sides sweeping across his face.

"I'm going to fold the laundry, honey. Let me know if I don't hear the beep?"

Zachery nodded without looking up, and Maxine let her stare linger a moment longer on his brown eyes downcast on the book, the lashes thick and full like her own, like Frank's had been. Through the window behind Zach, she could see the birdbath Frank had installed. A brown finch flitted about in the shallow water. She refocused her gaze on Zach's face, his high cheek-bones, the dark thickness of his eyebrows and then she looked away. Frightened, briefly, at the feeling of looking at Frank, but not Frank, Zach. Her baby boy, her husband's son.

\*

The doorbell rings and Maxine jolts upright in the armchair, nearly upsetting her glass of pinot grigio, her reverie broken with the familiar dong. She doesn't see a figure at first, but there's a red Jeep parked along the street, and she remembers that she'd told Norman Williams, the Unitarian minister, that he could stop by to go over the service for Zach. The doorbell rings a second time and Maxine gets up slowly to answer the door.

"Oh, Max—how you holding up?" The warm, creased face of the minister greets Maxine, and she finds herself drawn into his arms, feels the pressure of his fingers on her shoulder blades.

She pulls away gently and smiles, avoiding his eyes and their pooling sympathy. "Thanks for coming, Norm. I just haven't felt so much like leaving the house."

Norm nods and follows her as she walks toward the kitchen. "Can I get you something to drink?"

Norm shakes his head, "Nothing for me, thanks."

Maxine stops when she gets to the kitchen island and then gestures for Norm to sit at the table as she moves to pour herself a glass of water from the Brita.

"I wanted to make sure you were okay, Max. What with—" Norm raises his hand in the air then fans it out gesturing toward the front yard.

Maxine nods and leans against the counter, drinks the water, and feels the delicate muscles in her throat move as she swallows. "It is what it is."

"I didn't think anyone could be so indecent." Norm doesn't look at her, looks down at his brown loafers, as if he too were to blame.

She puts down the glass of water and pulls a green grape from the bowl where they sit clustered on the island and places it in her mouth. She gestures the bowl toward Norm, but he shakes his head.

"I mean, a child is dead, how could anyone think to do something like that. But you know what, it's probably just another kid, someone with a lot of feelings they don't know what to do with. Oh, Max. I'm sorry."

Maxine watches as Norm tenses his hands into almost fists. Her mouth is partially open, and for a moment she tries to see herself as he sees her. The thin robe, the slim ankles exposed, the bare feet. Her nipples just slightly erect in the cooler than average April morning.

"It's a handful of people if anything. They're scared of what they don't understand. They want something to blame. Most people have been fine. Kind. Normal, you know." Maxine sighs. "Should we talk about the service?"

"Right. I'm sorry, Max. I just thought, you know—we were better." Norm closes his eyes and shakes his head again. A display of righteousness, she thinks.

Norm isn't handsome like Frank, instead maybe bulbous, this might be the word she would use if it didn't seem so cruel, so petty. In this moment, sitting across from her, she can sense his discomfort. That he doesn't know what to do with himself, his hands, his feet, his concerns about their shared humanity. And then it strikes her, as if a slap to the face, how much he's like them, those mothers. That he wants her to dispel the rumors for him. He wants her to say out loud that none of it's true.

"Norm?" He raises his head and looks at her, looks her square in the eye. She opens her mouth slightly and then purses her lips and frowns. "Are you sure I can't get you something to drink?"

*

On the one-year anniversary of Frank's death, Maxine made a special dinner for herself and Zach. She didn't remind Zach of the date or the reason for the elaborate meal, but she figured he might guess, as they had grown close in the preceding months, had begun to develop something of a secret language, a way of communicating that didn't always involve words. With Frank's life insurance policy, Maxine was privileged to continue working only part-time for the local plant nursery, as she had done before his death, making use of her degree in horticulture. After soccer practice, Zach would walk the short three-quarter mile to the Grendel Nursery and meet his mother just as she was finishing her shift. Then they would drive home together, sometimes stopping for pizza or ice cream or groceries as need dictated.

On this particular Wednesday, Zach arrived slightly later than usual, and Maxine could sense something fidgety in his movements, the tossing of the backpack into the SUV or the way his hand glided back and forth over the radio presets looking for something to listen to.

"So?" Maxine waited to speak, waited until she and Zach were on the main thoroughfare that led past the strip malls and office parks of their community.

"So?" Zach echoed back, slightly higher-pitched, his fingers tapping an uncoordinated rhythm on the passenger side window trim.

"How was practice?" Maxine's eyes focused on the road but glanced intermittently at her son when it was safe to do so.

"Sucked mostly." Zach stopped drumming his fingers and leaned his seat back, his eyes closed.

Maxine said nothing, this being one of the few times she'd heard him speak this way, like someone else's teenage son. Like the ones you found on television, all reticence and snark.

"What's for dinner?" he asked, sitting up and putting his feet against the glovebox, something she'd ask him not to do before.

"Rotten bananas," said Maxine. She pulled into the left turn lane to enter the gates of Dew Meadows.

Zach was quiet beside her, but she could sense his desire to say something, to respond to her in kind, but she resisted looking at him and he stayed silent.

As they drove through the neighborhood, Maxine waved to two different couples walking their dogs. She made sure to keep her wave stiff and controlled, like a Miss America contestant. These were her tricks, her mood lighteners, same as the ones she'd used with Frank when he'd been grumpy or frustrated or depressed by ugliness at the firm. Now there was a silence between her and Zach, and in a way, it felt like a place she'd been before.

They arrived at the house and, wordlessly, she opened her door and headed for the porch. Zach trailed behind her, pulling his black Jansport by one strap and as she unlocked the door, he stood behind her quietly. She could sense that he wanted to speak, and as they walked in the house together, she glanced back and saw his mouth open, fumbling for words he didn't say.

"Do you want a snack? I won't have dinner ready for a couple hours."

Zach shook his head and started toward the stairs that led to the second story. She watched as he moved up the stairs, his shoulders slumped like the broken stalk of a crocus.

"Hey," Maxine called after him.

"Hey," he called back down to her. His eyes lingered on her

face, and she felt the sad, adolescent weight of his gaze. Then he turned and continued up the stairs.

In the kitchen, Maxine poured herself a healthy glass of wine and got started on dinner, the meal that had been Frank's favorite, chicken involtini with spinach and prosciutto. Pounding the chicken breast and listening to Bob Seger radio, Maxine could almost transport herself to another time, imagine herself in a parallel dimension where the permutations of death were rearranged, and Frank was still alive, about to walk through the door, a pink box from the bakery held gingerly in his hands, his lips about to press against her throat, his hands on the small of her back.

A second glass of wine and the frying pan out, sautéing the rolled bird, browning it on each side and then, as if by magic, Zach was in the kitchen with her, but his face was no longer stony, no, his eyes were slightly red, slightly puffy and his jaw was fixed and hard, trying not to cry, and so she hugged him tightly to her and he let her.

When she let go or he pulled away, he leaned against the counter and looked at her, and she felt almost embarrassed at his gaze, its sudden adultness. "So?" she asked again and then turned to swallow the end of her second glass.

"Can I have some?" He looked almost pleading to her, and for a moment she considered saying he could, but then she shook her head.

"We can't all the way fall apart." Then, "Here," and she opened the refrigerator and pulled out the orange juice and poured him a glass. "Same thing, basically."

He nodded and then rubbed at his eyes with his open palm. "Dad's favorite?"

Maxine nodded. "You can help with the potatoes or you can cut the ends off the green beans."

"Green beans, I guess."

He came and stood in front of the chopping block, so they were side by side. He was taller than her, but for how long had it been that way? The revelation felt strange to her in the small space of the kitchen.

"This is going to be delicious, I think. You think?" The room smelled like butter and white wine, rich and sweet.

"Jack and Andrew were talking about you before practice."

Maxine listened, didn't interrupt, used her tongs to poke at the chicken and then bent down to retrieve a glass dish for placing the rolled breasts in the oven.

"They said you—"

Maxine reached for the composting container and passed it to Zach. His eyes didn't meet hers. "Put the ends in here."

Zach nodded and she could see him biting his lip in her peripheral vision. "They said you were the reason Dad died."

Maxine nodded slowly. "How's that?"

Zach reached for his juice then put it back down. "It's stupid."

"I'll bet." Maxine refilled her empty glass from the box on the counter. "They just want a reaction is all. Anything they said isn't true."

"They were talking about the way you look. How you look good or whatever. How their moms were talking about it or something." He swallowed, staring down at his feet. "That you and dad *liked* each other too much, you know?" Zach's face was reddening slightly, perhaps, Maxine wondered, from the heat of the stove, the potatoes boiling now, the idea of his mother's sex.

Maxine reached out a hand and placed it on her son's head. She rubbed back and forth to feel the stubble of his fresh haircut, the tiny hairs swaying back and forth under her touch. Zach didn't resist, he let her pet him, and a moment later Maxine felt herself awake as if from a dream. Zach, beside her, had closed his eyes and was holding her hand, clasping it in his own, and she felt the strength of his fingers. They were just now longer, wider than her own, and they clenched her hand tightly, so tightly. It was the wine. Maxine shook her head to clear her thoughts, then pulled free of her son's grasp and placed the chicken into the oven.

"Dinner will be ready in twenty—why don't you get started on homework and I'll finish this, yeah?" Maxine bent down to retrieve the steamer from a lower cupboard.

Zach stared at her for a moment, then nodded and moved toward the kitchen entrance, its open vaulted doorway. "Sorry."

Maxine caught his eye, smiled. "I'm glad you told me." She forced her smile brighter as he left the room, listened to his socked feet as they moved up the hardwood of the staircase. When he was nearly to the top of the stairs, Maxine glanced toward the window where she could see her reflection in the glass. It was dark outside save for the streetlights; any starlight obliterated in the planned suburban sprawl. She moved her hands slowly from her neck to her hips, smoothing the fabric of her shirt, her slacks, feeling the shape of her figure. Making eye contact with her own reflection, Maxine bit her bottom lip until she felt it had grown red, redder, nearly lipsticked in its color, then, nodding to herself, Maxine turned back to the stove to finish Frank's dinner.

\*

Maxine and Norm agree to make the service a simple one. A chance for Zach's friends from school to say their goodbyes, nothing religious in nature, just a time for those in the community that choose to celebrate Zach's life to do so, openly and in public. Both Maxine's and Frank's parents passed away years before, and there's little extended family to speak of—the ceremony will be simple and true to Zach's nature—though as Norm points out— any funeral for a child is naturally more brutal, more confusing, and therefore, in many ways, impossible to get right. The point is to try your best.

Maxine has finally convinced Norm to accept a cup of coffee and now, somewhat regretting her insistence, they sit together in the front living room, she on her velvet chair and he on the sofa with its dainty clawed feet. She's put some stale Oreos on a plate between them and the minister slowly spins one of the cookies in his hand.

A silence has developed after Maxine asked about Norm's experience with funerals for children and Norm's subsequent slow, careful answer that, yes, he's presided over a handful in the twenty-three years of his ministry. Now, Maxine stares out the window, its view of the Turners' hedges and white pebbled driveway so familiar that the sight feels like a companion, an old friend.

"Maxine?"

"Yes?" Maxine turns to Norm, unsure of the time that has passed since he said her name into the still room.

"Had you thought about music? Maybe some of his friends would know a song or two to suggest?" Norm lifts his coffee cup to his lips and swallows.

"Yes, I'll find something. Maybe something from his iPod, I think."

"Good."

Maxine nods, tucks her bare left foot under her thigh.

"Max?"

Maxine looks at Norm and this time his eyes are downcast. "Yes?"

"I hate to ask this——" Norm hesitates, clears his throat. "Did you know he'd been drinking? Going to the quarry?"

"I did."

Norm cups his chin with his hand. "I'm so sorry, Max."

Maxine reaches for her coffee, then changes her mind and

leans back in the chair. "He told me he'd gone a couple times, that he liked to go there and think. Not that I didn't guess he was drinking. I mean—" Maxine stops speaking, digs the nails of her right hand as deep as she can into her palm. "I didn't think I could stop him."

"He was alone when it happened?" Norm glances at her, then looks away.

"As far as I know." She pauses, breathes in silently through her nose. "Two girls from another school found his car, after I mean. One of them was supposed to meet him for a date. I'd never met the girl." Maxine puts her hand over her face, can feel the awfulness of this feeling seething in her cheekbones, under the eye sockets. From underneath her fingers, she can sense Norm leaning forward in his chair and then a moment later she feels his hand on her back, moving gently back and forth like a metronome.

"I shouldn't have brought it up, Max. I'm so sorry for all you've had to go through."

It's okay, she thinks. We get what we deserve, she thinks. And then, aloud, "You just want to understand. We all do, I mean, we want to know."

\*

After the initial period of grief was when the real sense of loss set in, at least for Maxine, and she assumed, for Zach as well. A week, a month, three months, even six months after the death, to be grieving almost constantly was all right to most people. Most people who didn't lose their husbands or their fathers at such a young age could understand. Most people who had known real love and lost it—they could accept this version of another's suffering. But then eventually, the sadness had to end. At some point, come the one-year mark say, the grief needed to be hosed off, put away, except for on special occasions—Father's Day, anniversaries, birthdays—when it could be reignited in all its wet and messy feeling.

Still, a year, a year and a half after Frank was gone and Maxine still felt daily the absence of her best friend, her lover, her partner. Two or three failed first dates at the behest of other women in the neighborhood had only further cemented the idea that most people were not Frank, and that being still beautiful in her middle age made her desired, but rarely seen. She and Zach, unlike most of the other mothers with teenage sons in the neighborhood, had become increasingly close. They spent time together without complaint and enjoyed each other's company, liked one another as people, as family, as mutual beneficiaries of Frank's enduring love and memory, and though this closeness did not come without the occasional comment from the neighbors, for the most part, Maxine felt proud of their love.

For despite his relationship with her, Zach was also a normal-seeming kid, though not as much a kid now that he was just two months shy of sixteen. He helped her clean up around the house, and sometimes he made dinner, scrambled eggs or grilled cheese, his specialties. In the afternoons or on weekends, he skateboarded with his friends or played basketball and sometimes he brought friends over for dinner or hung out at the mall and went to see terrible movies. She had the sense that he liked girls, and that sometimes they liked him, too, though he was shier in this regard, at least with her. But what was most precious to her was how they were able to treat one another like humans, and sometimes, Maxine wondered if this was a gift, that if Frank had still been alive, Zach might have been darker, more selfish, more like the other boys who angered easily at their mothers' love. But not she and Zach, they had an intimacy that was rare, that Maxine lingered on sometimes, at night, when she was drifting into sleep, how lucky she was, despite the pain or because of it, that she had a child to love so much, a younger, newer version of the man that she had loved. A person to mend her heart.

Then on a Saturday night in early June, Maxine went on a particularly terrible date. The man was tall, relatively good-looking, a tax attorney and family friend of one of Zachery's friend's fathers. His name was Graham, and she felt like meat by his side. In response to his brutish stares and his unilateral command of the conversation over such topics as the problems with female CEOs and how she ought to invest Frank's pension, she'd gotten herself drunk, nearly stumbling drunk or definitely stumbling drunk, whichever kind meant that she was unable to drive herself home, and so let him do so at the cost of a rough grab at her left breast when they arrived at her house and his tongue, thick and chalky, jammed down her mouth like a fat, engorged bulb.

When she eventually managed to get herself out of his car, she staggered up her driveway and onto the front porch, got her key to work in the door and, finally, collapsed on the tile of the foyer, her purse open, its contents spilled and her head curled swan-like onto her lap. It was there that Zach found her, lifted her up, agreed to get her a glass of wine so she would stop crying, and helped her up the stairs to her bedroom, the bedroom she had shared with his father.

When Zach managed to get her settled at the foot of her king size bed, she sat swaying, gripping the glass of wine in one loose hand and using the other to hold his arm. It was then she could finally start to hear the question he'd been asking her, see the concern and confusion in his boy face as it peered down into her own.

"What happened?" he asked. His look so gentle, the nose and lips of another person, an earlier person blurred across the version of his face that she could make out in the spare light of her bedroom.

She shook her head, the words a series of scattered seeds stuck inside her throat. "Nothing happened." She reached back with one hand and managed to unzip her dress halfway, inching her shoulders free, the top of her black bra exposed. She closed her eyes, opened them a moment later and put her lips on the glass in her hand, left red lips on the rim of the glass and leaned back, spilling the wine onto her black dress, her bare clavicle. She closed her eyes then opened them, and he was in front of her again, so skinny but strong seeming in his shirtlessness. This strange version of her oldest friend in gym shorts.

His features swirled before her and she reached a hand toward him. "Stay with me. Okay, baby?" She thought about laughing but when she opened her mouth no sound came out, which seemed like something funny in its own right. And then he was beside her on the bed, hugging her and crying, and she said, "It's okay, baby. Really, I'm okay."

He was crying or his face was wet, and she kissed his cheek. He tasted like salt, then she kissed his mouth, like he was a baby, like he was her baby, and she felt her tongue against his teeth. And she was holding him down on the bed, and in her arms, she felt him go rigid, she felt him unwillingly excited against her, she felt him go limp, then the attempt to crumple up, to be so small, to disappear, to be a child once again and she let go.

"I love you, Frankie," she said and then darkness, her eyes closed, the room spinning and then nothing. Nothing. Then the morning, the bed empty. The house empty. Her dress sweet and crusted with dried wine. But no, it wasn't empty. He was still there, still breathing, asleep on the far side of the bed, and inside her gut, the most hideous bloom.

*

When Maxine finally says her goodbyes to Norman, he insists on giving her a hug and in his warm, forgiving embrace, Maxine briefly feels herself untether, slip away, lose all and any sense of why continuing to be a human being is worth anything at this point. But then he's gone, and she stands barefoot on the tile of the foyer, in her empty house, far too big for a creature as small as she. She continues to stand, feeling the cool tile, its coolness, the cool house, its windless silence until the mewing of the cat interrupts her thoughts, and the animal's hunger redirects Maxine with purpose to the kitchen.

More wine. As if it was ever the solution, but now, now it matters so little that filling her small-boned frame, drowning her organs in Chablis, in sauvignon blanc, is finally no one's problem but her own. But again, the box is almost empty, and this will mean a need to leave the house, to venture out into the world, to chance a meeting with the one or two or three mothers who have seized on her trespass, however unbelievable, intuited her as the worst kind of rot in their clean, wholesome community, and how, with what evidence?

The wanton lie, the accidental truth, the casual peeping tom who may or may not have seen mother and son in the backyard, she tanning in her orange bikini and the son, her son, his eyes unhealthily fixed on her body. Or maybe even it was Zach, a slip to a friend that sometimes, yes, sometimes, she let him sleep in her bed. That sometimes she fell down drunk and it was he who undressed her, he who brought the aspirin, who rubbed her swollen legs from where she'd stumbled. Together in bed, clothed but tender, tenderly together, anything not to be alone, to not have to forget the feeling of another's person's body, the smooth skin, the muscles moving like shoots sprouting toward light, involuntary. The mistake. Then the death. No, the accident. But she, the culprit, regardless, her guilt licking her insides clean as a chicken bone, clean as something that could never be clean again. Her baby, dead. Her baby gone, her sins, her selfishness, his undoing.

But this is her kitchen. This is the counter under her fingers. This is the liquid sloshing in her belly, her lack of belly. This is her cat, Georgie, who must be fed. Maxine goes to the pantry, takes out a tin of cat food and empties it neatly into the cat's food dish. To feed the cat, this had been Zach's first chore, his first responsibility in the days of she and Frank, in the days of parenting, in the days of keeping it together.

She has not been in Zach's room since the death, but Maxine decides she will go there now. Thinking of her words to Norm, she realizes she will not find his iPod, it was on his body when he died, but she will find something, some sound, some trace of the person he could have been.

Maxine takes the stairs slowly, lets each step feel like something solid beneath her weight. When she reaches the landing, she pauses, then says the name out loud to the empty house. "Zachery."

Without thinking, she knocks on his bedroom door before entering and when she enters the smell of him is so intense it nearly cripples her to the floor. Her mouth is dry. Her teeth, the deepest recesses of her gums, they ache, pulse with the blood of feeling. It is too much. Maxine slumps down to his bed and fingers the dark blue comforter, closes her eyes.

Two nights before his disappearance, his death, Zachery had come into her room, late at night, smelling of cheap beer, not turning on the light and wearing only boxer shorts. He had entered her room as he had sometimes done in the last year, in the time since her first attempt on his body, and he had sat on the edge of the bed, her bed, and put his hand on her face, waking her. "Maxine." He said her name, as he had sometimes done recently. The word in his mouth did not sound like Frank's voice. There was a bitterness, a sense of loss that made her weak, a falling out of the bottom of her stomach as if driving quickly over a hill.

"Are you drunk?" Her face remained on the pillow, her eyes partially closed.

"Maybe." He sighed, a deep chasmic sigh that Maxine felt herself falling into, a sigh where Frank lived at the bottom, as if in a well. A child lost and trapped.

Maxine stayed quiet, slowly she tried to rise, but Zach put his hand on her shoulder, held her down gently, but firmly.

"There's a girl I like."

Maxine nodded, pushed herself against his hand and this time he gave way. "Oh? What's her name?"

Zach shook his head. He put his hands over his face, over his eyes, and rested his elbows on his knees. Maxine waited, slowly reached out a hand to rest on his back.

"I don't know her name yet, but I saw her." His face was still in his hands and Maxine began to gently rub his back.

"Does she go to your school?"

Zach shook his head. Under her fingers, she could feel the heat coming off him, the feeling of dried sweat on his bare skin.

"She goes to Lincoln. I saw her when we played them. Her friend is going to set us up."

"Good." Maxine stopped moving her hand, started to pull it away from him, but Zach reached back and grabbed her fingers, pushed them down against the bare flesh of his shoulder blade. Maxine hesitated, felt the cool air conditioning under her thin nightgown, closed her eyes, then opened them. "You deserve someone good."

Outside the window of the bedroom, Maxine thought she could hear an owl, then nothing, then a car driving too fast down the street, past her house and then onto some other street, some other place.

"I won't tell her about us." Zach still held her fingers, pressed them down firmer now into his skin, pressed down the nails, so she wondered if she was hurting him.

"There isn't any us, baby." Maxine felt her body, its edges and lines, blurred somehow, like shame smoothing away the limits, nothing between her and her son but loss, a misplaced need. The softness of her mother heart beating in her chest. She was his mother, still.

"Do you wish I was him?" He dropped her hand and it fell back to her lap like a petal. "I could be him if that's what you want."

She looked at her fingers, how hollow they looked in the light-less room.

Zach looked at her, then away. "All my friends talk about fucking you."

Maxine pulled the comforter around her, sat farther up in bed and looked at her son, held the space between their bodies in her mind, like a rock, a jewel, then leaned forward to touch his hair, to let it fall through her open fingers. "I'm sorry, baby."

Zach was quiet. The room was quiet. Outside, if she strained hard enough, Maxine thought she could hear birds sleeping, readying up for their morning songs. It was a sound she had never thought about before.

"I'm tired, Mom."

"I know, baby."

"I miss him."

Maxine nodded, leaned forward and again touched her son's

face, his hair, its feeling just slightly greasy, and then his arm, the muscles in his slim arms and then, again, she made herself let go.

"Can I sleep here tonight?" He turned to look at her, his eyes, brown, glossy, red-veined like his father's had been when he was just done, so done with the day, with it all.

"I don't know, honey."

Zach stood up and walked to the far side of the bed, the side where Frank had slept and he pushed aside the sheet, the comforter and crawled beneath the layers, and in a moment, she knew she would turn to him, move toward, hold him, her baby, and he would hold her back, be unable to resist, neither of them safe from letting go, neither of them safe from what it is they'd felt, neither of them free from Frank's love.

In his bedroom now, in the light of day, Maxine comes to. Her own hands digging into the soft flesh of her upper arms, the nails indenting the skin in crescent moons. Outside, the sun brightening, the clouds dissolving, dissipating so they might no longer weaken the light's path through the open windows of her empty house.

She closes her eyes, feels her guilt like the thick loam of the earth mounting her, piling around her in a thick, confusing agony. She drops her hands down, her chest collapsing against her knees, and from the ground by her feet, takes a dirty shirt from the bedroom floor, the fabric soft in her fingers and presses it to her face, her baby, her boy, a smell like fruit so sweet, so ripe, its bruised flesh in her fingers, nothing she could have known she wanted, until. Bright sunlight against her closed eyelids like milky white light on a Sunday afternoon, its color the end of everything, but it reaches her here, deep below the earth, and she calls his name, both their names, sweet tendrils of sound, of longing, rising upwards in her otherwise empty home.

# First Date

On a first date, Jamie is learning what to say, and it isn't the truth; it isn't the story of redemption, his own, or the difficulty of childhood, he's fifty-eight, or the way that prison teaches a man something about living that nothing else does, no. On a first date, Jamie is supposed to be attentive, is supposed to let them see the gentle meat of his gray eyes and the lines in his face that they can trace with a finger, later, when they know him, later that night or in a few weeks or months, but just later, when they know that he's the kind of guy they could love, that they could trust, that would give anything, yeah, anything, for their affection.

And, of course, when they meet him, they should feel safe. They are safe, anyway, so it's just a matter of them knowing it. Them, the girls, no, the women. They should feel safe with Jamie, they have every reason to feel safe. And yet, the murder has a way of looming. The thing you did when you were an idiot kid that every day since you regret, but it's there, in the news, on the internet. In your heart. In the meteor of shame and guilt inside your belly. The act is there, is never not going to be there.

The homicide of his father is never meant to be first date conversation. Still, it's the kind of thing Jamie can't not say for too long because then the women feel baited when, eventually, they figure it out. How to be a person first though, without the blood ruining it all? It's the kind of thing that almost makes a guy want to give up, but then the drawer at home with only two forks in it, and the way the moon hits the wall by his bed where there isn't any kind of poster, and the carpet by the door where his brown work boots sit alone, and he will always feel worse in the end not at least trying. Because at least with Jamie, the mess is already out on the table. At least, with him, the scars are there, are right there waiting, no needing, to be known, to be dealt some love, just anything, just a chance.

Doreen is the latest woman to have responded to his messages on Match. She's fifty-two, divorced with two children, both in high school, both boys. She works as a paralegal and has dark, curly hair that, from the pictures in her profile, nicely frames the round cheeks of her face. They messaged back and forth for a few days and then she'd put a winking smiley which Jamie knows to interpret as an okay, let's try this in the real world. So, he asked, and she said, yeah, all right, let's meet for a coffee or maybe a wine.

This is in Maine. In the state where Jamie had been sentenced to life in prison with the possibility of parole after twenty-five years for the murder of his father, and where he'd been, somewhat miraculously, paroled after serving a total of forty-two years. It's the kind of thing that could also not have happened and he could have continued to be a person who lived his life in prison until the life was all used up, like one of those yogurts that you squeeze from the bottom that he hadn't known existed until two months after his release, back when he was staying with his elderly aunt who was kind, so kind to him, it hurts, even now, to think of what she's done for him.

But Doreen. Even the prospect of Doreen would not have been possible if it wasn't for Selma and Markus and Dwayne and all the good, kind folks who helped guys like him who got out and didn't even know what the internet was, except it was this all-powerful force that had swallowed up the world, when they, the guys like him, were being preserved in a vat of brine, just pickling in those walls, each day more obsolete and useless and shrunken, and then you get out, and thank god there's a place like the reentry center where they teach you how to be a person in the modern world, so you don't just end up on the street. But no. None of this is what he can say to Doreen. Not at first.

Doreen knows what, after all. He's fifty-eight, he has no kids, he has short graying hair, but he still has hair, which is another miraculous thing. He has a steady job doing maintenance work for the hospital, and he has most of his college degree. He likes fishing, taking long walks through the woods, seeing all the colors, there are so many colors, and his dog, Albert, the Rhodesian ridgeback, and, of course, that he likes to read poetry, which is true it's good stuff that gets in your bones and almost, maybe almost, can make you feel like there's a woman beside you, but no, maybe not tell Doreen that part.

In the small kitchen of his one-room apartment off Williams Avenue in Bar Harbor, Maine, Jamie prepares himself for the evening ahead. It's Friday night, so he got off work at 4:30 p.m., came home, took Albert for a walk, microwaved a frozen burrito, ate it standing up in the kitchen pouring tabasco on each bite. Then he showered for the second time that day, shaved his stubble, only cutting himself in one tiny spot because he was nervous, and then sat on his bed, staring at the clothes in his closet and jamming his tongue nervously against his bottom row of teeth before finally picking out a white undershirt, a pair of boxer shorts, a pair of dark blue jeans and a red and yellow flannel shirt that he had bought at Goodwill. Sitting on his bed, Jamie finds it hard not to recall the sensation of getting ready for a date in high school, but back then his nervousness was overwhelmed by a false cockiness, an innate knowledge that the girl, his high school girl-friend, Karen, wanted him so badly that whatever he wore was beside the point. Back then they were in love. Back then he was a normal guy. There was an innocence, back then, they could both believe in.

He and Doreen are meeting at the Bean, a coffee house that also serves wine and beer, so that if the night takes that course, they can take it. They're meeting at 7:30 p.m., and Jamie figures he will need to be there at 7:20 p.m. so that he's early, but not too early, but maybe politely early. He'd tried to read some articles online using the library's computer about how to handle a blind date, but most of the advice he found was for women and how to protect themselves against a potential creep, and Jamie couldn't help but wonder if he was the creep they were describing. A polite creep. A creep only in the sense of omission, but it isn't even a permanent omission. It is—it's something he has to wait to say.

Jamie has now been out of prison for one year, and six months into that year was when he first started trying to date. When he first got out it was all so blinding, that the basic normalcy of adulthood, each moment of it, was like some kind of unknown jewel fallen in his hands that needed to be held and admired and saved. He'd seen a prostitute, two different ones, in the first month, mostly to be sure that everything still worked, but the act had made his heart hurt, and, besides, risking his parole seemed like a terrible idea, and the girls, these were girls, didn't like him and he knew it. He was a chore to them. An old, sad guy with gray hair and a lined face and muscles where the skin over top was just beginning to sag.

But now in his kitchen, Jamie pours himself a glass of water from the tap and drinks it slowly, his left hand reaching down to rub Albert's forehead and ears. He hasn't yet told Doreen about his time served, which is intentional, only because the last few first dates he found himself blurting it out as if to warn them. But Jamie isn't violent, no, he isn't violent, even though, yes, he's done a violent thing. The blurting out, the redness in his face when he said something like, I have to tell you something, and they'd ask, what, and he'd say, well I spent a lot of my life in prison, and, for what, they'd say, and, for murder, he'd say, and, oh, they'd say, and then a pause and then, of who, they'd say, and, of my father, Jamie would say, and then there wasn't much left to do but pay for the coffee or the beer or the frozen yogurt and say his goodbyes.

So, with Doreen it will be different. He'll wait with this one. Because saying it on the first date, or in the online message before the date, or even saying it in his profile hasn't seemed to work, has only seemed to scare the women away and for good reason.

"Hi Doreen, I'm Jamie." These words, said aloud in the small kitchen feel small but feel right. When you spend decades without a space to talk aloud, the inside of your head becomes a well-groomed chamber, a place to place your thoughts, organize them, keep yourself sane. But it is just now seven which means it's time to go.

Jamie glances at himself in the mirror, combs his hand through his hair, gives Albert a Milk-Bone and leaves the apartment, locking the door behind him and placing the key carefully in his jean pocket.


Jamie arrives ten minutes early as planned, waits to order sitting nervously at the small two-top. He counts the sugars in the sugar caddy twice and then five minutes past 7:30, Doreen enters the coffee shop. He can tell it's her because of her hair and because she'd told him she'd wear a red shirt. Her face is prettier, softer than what he'd expected from the photos, and her lipstick is red like her blouse, with just the smallest dab of it on the corner of her slightly yellow left front tooth, a fact which Jamie only notices later in the evening when she smiles with full teeth for the first time.

He rises to meet her and extends a hand which she takes limply in her own.

"Hi, Doreen?"

She nods and motions toward the counter. "Should we order drinks?"

Jamie smiles and follows her to the register to place their order. Doreen orders a chai and so Jamie orders himself a cappuccino, something he's learned to do in previous moments like this one. When Doreen starts to open her purse, Jamie lightly puts his hand on her arm while simultaneously pulling out his own wallet, and she half smiles, but he can't help but feel her slight recoil beneath his touch.

When they're resettled at the table with their drinks, Jamie puts his hands together, careful to keep his elbows from touching the table. "So, you're a paralegal? Was that something you always wanted to do?"

Doreen shakes her head and half smiles. "To be honest, not really. It was more like something I fell into before I had kids, and then when I knew the Father and I weren't working out, something I could return to. Pretty romantic." She pauses to blow on her chai and Jamie nods.

He can feel his chest tensing. In his mind, he tries to ignore the sense that the silence between them could easily become permanent.

"What about you? You do maintenance work, right? How'd you get into that?" Doreen asks without meeting his eyes.

"I do—It was just something I got training for, so I guess I picked up the skills and all." Jamie can feel his feet inside his boots and concentrates on the feeling of his toe against the tiny hole in his sock. "Still, working with the law, that must be interesting stuff?"

"It can be."

Jamie can smell her perfume, a hint of lavender. He opens his mouth to comment on this, but decides against it as he watches Doreen press her fingers into the sides of her ceramic cup.

"I'm sorry, I'm low energy tonight." Doreen shakes her head and sighs and Jamie hears the sigh, can almost see it in the track-lit room.

"You're fine."

Doreen raises her eyes from the mug and looks at him and Jamie can see that her eyes, unexpectedly, are green.

"Long day?" He's still looking at the greenness, like small meadows.

"You could say that." She swallows another small sip of the drink and Jamie notices the red smudge of her lipstick on the rim.

"You can be honest."

Doreen raises her eyebrows just barely. "What's that?"

"It's okay." Jamie rubs his thumb against the back of his hand. "I know I'm not as tall as you would have liked." He glances back to see her reaction and her lips are just barely pursed.

Then, she's nodding. "Yeah, you might be a little shorter than I normally do."

"Yeah?"

"But it's rare you get a guy over seven feet in Maine."

Jamie nods, biting the insides of his cheeks slightly to stop himself from smiling and looks at her to see her looking at him. "So why the long day?"

"You don't want to hear about that."

"No?"

"It's not the best first date chitchat is all."

"Then what are we supposed to talk about?"

"Huh. Pets? Jobs? The basics."

Jamie feels himself relaxing, feels the blood moving around his body in gentler waves, tastes the bit of foam in his mouth just slightly souring. "I want to hear whatever you feel like telling me. Honest."

Doreen again raises her eyes to his. "You look a lot like your picture, you know?"

"Yeah?"

"Not all the guys do. But you do."

"Well, good I guess?"

"Yeah. Good."

Jamie takes another sip of his coffee and looks at Doreen again, this time more fully, lets himself really see the hair, its dark brown almost black color, likely dyed that way, and the way it floats in airy tufts around her face, and her breasts which are prominent but not showing any cleavage. "So, we talk pets now?"

Doreen laughs and Jamie hears the sound, small and sharp and jewel-like.

"My day in two words: teenage boys."

"Yeah?"

"My sons, fourteen and sixteen. The older one, of course— oh forget it. On the way here I told myself I wasn't going to talk about it." She shakes her head, raises her hand to her brow.

"It's okay."

"Yeah?"

"Yeah." Jamie nods. "But maybe you want something a little stiffer to drink?"

Again, Doreen laughs. "That'd be alright."

And Jamie is on a good date, maybe the best date he's been on since he started this process, or the first one where he's been funny and not just nervously waiting to talk. And the strange part is how normal it feels, how all of a sudden he's a guy who a woman might like to talk to, might even want to holds hands with, and not some asshole just waiting for the chance to feel a woman up, not a bad guy who did a bad thing and should never be offered the chance at love. And even as these thoughts start to percolate in his brain, he tries to quiet them and stop thinking and just be there, be honest, be plain, be himself, and more than that listen, listen to this woman who's in front of him and is, herself, kind and funny and human.

Doreen stays for two glasses of wine and they talk about her kids, her son who's rebelling (drugs, a DUI), and the younger one who's angry at her for the older one's rebellion, and the ex-husband who's more interested in his new girlfriend's kids than his own, and her parakeet, Stacey, and Jamie's Rhodesian ridge-back—what is the deal with the ridge anyway? And so, they talk for almost three hours, and it's easy, and Jamie doesn't lie to her, no, but also he doesn't mention his time in prison, but not by lying, just because it doesn't come up. And so they end the date, they part ways out front, and they hug, and she feels soft in his arms, but also strong, not limp, and he tells her that he'd like to see her again, and she says this is good because it's what she wants, too, and then Jamie is driving home and he gets home and he takes Albert for a walk around the neighborhood, and he lets the dog sniff anything and everything he wants to sniff for as long as he wants to sniff, because Jamie feels good, feels generous, feels like this is what it's like to be a free person, and it's nothing like the air in a cell thick with the breath and loss of a hundred desperate and waning men.

In the morning, Jamie is consumed by his routine. The guiding principle of his survival during the time of his incarceration was routine, living by a strict schedule, giving each hour over to a

precise activity or task. This same way of living is what's made
the transition to the outside world possible. On the weekends,
when he doesn't have to be at work, he rises at 6:00 a.m. and
does fifty push-ups and seventy-five crunches and twenty pull-
ups. He reads for thirty minutes before washing his face, brushing his teeth, and combing his hair. When he's finished cleaning
up, Jamie goes to the kitchen, feeds Albert, takes him outside for
a walk around the block and then back upstairs to make coffee
and oatmeal for his breakfast. He drinks his coffee black and eats
the oatmeal with a ripe banana or some frozen blueberries, a
luxury he didn't have while in prison. When he's finished eating,
he takes Albert for a three-mile walk, returns home to write letters for an hour (to his friends who have not been released), then
he goes grocery shopping and on any other errands that have
accumulated during the week. After lunch, his afternoon is taken
up by practicing guitar, a trip to the dog park with Albert, a visit
to his aunt where she lives now in the nursing home, and a trip to
the library to check his email. Jamie's saving up for a computer
but hasn't purchased one yet. In the evening, he eats dinner and
watches television, unless he's made plans to see a woman. To
this point, Jamie had not had the prospect of a second date, and
it's this nervous energy that makes this Saturday feel different
than the others.

At the grocery store, touching the avocados, or at the dog
park, watching as Albert plays tug with a standard poodle, he
can sense a feeling like hiccups in his bloodstream or, yes, maybe
butterflies, the prehistoric sense of a crush, something he has not
felt since his youth, and for clear reason. Jamie's not entirely sure
why this date feels so different from the others, though he's aware
of his omission and its role in their seeming connection. On past
dates, had he not made the women laugh, only to spoil it with
the slip of I-committed-a-violent-crime-when-I-was-sixteen-for-

which-I-spent-my-life-in-prison. It was a lot for any person to take in, and maybe it wasn't even a question of timing, maybe it was a kind of flag on the play that meant he was forever out of the running, at least to the average woman.

At 3:30 p.m., Jamie, as per his usual Saturday routine, takes the pound cake he'd purchased that morning at the grocery store and heads to the Future Dreams Retirement Facility to visit his aunt, his mother's younger sister, Gloria. Gloria, who'd taken him in after his release, who he lived with for five months before getting an apartment of his own, whose own health had since deteriorated, leading to her move to the retirement facility and her gifting of her car, a 2003 Buick LeSabre, to Jamie.

Knocking softly on her door, Jamie enters after hearing her scratchy *Come in.* He gives his aunt a warm hug and a kiss on the cheek. In preparation for Jamie's visit, Gloria has seated herself at the small table in her suite. Using her water boiler, she prepared a pot of tea for the two of them. Jamie's aunt is a smallish woman with a wreath of white hair and a slight hunch to her back. Her husband, a lobsterman, passed away nearly twenty years prior and the two had never had children. Gloria is the most kindly religious person Jamie has ever known, and a particular lover of animals, so that Albert's adoption had initially been at her suggestion, and the subsequent naming in honor of her late husband.

In the sizable suite, Gloria looks on Jamie with fond eyes, and Jamie smiles, settling himself at the little table and slicing the cake he purchased for the occasion.

"I got cinnamon this week, how's that?"

"Looks delicious. I'll take a big slice, honey."

Jamie nods and cuts into the buttery cake, placing a large slice on the small, porcelain tea plate and handing it to his aunt.

His aunt lifts the teapot to fill a cup for Jamie. He holds the delicate vessel in his large, calloused hands.

"You seem good today, honey. How you feeling?"

Jamie nods. "I'm good. Been a long week, but I can't complain. How about you? You seem good, too."

"I do, I feel good today. Not doing the stairs anymore is really helping I think."

"I'll bet." He sips his tea, lets the easy quiet build between them.

Jamie appreciates the fragility of the space he shares with his aunt and the sense of trust that this tiny, delicate woman gives him. It's a hard to describe feeling and he's never really tried to describe it, but there's something precious in the bones of her hand and the loving way she sees him, like they're just two people together in this room with its afghans and its china and its photos, framed and placed like windows all around the pale yellow walls. It's like Jamie can be with his whole family in this space, and they can look at him and he can look at them, and it's quiet, and not angry, and safe.

"I dreamed about Margaret again last night. She was telling me how much she loved you, sweetie." Gloria slides a large bite of cake into her mouth.

Jamie nods, closes his eyes, not meaning to but trying to picture Margaret, his mother, even still.

"I've been dreaming about her a lot lately, Jamie. I don't know, what do you think that's about?" Gloria looks toward him. Her eyes appear magnified through her glasses' lenses.

"You miss her? I'm not sure." Jamie takes a bite of cake, the flavor of cinnamon briefly tingling his nose.

"She was alone in the dream. I mean it was just the two of us and we were back on Mulberry Street where we grew up. Remember that house?"

Jamie nods, studying the teapot with its small painted flowers that are maybe lilies or, if not, lilacs.

"I don't know why I keep seeing her. We're not girls in the dream either. We're both grown up, but we're back at the house. Funny, huh?"

The flowers look hand-painted, and it's possible that they are hand-painted. They look so delicate to Jamie and almost realistic.

"You know she loved you."

Jamie nods.

"She forgave you. I know she forgives you, honey. She——."

Jamie takes his aunt's hand in his own and gently squeezes her fingers. His aunt's eyes rise to meet his and they smile at one another for what is maybe a long moment, and then he places his aunt's hand back on the table and he reaches for a sip of his tea.

"This cake really is delicious, honey, thank you for bringing it."

"I'm glad you like it. Maybe we do chocolate next week."

"I'd like that."

An hour or so later, after a few hands of rummy, and a walk around the gardens, Jamie says his goodbyes and makes his way out of the home and back to Albert and the rest of the evening. In the car, on the short drive to his apartment, Jamie decides that he'll call Doreen when he gets back and see if she would like to see him again the following weekend. He imagines their voices on the phone, and he can almost hear the lilt of her voice in his head, the potential that could come out of this for both of them and briefly, for a moment, Jamie lets himself feel confident that maybe this one could work.

The call to Doreen is successful if the slightest bit awkward, but she does seem happy to hear from him, and though he wonders if he's a bit too eager, they make plans for the following Friday. So then it's just a question of getting through the week and not getting too obsessive over what the date will be like and whether she'll look him up online in the time between (which he has heard is something that people do to one another) and whether he'll find a good way to say the unsayable, and whether waiting till the third date is just a recipe for this connection, like all the ones before it, not going anywhere, but for lack of honesty instead of honesty, full frontal and present.

When Friday finally arrives, even Albert seems aware that something is at stake and his fervent licking of Jamie's face upon his arrival home from work seems intent on expressing good wishes and an excess of love.

Jamie follows much the same routine as the previous Friday minus only the eating of the burrito, but still the walking of Albert, the showering, the shaving, the tiny cut and the selecting of clothes from his closet are parallel actions. Jamie's apartment is kept almost compulsively neat, largely from habit and the practice of living in a small, sometimes shared, space. In his kitchen, drinking his requisite glass of calming water, Jamie accidently lets himself think that this neatness will pay off should this woman, Doreen, care to enter his home at some point this evening or in the future.

Again, Jamie offers Albert a Milk-Bone prior to leaving his apartment and then makes the short drive to El Tractor Azul, the Mexican restaurant where he and Doreen have agreed to meet at 8:00 p.m. Jamie, arriving at 7:50 p.m., is escorted to the table, a booth, by the host and then waits for Doreen to arrive, drinking his water slowly and not yet eating any of the tortilla chips from the basket placed in front of him by the server.

At just past 8:00 p.m., Doreen arrives at the restaurant, and Jamie, on seeing her, feels his heart flail just the tiniest bit. He rises and they hug and then they're seated again, and Jamie feels a brief thump of panic in the moment before conversation begins, like what, again, if he has nothing to say except for his small piece of truth? But instead, the conversation flows smoothly.

"And so your week, how was it?"

"Good, you know, long. But thankfully, the boys are with their father tonight, so I get a little bit of a breather."

After the second margarita and during the guacamole stage, Jamie feels comfortable enough to tell Doreen that he likes the way she smells, her perfume, the lavender again.

"You smell good, you know that?"

"Do I know I smell good?"

"Yeah, I mean your perfume or whatever it is. You wore it last time, too. I remember it."

"Well, thank you. You smell good, too I bet, but I can't really smell you over all the food."

"That's not the food, that's me. I dab myself with avocado every day."

"You know I thought that, but then I didn't want to be rude if it wasn't the case."

When the food arrives, steak fajitas for Jamie and spinach enchiladas for Doreen, they're laughing, grinning almost. Jamie has even reached across the table to touch her hand and she's let him. She held his gaze and then laughed and said something about how he was wooing her and it was all too much, too much.

For his third drink, Jamie orders a beer and Doreen gets a glass of sangria, and they concentrate on eating for a bit. Then, shaking her head, Doreen looks at him and says, "It's a little strange dating at our age, isn't it?"

Jamie pauses, swallows the bite of refried beans and rice and starts nodding, "Yeah, I see that, I think."

"It's like we're playing or we're getting to play at being young again."

"Yeah. It is a certain feeling like that. Like adolescence

maybe." Jamie reaches for a chip and submerges it in the salsa before bringing it to his mouth.

"It's just, I mean I did love my ex, but I also feel like so much of my life got all swallowed up in that and when it was bad it was bad and then kids and all. If it didn't sound so cheesy, I'd want to say, where did my life go, ya know?" Doreen closes her eyes for a moment then reaches to take a long swallow of her sangria. "God, I'm sorry. It's the drinking."

Jamie shakes his head. "No, you're fine. I mean, I know the feeling."

"You never married, right? Why is that, can I ask?"

"I just, I don't think I was ever ready for it. I wasn't mature enough, I—." Jamie reaches for his beer, swallows some. "I, I got to tell you—."

"You ever sad you didn't have kids? You don't have kids, right?"

"No, and no, I don't know, again it's that—."

"Maturity? God. If only more people thought they needed to be more mature to have kids. Maybe if I'd been more mature I wouldn't be dealing with what I'm dealing with."

"I'm sorry."

"Aww, don't be sorry. I'm not sorry, that's just life, right?"

Jamie nods and again reaches forward to touch Doreen's hand, to feel her fingers between his own and she looks back at him, her lips closed but her eyes, bright and wet and focused on him alone. And later, Jamie will know that this is the moment she decides to sleep with him that night, or so he thinks about it later, when they're leaving the restaurant and she says, hey wait, maybe I can come over and meet your puppy, see that ridge and he says, okay that would be okay. Okay, she says and no, he meant that would be great, he says and what he doesn't say, he doesn't say, but not for lack of trying at least a little, and before he knows it she's following him back to his place and his heart is a big fat knot.

At his apartment, she comments on the neatness and the lack of decoration and he explains that he's recently moved, and she laughs and says, okay, as long as he's not secretly a serial killer, and he lets himself laugh at this one with her.

In his bedroom, after meeting Albert and giving her a beer and briefly stepping outside to let Albert do his business, they sit on his bed and he wonders, briefly, if maybe she's too drunk and this is a mistake, so he asks her.

"Are you sure about this?"

And Doreen laughs, that ruby sound, and she kisses him, and it's an incredible feeling to be kissed by someone who wants to kiss you and to feel those lips pushed up against your own, and all that that means right there, felt in that pressure, in that softness and heat.

Jamie undresses her, slowly, carefully, sees the white flesh of her belly and the stretch marks on her arms and sides, and it's all so different from when he was young, but still beautiful, more beautiful, maybe, because of what it means, now in his age, and place in life. They make love, twice, slowly, carefully, using protection, and then Doreen yawns and presses her face into the soft pillow and closes her eyes and asks him to hold her, please, just hold her until she falls asleep.

An hour later, Doreen is asleep in his bed, her naked body covered by his red comforter, but Jamie's still awake. Gently, he pulls his arm from around Doreen, doing his best not to disturb her. He pulls on a pair of boxers and walks to his kitchen to get a glass of water. Albert, who's been asleep by Jamie's side of the bed on the carpeted floor, gets up to follow Jamie to the kitchen. Jamie drinks his water and looks out the window to the right of his refrigerator. The streetlight obscures any stars and the view is not unlike the view from his window in the prison, the last room he lived in before his release, a private cell, luckily, and one with a view of the exterior, a tree, some barbwire and a lamp pole with a light that burned all night long.

When he finishes the glass of water, Jamie walks to the bathroom, but before he does, he looks into his bedroom to see Doreen there, vulnerable and pale in his bed with the moonlight gently embalming her visible skin, the arm tucked around her head and the toes, painted a deep purple and poking out from beneath the bottom of the comforter.

Jamie continues to the bathroom and quietly closing the door behind him, sits down on the toilet to pee, something he does sometimes now, in his late fifties, something he didn't do in his youth. The urine quietly hits the inside of the bowl and Jamie rests his head in his hands and closes his eyes and tries not to think about it but does anyway because it's the thing that is always there.

He had not planned to kill his father. It was not premeditated, which ultimately helped with getting parole, but the act was done with a shotgun, a burst of hatred and anger and violence that eclipsed all reason and led to two shots through his father's chest in the living room on a Sunday afternoon in late February. His mother wasn't home, but his younger brother was outside practicing his lay-up on the hoop outside their suburban home. Later, his younger brother said he heard the shots, later his younger brother said he had always known Jamie was broken, was evil, was not a good person at his core.

He and his father had never gotten along, not even when he was a child, but there was no clear external abuse, there was only the below-the-surface tension, the spite and distaste his father had for him from birth, the jealousy or envy or whatever it was that everyone in the family silently acknowledged but never spoke about, and then there was Jamie's own immaturity that wasn't a lie to Doreen when he said it, that was the truth. He was not mature, maybe not even now.

He'd been hunting with friends that day, had come home with the shotgun, had seen his little brother out front with the basketball and gone upstairs to clean the gun and put it away, and his father had been there, said something, nothing important but something cruel as usual, and Jamie didn't think, didn't even know he did it till it was done, but the bullets sprayed the chest, the face screamed and turned white, and the mouth hung open as the man fell to his knees then to the ground and then the blood, so red and perfect, came out in beautiful rivers on the white, Berber carpet. And the thing they don't say is that shame and fear and regret are instantaneous, are there even before the fugue state lifts and the sound of the gunshot hits your ears and Doreen, Doreen, this is what it was like, but tell me can you love me now, ever, tomorrow?

Jamie shakes the drops of urine from himself and stands up, flushing the toilet as quietly as he can. Outside the bathroom door, Albert whines quietly. Jamie washes his hands, opens the door and squats down to pet the animal and to feel the ridge along his beautiful, tawny red back. Then Jamie stands up again, straightens himself and enters his bedroom, where as gently as possible, he gets back into the bed, pulls the comforter over his body, and reaches out an arm to cradle the sleeping, innocent body beside him.

# Sweat

My dog, Gus, has started to sweat. I noticed it first on Tuesday when I was getting him ready for our after-dinner walk. Justine, my girlfriend, was mumbling something to herself and giving me a dirty look, which I could understand what with the fight we'd just had. But then I got distracted because I was standing over Gus, and I noticed he was wet. Like there was something on the back of his neck and around his shoulder blades. He's a Weimaraner, so it shows up real obvious on that gray fur. The floor under him was wet too, just the smallest puddle. Naturally, I was disgusted.

"Gus," I said, "Did you piss here?" And he wagged his nub at me, like hey buddy, I don't speak English.

"Get the fuck out," said Justine. Her head was down, and this was maybe what she was mumbling a moment before, but now I could hear it.

All the same, I bent down to smell the floor, which might have been disgusting, but I wanted to know if the dog was all right.

The puddle didn't smell like anything though, so I figured Gus must be drooling was all. Justine was crying by then, and I could hear her sniffling, which I think sometimes she does more as a performance than to stop the snot from coming out of her beautiful nose. Her nose is beautiful. I take careful note of that when we fight.

But all the crying was making me feel shitty, so I said, "I'll be back," and she said another curse at me, and then I was moving Gus to the door, and he was so excited, me putting on his collar and his leash, and to be honest, I was a little bit excited, too, just to be out of that house.

Me and Gus took our usual walk, following the sidewalk on our block till it ends and becomes grass, and picking it up again on the next block where there's sidewalk again. The sidewalk comes and goes in this town. It's not something I've ever understood.

As I was walking, I started thinking about Gus's wet fur and what might be causing it and like on cue he turned back to look at me, to check in. Then he squatted to piss on a bush, his leg raised like a dancer's, all delicateness and bone.

This got me thinking about Justine, and why I'd gotten so mad at her earlier, like if there was a reason to my getting pissed at her other than being three beers into the evening.

We'd been talking about work, and I was telling her about the oven and how it's been acting all uneven lately, and so I burned a pie, two pies, and that's not something that happens to me. And I was talking, and I looked at her face, and I just happened to catch her rolling her eyes, her little internal conversation with herself, and it just got me going. How you can be talking to a person who you love and they at that same time are thinking how you sound like a moron. So, I grabbed her wrist, just to feel the boniness of it, just to remind myself of how small she is. But still, somehow, it got going from there.

I have been trying not to do this where I let it get going, but sometimes it slips away and then we're at each other's throats.

But thinking about this made me feel shitty like before, so I tried not to think about it and instead I thought about what it is I know about dogs and sweating. And how, to my understanding of it, dogs don't sweat. They pant or they let it out through their ears. And so what did it mean for Gus and was he okay?

Sometimes, Gus will start howling when me and Justine fight, and the howl makes me remember there's an innocent there, and sometimes it works, and I stop whatever it is I'm doing. But then sometimes it doesn't, and I don't think about Gus, what it's like to be a dog, an animal that can't do anything about the things that happen around them, and I wonder is that what it's like to be Justine? But like I said, I just don't know.


Me and Gus took the long way which leads us past Georgie's house with the willow tree in her front yard. I always get a little mixed up by this house because we had a tree like this in the neighborhood where I grew up. It was down the street, and I used to go there to wait sometimes when stuff was getting out of hand at home. I always liked this kind of tree, how its branches were always moving with the wind, just going along with things. Just doing what it did.

"Hello, Matt."

It took me a second to understand who was talking to me, but when I looked up, there was our neighbor Georgie kneeling down in her lawn and watching me staring at the tree in her yard.

She had gardening gloves on, and she was squatting down kind of running her hands through the grass. She's an older lady, but she's put together. Her hair's gray, but you can tell it's dyed, just dyed a different shade of gray from what it would be if she didn't dye it. Or at least that's what Justine says.

"What're you doing?" I asked her, and she didn't look at me, she just kept running her hands through the grass.

"I'm looking for glass."

Gus pulled a little on his leash, so I pulled back. "Yeah?"

"I stepped on glass earlier, so I'm trying to find other pieces. Shelly's bringing the kids over tomorrow and I don't want them stepping on it."

I thought about how whoever broke a bottle or whatever probably didn't give a shit about somebody else stepping on the pieces.

"Animals," I said aloud. And Georgie looked at me confused, and then nodded I guess to be polite, but I don't know she was thinking what I was thinking.

I watched her for another moment as she ran her hands back and forth through that grass, it being so bright green, like the color of grass kids draw on those pictures of their houses with the mom and the dad standing in front of them, and then I nodded again to her and said goodnight and kept walking. I would have stayed longer, just to see the way the willow branches touched her back when the wind blew, but I didn't want her to think I was a creep or slow or something. Besides, Gus, he was ready to move along. There was a whole lot of things for him to smell, and the sun, it was setting and fast.

\*

On the walk back I was trying to think of something I could say that would make Justine less angry and less hurt feeling, but there wasn't much I could think of beyond I was sorry and that I loved her, now more than ever.

Back in the house, I let Gus off his leash and out of his collar. Then I poured myself a glass of tap water in the kitchen, and even though it was lukewarm, I drank the whole thing down. I guess I was a little bit nervous to see Justine.

I found her in the bathtub, only, all I could see was her lips and her pretty nose and the top of her forehead where the widow's peak begins.

I sat on the toilet with the lid closed. "Justine?" I said.

"I thought you were serious about working on this shit."

I was serious, I thought, but I knew she didn't want to hear that, so I kept quiet.

"You make me look like a real asshole, you know that, Matt?"

It was strange hearing the words come out of her, because they were sharp, they were angry, and yet her face was so calm all tucked into that mass of bubbles.

"I know. I'm sorry." It was true when I said it. And true most of the time. I was sorry. "You know I'm the asshole." I rubbed my hands against a spot on my jeans. "You look beautiful, J."

I could almost see the wave of frustration cross her face and then it ended into the water. "I don't know," she said, and it was almost more like she was talking to herself than to me.

I didn't say anything back to that because it wasn't for me. Then she opened her eyes, they'd been closed, and she said, "Your sister called."

"Yeah?"

"Yeah. She called me because she said you hadn't been answering your cell. I told her you were out." Justine glanced at me, then closed her eyes again and settled back into the water. I wondered if the water was still warm, but I didn't want to touch it and mess up the bubbles. "You should call her back," Justine added, and then she was gone again into the bit of peace she had created in the tub.

"Okay," I said. I felt like a kid then, sitting on the toilet and talking to her. Like Justine was a mother or my mother or something.

"Is Gus okay?" she asked, and then she rose up a little and looked at me, and I swear there is nothing like her face. That nose and the eyebrows, plucked so thin, and her fat lips which she always tries to keep closed to cover these big chiclet front teeth of hers, and I'm in love.

"I think he's okay."

"Okay."

Then I left the room and I stripped to my boxer shorts and turned on the TV in the bedroom, and I was in bed, relaxing and watching *Bones*, and I thought about calling Amy, my sister, but I didn't. Gus came around to my side of the bed where he likes to sleep and dropped to the ground on the carpet there, and it was good. It was good. It was all good.

\*

The next day we didn't fight at all which was not uncommon after things got ugly. Justine works at the bank as an assistant manager, and after our lunch rush I brought her a pie I made, half-pepperoni, half-mushroom, her favorite.

She smiled at me, but I could tell it was still on her mind, the things that had happened the night before, and I could see the makeup, the powder on her wrist to cover the bruise was almost half brushed away, and I felt shame then, which was definitely what I deserved.

She asked me if I'd called Amy and I said, no, because I hadn't and not because I was ignoring her, I just didn't want to hear what she had to say.

Justine said this was the definition of ignoring, and I let that one go on account of the fact that she was right and that she looked extra delicate behind the bulletproof glass, even though it should really show how safe she was—how protected.

I went back to work. I'm the day manager, so I spent the rest of the afternoon prepping dough and cleaning up around the ovens. Those ovens need a good cleaning every so often, but they don't always get it and it's a shame.

When I got off, I decided to stop by the Giant and get a few things, some flowers for one, and then some salmon fillets because it's Justine's favorite kind of fish. She likes seafood a lot, so I thought this could be a nice thing that I did for her. I couldn't remember which was her favorite flowers, so I got yellow roses, because they smelled nice and I figured you can't go wrong with roses.

At home, Gus was waiting for me by the front door and he leapt up and put his paws on my stomach and he kissed my face all over. His fur was dry, so I figured the other night must have been a fluke, and I let him out into the backyard, which is tiny but also, we keep it neat. I threw a ball for Gus and he chased it, and then I went to put the flowers in a vase only I don't know where Justine keeps them, so I used a glass jar which I thought looked pretty good.

When J got home just after six, I was waiting in the living room, showered and clean and playing with Gus who was rolling on his back, hungry for pets. She pulled into the driveway, and I waited for her to get out of her car, but she didn't right away. I got up and pushed the curtain back to see her, and there she was just sitting in the car with both hands on the steering wheel and her mouth open so you could see her teeth and they looked bigger and whiter than ever. She stayed that way for a long moment, and I couldn't help but feel that I was the reason she didn't want to be home, and I have to say it made me feel sick. It took a lot of what I had not to get angry, and to go outside and confront her, but I didn't go outside I stayed put.

Because I was going to be different. This was what she meant the other night about being different, because I was learning to not take the stuff that hurt me and react, but to take the stuff that hurt me and think about it like it was marbles. I could learn to say: Matt, this fact of Justine sitting in the car is because she is feeling things and it is not because you are a worthless prick and so do not force the situation. You just need to let the marble be. Let it roll toward you or away from you and forcing things is not always the best way to go.

This was the mantra that we had been practicing. The last time J threatened to leave, the only way I could convince her not to go was to agree to watch this YouTube doctor she'd found, and so came the mantra and so came the better Matt. A more and perfect Matt. A Matt who collects marbles and does not hurt the ones that he loves, and like Justine said, "If you can believe this Matt exists, so will I."

So I sat patiently on the couch and distracted myself with Gus who was rolling around and wiggling his hips and letting his tongue loll out of his mouth like a Fruit Roll-Up. I pet his belly, and I could almost forget that J was outside, and then before I knew it, she was inside, and I was jumping to my feet and feeling nervous like she was what I've been waiting for my whole life. Which she is.

Gus made no fuss about showing his love and he was all over Justine, and so I waited my turn and when I did, I gave her the gentlest kiss I was capable of. She kissed me back but there was that hesitation, and I told myself well at least it was not a recoil. At least she didn't give me the cheek.

"I bought some salmon fillets, you want me to grill them for dinner?"

"Yeah. That'd be okay." Justine looked tired then and like all she wanted to do was sleep or get away from me, and I held the feelings I was feeling inside and did not let them out.

"You want me to bring you a glass of wine? Relax?" My face felt earnest in a way that I was not sure I would have recognized myself, if not for the fact that I had been doing this a lot lately. What with how hard it was to change and to be a good man and not just some of the time but all of the time.

"Yeah, that sounds good." Justine dropped her purse and moved to the bathroom and I leaned back slightly to give her room to pass.

I went to the kitchen and poured a glass of white from the box in the fridge, and then I waited for her to get out of the bathroom. I heard the sink water going and then the flush of the toilet and I was waiting in the kitchen, my hands concentrating on how thin the wine stem was and how I didn't want to break it on accident if that was possible.

When she got back to the living room, I gave her the glass and then she dropped to the couch like she was beat.

"You beat?" I asked, but her eyes were closed so I let a pause develop in which I could only guess that yes, she was tired. The room was quiet, and I tried to be quiet too, but I could hear myself breathing it felt like, and then Justine spoke.

"Jesus, Matt."

"Yeah?"

She sat up and took a swallow of the wine then put it down and sank back into the couch. Our couch is brown and soft and has white pillows on it that Justine says are tacky even though it was her mom who crocheted them for us last Christmas.

"It's like I see you getting better and thinking more before you do stuff and then last night happens and fuck." She looked at me, right at me, and then she shook her head and held the glass in both hands and swallowed. "I mean, I'm an idiot."

She was making fingerprints on the wine glass. I could see the smudges as the light hit through the rim.

"I mean, how long is this shit going to happen, Matt? I don't even know what I'm doing with you half the time." She put the glass down and pushed her fingers against her eyebrows and her fingers traced the skinny lines.

"Nine years. We've been doing this nine years and I must be crazy at this point. I must be fucking crazy to still be here." She closed her eyes and leaned back. "Bertie was asking about us at work and I just felt so embarrassed because I knew she knew what was up, and I had to say it was nothing. And I'm asking myself— who am I protecting here? What the hell am I doing, again?"

Justine took another drink and shook her head and then I saw her shrink, like she became smaller in front of me, and I wondered if it was out of fear, but I kept not saying anything. I didn't know what to say that was any good, and I didn't want to say the wrong thing and listening was good I knew this, and she was a marble and I was letting it be. I was letting her words be the ones that were heard.

"Goddamn you, Matt. Sometimes that's all I want to say. You break my goddamn heart."

I noticed then my hand was wet and there was wetness on Gus's head and behind the ears where I had been petting him. I pulled my hand away and there were little drops of water falling away.

Justine was looking at me looking at my hand, and I wanted to say something, but I couldn't get the words out.

"And please, Matt, call your sister." Justine picked up the glass and downed the last of her wine, and I could almost see a dullness start to enter her brown eyes. A protective film or something that separated her from me.

I nodded, but I was thinking about Gus, and I leaned forward to look at his face to see if he was looking different but there was just regular dogness there. I pet him again and he was even wetter than before. Then he whined, and I looked at Justine who was looking straight ahead toward the TV, which was off, but that's where she was looking.

"Gus is wet again." I knew the words I was saying weren't what she wanted to hear, but Gus was wet, and I didn't know why. I raised my hand up to show the wetness, like it was proof or something, but she wasn't looking at me she was looking at Gus.

"Come here, boy," she said, and Gus got up, real obedient-like, and went toward her and she started to pet him, and I could see her hands getting slick and wet. "What is this?"

She raised her hand to her nose and sniffed once, delicately with her delicate nose and then shrugged and wiped her hands on her slacks. "It's like he's sweating or something?"

I got up and I sat next to Justine on the couch and put my arms around her and she let me, and I thought about the frailty of this, of her, of us, and of Gus and whatever was his problem, I don't know.

"I love you, Justine." I didn't mean it to sound like a script, but I knew it did and this was when the words I had weren't any good, and I knew it when I heard them, but still I knew saying nothing was worse. "I promise you, J. I'm sorry. I'm going to be different and I know you have no reason to trust me, but I love you."

Justine let me hold her and Gus was pressing against my legs and I could feel it, the heat from both of their bodies and it was special and I knew it. So I didn't let go. I didn't let go until I had to.

Eventually I cooked the salmon for us and Justine looked up "wet dog" on the internet. We ate dinner and didn't much know what was going on with Gus, so we decided to wait and see if it kept happening or if it was just a two-time thing. I went out back after dinner to call Amy because I knew it was something I couldn't keep putting off.

I stood in the backyard near the grill, and the air was cool, it being late September.

"About time, Matt."

Amy's voice was high, and she was pissed, and I got it because it had been two weeks she'd been trying to talk to me and I kept not calling her and I knew, she knew, my reasons weren't good.

"I'm sorry. I've been real busy at work and you know."

"Right." She breathed in and out loudly, and I could tell she was practicing keeping her cool with me. I was her little brother and she had been practicing this for years, thirty years at least.

"You free for lunch tomorrow—Justine told me you're off, and I'm going to be down by you guys tomorrow." Her voice was bright now, like she was trying to be both friendly and casual. "There's some stuff I need to talk through."

I listened to how the wind was hitting the trees and how my own breath sounded, calm, slow. "Yeah, I don't know. I had some errands I was going to do—"

"How's noonish? At that sandwich place you like?"

In the kitchen, Justine was washing dishes and Gus had his front paws pressed against the window wanting to be let outside. I opened the door and he ran outside and did a quick lap around our little backyard.

"You know I'm working through this shit and there's stuff that you and me need to go over."

I paused for as long as I could before it got to be awkward, and then bending down to grab a ball for Gus, I said, "Yeah, okay. I'll see you there."

We hung up a minute later and Gus was running all around and leaping and it's beautiful the way his body can lunge in the air almost like he's a gymnast or a dolphin or something.

I knew why Amy wanted to talk, and I knew I didn't want to do it, but this was one of those things that Justine would say was me working on myself and my issues, so I knew there was no way out. It was a thing I had to do if I wanted to keep what's good around me and maybe become a more decent guy.

I called Gus inside with me, and I came up behind Justine and I held her, and even though she was laughing and saying, "Hey, I'm busy here," and the soap was all over her hands and the water was running, I didn't let go, and I could feel her, just the smallest bit melt into me, and I knew again she was the best thing I had in my life, would ever have.

*

The thing I knew was that Amy wanted to talk about Dad. Our dad, Mitch, who died last year before Amy got to confront him about all of the stuff that happened when we were kids. The stuff that happened before Miranda, our mother, moved us away and divorced the guy and he stopped, in most ways that mattered, being our dad.

This process of Amy's healing, what she called it, had been going on for at least five years, and so sometimes she said she needed me so she could verify stuff, or that's what her shrink or whoever it was she talked to said she needed to do. She thinks

I'm a witness, too, so I got to talk about this stuff, and I don't think it does much good, but Amy thinks that's why I'm the way I am with Justine, and Justine agrees. Justine said we couldn't think about having our own kids unless she knew the "cycle" was broken, and I said, okay, who said I want kids anyhow, but okay. I hear you. Amy said I'm not near as bad as Dad, but still, sometimes it makes her want to kill me to think about how I get with Justine, that I could ever be anything like him, and I guess, in the end, I can't blame her.

I was ten minutes late, and Amy was there sitting at a little two-person table drinking water from a little plastic cup. She stood up when she saw me, and we hugged.

We look the same pretty much, the same brown hair and we're both on the shorter side with smaller builds. But I have a mustache now and she doesn't, not that I could see. She was more dressed up than me too, which made sense because she's the lawyer, she's the successful one in the family.

"You look good," she said, and I nodded the same to her and we ordered sandwiches and then sat down to wait for them.

I got a Coke and I sipped this slowly as she started to tell me about what she was working through. I put my elbows on the table, and I leaned forward to sip through my straw. She looked like she was taking care of herself, but she looked tired just the same.

"I've been thinking about Mom a lot, you know. Like I hadn't really thought about her other than she was the one that saved us from him and all." Amy sipped her water and glanced toward the counter. "But I don't know. I've been thinking about her more lately and how long it took her to do anything, you know?"

"She did her best." The Coke was sweet on my tongue. Justine and I don't drink soda at the house, so this was kind of a luxury.

"Yeah, I know that's what we always say. But like, I've been feeling angry lately. I don't know. You never get angry at her?"

"I don't know. I don't think about it so much."

Our sandwiches arrived, mine a meatball and Amy's a turkey and swiss. I picked up my sandwich and took a big bite, so my mouth was filled with bread and cheese and sauce and meat. I looked at Amy like I was sorry I didn't know what to say.

"Well, I think it's okay for me to be mad. For us to be mad. My therapist—she was saying it's normal to have this reaction and for it to come latently. You know? Like first I had to work through my anger with him and all."

The sandwich tasted so good that I took another large bite and again my face, my cheeks were just stuffed with the deliciousness of the sub.

"I mean, it took her twelve years to leave him—you were still a kid at least, but I wasn't then. Why'd it take her so long?" Amy raised her sandwich to her lips, then put it down. She took another swallow of water. Then she looked at me, a long cool look, and I felt my stomach kind of turn.

"Justine and I talked the other day when you weren't picking up. She says you're still having trouble with your anger."

I nodded and swallowed the bite in my mouth. There was only half my sandwich left and I wondered if it was like an hourglass telling me how much longer this was going to go on. "I'm trying. I mean, we're working on it."

"She says it's like you're a different guy sometimes—she almost can't recognize you."

I stuffed more bread into my mouth. "I mean, I get loose is all. I don't know what happens. It's like—" I put my hand up to cover my mouth, thinking of the way it must look to her, my mouth all full and everything. "I just get going and I'm not me. It's like I take all the shitty stuff I feel about myself out on her. I don't know. I push her a little." I swallowed. "You think I don't disgust myself? I do."

Amy nodded and picked up her sandwich and took a bite and we chewed quietly, both of us, for a minute. Then Amy swallowed real dramatically and shook her head like she was remembering something ugly, something not good.

"Do you hit her, Matt? She wouldn't tell me—she just said rough—like she knew you loved her, but you were rough with her." Amy's eyes were big now, widening and wet around the edges.

I took a long pull on my Coke, and then I shook my head. "No. I haven't. I don't. I don't do that." The cheese was congealing on my bread, hardening into the sauce which dripped red onto the paper plate and my fingers.

"You make me worry, Matty." Then Amy was reaching out her hand and rubbing my shoulder back and forth and it reminded me of being a kid, just briefly, just the feeling of her having to be there for me because sometimes she was the only one.

I closed my eyes and tried to picture the worst thing I'd ever done to Justine, and it was like in my mind I could feel my arms like his arms and my face all shiny and red like his used to get. Something about Justine's lying to Amy was rigid in my gut. And I thought, of course, she protected him as long as she could, and I didn't even know the she I meant if it was Amy or Justine or my mother.

"I know I need to be better."

Amy's hand was still rubbing my shoulder, but then she dropped it to the table, and it rested there like a fallen bird or something. "If not for her, Matt, then for you."

I nodded, and I felt myself almost choked up or something, and I tried to smile but I couldn't help it, I started to feel angry that she'd made us talk about this crap. And I felt angry that I was picturing him in my head because I hate that asshole, and I hate even more seeing his face in my mind when he's dead, and he shouldn't be anywhere but in a coffin or scattered somewhere like dirt.

But Amy must not have known what I was feeling because her face looked brighter now, and she was munching on her sandwich now, and so I pushed away all the feelings I was feeling because if she was okay, I was okay.

"Hey, Amy," I said, "Did J tell you about Gus and the sweats?"

*

The next couple weeks were easy, slow. Me and Justine were getting along good, and it reminded me that most of the time we did get along just fine, and most of the time there were no worries at all between us. I mean, there's a reason we've been together so many years, and it isn't settling, it's love, it's simpatico—that's what we are. Simpatico.

I took her on a date to this sushi place she liked, and we went dancing at this cheesy country western bar where we both didn't fit in which made it funny. She cooked my favorite meal, chicken cacciatore, and we watched television together and it was all right. Gus seemed fine, too, but I took him to the vet anyway because I figured with a dog as sweet as him, I didn't want to risk losing him. The vet said what I described didn't sound like anything he knew, and that Gus was just probably getting into something—the toilet—and so we shouldn't be worried. He said if it happened again take him in right then and there because otherwise it was maybe impossible to diagnose.

Even me and Amy were talking more regularly, and I told her, that yeah, okay, I might be willing to see someone professional if that was going to make a difference for me and Justine, and she promised me that it would, and I said, well then of course I'd try it out.

Then, it was Wednesday, three weeks after Gus first started what we'd decided to call "the sweats," and somehow things got going all wrong. I think what it was was that I had a shitty day at work. I'd been the day manager at Nino's for a little over a year and sometimes I'd work at night when they needed me to. It was an okay job, and like I said I was good at it which counted for something, I hoped. But the owner decided he wanted to switch me to nights full time, and I tried to tell him that I couldn't, that I had a routine and me and Justine had a routine, but he didn't care and so that was it.

On the way home, I stopped at Rick's Pub which I knew was not the right thing to do, but I felt out of control, and I figured one or two drinks wouldn't hurt me and might make me calm down. And it's not like I hadn't been drinking the past few weeks with Justine, so it wasn't like liquor alone was a problem. I had two bourbons neat and a pint, and then I headed home because I didn't want to stick around and get sloshed.

At the house, the front door stuck, and I couldn't get the key to work, so I ended up climbing the fence and going in the backdoor. Gus greeted me, and I started to feel better what with all of his unconditional love. The refrigerator was empty or almost empty, which was as much my fault as Justine's, but at that moment made me feel ticked. I turned on the TV in the living room, and I slumped down, and Gus came over and I pet his furry head. I watched a rerun of *Wheel of Fortune*, but I couldn't guess any of the puzzles. Just one of those days.

When Justine got home thirty minutes later, I could tell she was in a shitty mood too, and we didn't say much to each other. I listened as she went around throwing down her purse and taking off her shoes, going into the bedroom to change, and then I heard her opening the fridge, then the cabinets and having the same epiphany as me. She went and poured herself a wine, and I called to her, asking her to bring me a beer which she did.

She thrust the beer into my hands and a few drops landed on my knuckles.

"Hey," I said.

"Hey yourself."

Justine went and sat on our knockoff LAZ-boy, and I felt her looking at me, but I ignored her because I didn't want to get upset. I looked at Vanna White's smile instead, and I concentrated on those rows of teeth all even and straight and whitened.

"Matt."

I didn't look over at first. I kept my eyes on the TV.

"Matt. Weren't you supposed to go to the store? What're we doing for dinner? There's spaghetti, but we're out of sauce." Justine was wearing sweats and she had an emery board and she was half looking at me, half looking at her dainty nails.

"I didn't know you wanted me to go to the store. What is it you want to eat?" I kept my eyes focused on the letters, the big letters lighting up and swiveling. I tightened my mouth into a smile. "Why don't we order something delivery."

Justine sighed. One of these theatrical sighs she thought made her sound like an important lady. Like a bigshot. "I thought we were trying to be on a budget, Matty."

At this I shrugged because yes, we were supposed to be on a budget. But also, yes, life comes at you in different ways.

"You never stick to anything." Justine shook her head and stretched out her fingers, dainty, so dainty.

"What?" I said. There was a commercial on and the volume got louder. Some celebrity was talking about rental cars.

"I said, it's typical is all."

"Huh?"

Justine dropped the emery board. "Can you mute that shit?"

I decided to ignore this request, and instead I swallowed the rest of my beer in one long chug.

"So you're going to get drunk, too?" Justine picked up her wine, then put it down. "You can't follow through on shit."

Gus whined, one shrill sound, and then he got up and went over to Justine.

"Did you feed him?" Justine asked me.

But I didn't want to answer her. So, I didn't.

"Typical," Justine said, and she got up and Gus followed her, and I heard the sound of his water bowl being refilled and the scoop of dog food scattering and pinging against the metal food bowl.

I took this moment being alone in the living room to think about the marbles, to practice my mantra. I thought, we are both not at our best. I thought, this does not have to be something. I thought, this can be just a regular thing. A fight, but a regular fight. Then, I thought about the way marbles looked, all blue or green or red and clouded so you couldn't see their insides. They were mysterious.

I decided when Justine got back in the room, I was going to tell her about what happened at work and why I didn't feel so good.

Then she was back in the room, but she was crying, and so I was confused. "What's going on?" I said, and I stood up and I faced her.

She shook her head and then she used the back of her hand to wipe at her eyes and her nose. "I just," then she stopped.

I felt nervous, so I moved toward her, and I reached out to touch her, but she pulled away.

"I just don't trust you anymore." She sniffled then and her little nose twitched. "I mean, I just think—I can't even get mad at you because what might happen? That's bullshit."

"You can get mad at me." My heart was stepping now, like I could feel it marching in my chest or something.

"No. I can't."

"Yes. Get mad at me. It's okay, I promise." I reached toward her again, and she moved away, so I crossed my arms like it was what I meant to do all along.

"I just—" she sniffled again, but this time it was a deeper sob, and I felt my stomach dropping and I felt like a little kid, almost like that. "I just don't know how this can keep going when anytime I feel pissed, I also feel like you might come after me. Like—" She stepped back and wiped her eyes and her hair was falling down all over her face and she looked like a mess. "Like how can anything ever be good with us when I don't know what's going to happen next?"

I shook my head, like I didn't know what I was supposed to say to this. "But it's been good—we've been good, right?" I took a step toward her.

"I don't know what we've been. I just, I can't breathe around you sometimes." Justine was crying less, but her breathing was staggered like she was out of breath or something.

"But you love me," I said and somewhere in my veins or in my gut I felt him. Like something was coming loose. Like something was scratching at the inside of my throat or my brain.

"I mean, I guess. But what does that even mean anymore?" And Justine was looking at me almost clear-eyed.

"But you love me," I repeated and the veins, my veins, they were like a violin, a tuning fork.

"I just don't know." Then Justine shook her head, and she looked at me with the saddest, worst looking eyes I'd ever seen. And then I don't know what happened.

I guess I pushed her down. I pushed her down, and she was so soft and so easy to push down, and then I fell on top of her, and something inside me said, just once, just once you can do it, and so I punched her in the collar bone and I could feel that soft skin under my knuckles. But the bone, the bone was like rock against my fist, and then I leaned back, and I smacked her as hard as I could in the face, and she was just like stunned. And she shut up. She wasn't crying anymore she was just all shut up. And then, I leaned back, and I did it again, but it was my fist this time and her face, her perfect face and her perfect, ugly nose. And I could feel saliva in my mouth. Like I had just eaten something delicious, like a filet mignon, the meat juice dripping down my tongue and my throat, but then, a moment later, it was bile. And I stepped back, and I was Matt again, and then she started wailing. Like ugly. Like wailing. But it wasn't just her, it was Gus, too. I looked at him and he was soaked. Like he had just taken a bath and water was dripping off his legs and everywhere. And he was cowering behind the coffee table by the sofa, and he was cowering. And I looked at both of them, and I didn't understand because I loved them. I loved them so much.

"I love you," I said to Justine, but she was crying so much, I didn't know. I couldn't even tell if she heard me or not. And I felt the sick feeling inside of—I knew what I had done, and I couldn't make it not done. And so I felt even sicker. And that was when I got the angriest. When you knew you were the piece of shit that everyone thought you were, and there was no corner to turn to in your mind that let you escape from this. And if there was nowhere to turn, then you lashed out. That was just the animal part of it. That was just the biology of the thing.

I walked backwards out of the room to the front door, and I called for Gus and he slunk toward me, and I've never hit him. I have never hit him, but he was so scared looking it made me sick, almost angry, so I grabbed his collar and his leash. I said nothing as I left because the house was just Justine's crying, that's all it was and what was that to me.

Outside the sun was going down and there was a briskness to the air, and me and Gus were walking fast, like I wasn't letting him stop like I normally would. I was walking and going, and I didn't know what it was, but I had to keep moving.

Five blocks from our house, I started to think what did this mean, but I didn't like that, I didn't like thinking that so I decided it would be okay, it had to be okay. Because in the end love was the most important thing, and even if I had problems, I had more love than anything else and I had to give it away, you can't hold onto love like that, which meant I had to give it to Justine.

And then, somehow, me and Gus were in front of Georgie's house with the willow tree, and it was like I was heading there the whole time, but I don't think I knew it.

The sky was a pinkish red and it was like candy melting over the thin, green willow branches, all hanging down over the lawn. The yard was empty, and I was thankful it was empty because I didn't want to see anyone. I just wanted to be alone.

Then I was sitting on the grass or sort of kneeling more like, and I was feeling these branches, what with the wind and how they brushed against my back as my hands searched in the grass for something. I could feel the branches brushing the sides of my face all rough and kind of scratchy. And then I thought of something I hadn't thought about in years.

I was walking home, and I was a kid. I was little, not even ten, and I was holding a branch from the willow in our neighborhood. I was bringing a switch for Dad, and I was thinking I knew it was because Amy was in trouble. I knew it. I could see her face. I could see her lips where she bit them and there was blood from her own teeth. And then I was in the house, in the laundry room and Amy was kneeling on the tile, and she was crying, and I was crying, and Dad was taking the branch from me even though I was trying to hold it away from him. I was telling him not to do it, but then I was on the ground somehow and my lip was bleeding, and Dad was hitting her with it, with what I brought him. And then I was trying to get in front of her. I was trying to get between them, but I couldn't. And Amy was yelling at me to go away, and Dad was calling her a bitch, calling me a waste, and neither of them would let me help, and it was my fault. It was my fault he was doing it to her and my fault that she didn't think I could help.

And the grass on Georgie's lawn was prickly, it wasn't soft like how I thought it would be, but I kept running my hands over it, feeling it, like there might be something in it for me. My face was wet, and so I wiped it against Gus, but it didn't do anything. It was just getting more wet because he was wet. Then Gus was licking my face. A dog's tongue is dry, so Gus was helping me, and I didn't deserve it. I tried to say that to him, but I couldn't say it. The words they weren't coming out. But I loved him. I loved him. And her too. Justine, of course. And I loved Amy, I know I did, and I think I'd even loved him, but I wish I hadn't.

Because there isn't always enough of it, enough love and it matters. Love is the only thing that matters. I need to believe.

# Harold,
# Protector of the Children

At night, Harold dreams of children. Their faces young and innocent. The blondes, brunettes, the ones with dark, tightly curled
hair who he lies beside and they tell him—I could love you. Their
mouths open and then curl closed in pain. The dawn approaches
and an angry god sets in. Oh, Harold, he beseeches, do not of the
innocent mind corrupt. Another day, another painful layer added
to the ball of shame in Harold's gut. I am an awful thing, thinks
Harold. The objects in his bedroom turn away. The lamp. The
table. The Magritte. They cannot bear witness to his pedophilic
lust. But lust, says Harold, is not the same as action. To act is not
the same as biology. The pillow is gripped tightly and the night,
it ends in daylight.

   In the morning, in his bedroom mirror, as coffee brews in
the kitchen, Harold watches his own eyes as he carefully combs
his hair into a neat part. The polo he wears, with its SunTrust
emblem prominently displayed, hugs tight to his middle. He pulls
an errant hair from his shoulder, and turns away from the mirror,
setting his comb on the nightstand. Harold is twenty-six, but his
small stature and large-cheeked face give him a lasting sense of
boyishness. From the bathroom down the hall, Harold hears the
sound of public radio's *Morning Edition* and then a groan, followed
by the word "Shithead." Darlene, his roommate, is awake.

The bathroom door creaks open and Darlene calls from down the hall. "Hey—can you pour me a travel mug? I'm running late."

Harold nods, an action Darlene cannot see, and heads to the kitchen to pour the cup. He pours himself one as well then adds a splash of soy creamer to Darlene's mug and passes it off to her as she enters the kitchen.

"Thanks." She pauses to take a sip, her dark hair pulled up into a network of braids, impossibly complicated in Harold's vision. "I fell asleep with this hair—you think it works?"

Harold nods again, smelling now the strong floral spray that Darlene has generously applied in lieu of a shower.

"I know. I'm gross."

"No. I like it. Like I'm in a meadow or something."

Darlene laughs and rummages through her purse. "You going to the Taproom after work?" Darlene holds open a compact looking at her face and scrunching her nose so it touches her upper lip. "I think Leah said she'd be there." She glances toward Harold, and he catches her eye in the small mirror of the compact.

"You look fine." Harold opens the cupboard and pulls out a bowl, then grabs the Cheerios from the pantry. "And yeah. Okay."

"Good. Me and Stella will be there, too." Darlene pauses to take a long swallow of coffee. She opens the fridge, pulls out the creamer and adds a splash to the mug. "Maybe change your shirt before you meet up?"

"I'm sure."

"I think she's a nice one." The compact snaps shut and Darlene pulls out car keys. "Okay. I'm out. Will you feed Angie?"

Harold nods. Darlene is out the door, keys jingling loudly in her hand. The trace of her lingering in the small kitchen. Harold pours his cereal, his milk, and stands chewing the familiar cereal, its taste a chemtrail to childhood.

He finishes the bowl, wipes his hand across his mouth to remove any drops of milk, then whistles for Angie, pouring a cup of dry food into her food dish and supplying her with fresh water. The orange tabby wends her way toward him and Harold stops to pet her between the ears, kneeling down to accept her curious mews. She's a loving thing, thinks Harold. The creature purrs, rubs against his outstretched hand, brushes her forehead against his knuckles.

The dreams of the night before float ethereally in his mind, and Harold does his best to destroy the wisps. Though he cannot remember their content, the warm feeling in his belly is not one he trusts. The cat ticks against his hand and Harold closes his eyes, summons an image of the future, the one where he's happy, in love, surrounded by sweeping palms and beside him, a woman, a being whose unconditional support is too large even for his own special sickness. But then, she's gone. The kitchen cupboards surround him. The day, waiting.

Checking his watch, Harold gives the cat a final scratch and then gathers his keys, phone, and wallet. He departs the house, carefully locking the door on his way out.

The first time Harold felt an impure thought, he was a child so the pang was normalized despite its terrifying implication of sex. As his mother told him, the two together, folding laundry on his parents' queen size bed, "Even good boys have bad thoughts." He hadn't mentioned the specific feeling to her, the warm buzz in his stomach when his neighbor, Sally, also eight, had worn a yellow bikini in the backyard sprinkler, but his mother seemed to intuit much that was not said.

Later this logic carried with him to early adolescence, so that the mornings he woke up drenched in sweat were not altogether problematic, though the dreams themselves held subjects who seemed somehow misplaced. When his friends would speak of girls, more and more, Harold found himself biting his tongue. Because, for Harold, these girls did not mature. They stayed young, pure, children, while he himself became an unfamiliar predator. The stuff of fairy tales, but he was the witch, the one whose desire involved acts of cruelty. The wolf who, in satisfying his hunger, destroys the innocence of all around him.

At night, in his bedroom, Harold would imagine that a monster had taken residence in his belly. That he'd eaten something, a moldy cracker, a too pink hamburger, some sour milk—something that had poisoned his brain and made the objects of his lust so impossible. I am broken, thought Harold. I am no good.

Once, at age sixteen, Harold tested himself, agreed to babysit his cousin, a girl of six, and alone in the house together for an afternoon, Harold faced his demon head-on. He hadn't expected the temptation to be so great, the pull of his curiosity and desire so deafening in his ears. The girl, loud, rambunctious, red-headed and beautiful in her yellow tutu, and fawning over him: her older cousin, the boy, the hero. It took all of what Harold could muster to protect her from himself and later, complaining to his mother, he told her he would never babysit again. The irritation was too great, the child too annoying. And to himself, Harold vowed to avoid being around children altogether. He would invent a force field and no child would be able to penetrate the protective shield that Harold had constructed. It was the only way.

On more than one occasion, teenage Harold stumbled into the realm of pornography, but the regular, full breasted women felt a paltry substitution for his internal cravings. He tried watching men, but this too felt inadequate. And so, in shameful desperation, Harold experimented with watching children, tried to tell himself there was no victim in his gaze but as the months passed the horror of what he saw grew uglier and uglier in his mind. The savagery of his own lust manifested in his sleep. The innocents who suffered in his viewings entered his dreams to show him their ruined lives, their scars, the exploitation that his desire wreaked from their small bodies. So, with determination, Harold quit his viewing and slowly, over time, tried to smother his sex in gauze, the thing, his longings, so tightly wound that they could not touch the outer world. He Harold, in control, and the demon of his sexuality, a mere specter, difficult even to hear through all the many layers of dense shame he had compiled.

Through all of this, Harold remained silent, inwardly aware that this was the sort of secret one did not spill. His mother's love, though great, could surely not hold this wickedness in its wide net. Sometimes Harold wondered if there were other men or women born with this genetic abnormality, for where else could this desire have come from? His own past free of abuse, his own childhood untainted. But to try and seek these people out, even online, felt dangerous, felt like an attempt to justify a heinous longing. For appearances, Harold dated now and then, and often felt an honest attraction to the women who welcomed him into their arms, their bodies, but all the while, Harold felt the duplicity of his true self lurking within. Knew that to be honest would provoke disgust and so any intimacy was itself sheathed in lies. Drunk, at parties during college, in games of "I never," Harold sometimes wished for a slip, a release, a way to admit to the terrible thing so it might be dispersed like a dark bird from his psyche. But this never happened, and Harold knew it was for the best. The thing in him, so base, so awful, that for most people he passed, for those he knew, even for those that claimed to love him, the idea of his truth would never even manifest as possible. The bogeymen are elsewhere, not among us, or so his mother had promised.

\*

At just past five, Harold prepares to leave the bank. He performs his closing duties as banker, says his goodbyes to Kristin, the branch manager, and heads outside into the day's mouth, warm and waiting, unnaturally hot for the middle of October. The car ride is short, but the warm, sun-soaked interior of his black Hyundai makes the time feel long.

Once home, Harold changes his shirt, an effort suggested by Darlene with the hopes of impressing Leah, the woman with whom he's meant to have a first date this evening. Darlene, ever eager, that he, Harold, should find love.

The shirt he selects is a short sleeve button-down decorated with windmills, a mass of which are distributed in an orderly pattern across all planes of the fabric. He'd met Leah, a teacher friend of Darlene's from the private school, late the previous Saturday night, her small nose and smaller mouth making her a proportionate candidate for his own small statured self. That night, wasted, Darlene had flung them together, and Harold, equally drunk, had offered to wait outside the bar with Leah for her Uber to arrive. They hadn't spoken much, but they'd somehow come to hold hands, and Harold had admired the cleanness of her smell, the gentle feeling of her moist palm on his own. An echo of laundry and buttercups. Attraction, thinks Harold, is a worrisome thing.

When Harold arrives at the bar, the three women are midorder, the waitress stands at their outside table, partially shaded by a Guinness umbrella. Harold slides into the empty chair between Leah and Darlene and waves hello, orders himself an IPA. He turns to Leah smiling broadly. I'm a normal guy, thinks Harold, the thought a steady affirmation in his mind.

Today, Leah wears a yellow sundress and when she greets him, the thin straps tauten against the soft flesh of her shoulders.

"It's good to see you—you look nice." To which Leah blushes, slightly, and Harold inside senses a pang of want, of desire.

"I like your shirt," says Leah in response and across the table, Darlene laughs, a single fat *ha*.

The drinks arrive, beers for Darlene and Harold, vodka for Stella, and a bourbon with ginger for Leah who holds the glass in one small hand, sucking the drink through the thin red straw.

The table dissolves into chatter about the day, about work, about television and who has the best fish tacos and increasingly, Harold feels comfort in his skin. Leah scoots her chair closer toward the table and him, and soon he can smell her hair, the warm pleasantness of its girl scent, its flowery odor. More drinks are ordered, then French fries to share, a burger for Stella.

Across the table, Darlene rests her hand on Stella's thigh and Stella's hand travels down to interlace her fingers with Darlene's. The ease of their intimacy sends a pulse through his own clammy body.

Harold glances back to Leah, who looks down at her drink, stirring the remaining ice cubes in a circle. A strand of her nearly blonde hair falls loose against her face.

"So, how long have you been teaching?" Harold asks.

"I guess three years now?" Leah leans back in her seat and shakes her head. The soft yellow of her dress creates an almost halo on her pale skin. "It still feels like I have no idea sometimes."

Harold smiles, thinks about reaching to tuck the loose strand behind her ear. There's an innocence about her face that the cold beer seems to draw out.

"And you're in the high school, too?" asks Harold. "With D, I mean?"

"No, I actually teach second grade. Darlene and I met at a school-wide faculty meeting."

Harold takes a swallow of his beer and leans across the table to take a sweet potato fry. His tongue feels out the sharp ridges made crisp by the deep fryer.

"Yeah—I love it." Leah continues, her eyes, which he hadn't noticed were blue, looking up toward the sky that doesn't quite match their color. "It makes me feel taller, I mean being surrounded by all these little people all the time."

"I'll bet."

"Do you have younger siblings?"

"No, I'm the youngest." Across the table, Stella shows Darlene something on her phone and the two laugh. Darlene's hand grazes the back of Stella's T-shirt and Harold sees the hand like a hummingbird, tentative but alighting.

"Well it's like having siblings. Except the family is huge and they all want your attention all the time."

"That sounds tiring."

"It can be. But so can most things, right?"

"True." Harold can't stop himself from picturing Leah in the classroom. The image flits before him, the tiny hands clamoring for her, pulling at the fabric of her yellow dress.

"Do you like kids?"

"Sure. I guess." He swallows the last of his beer.

"It's okay. I find not a lot of guys think about it. Unless they're teachers or they have them, you know."

"Huh." Harold takes another swallow. He can see them, swarming him, the little legs and bodies, like blind puppies pushing toward sustenance, this otherwise wholesome display, made gross by his nature.

"I bet you'd be great with kids," Darlene says leaning forward, her elbows propped on the table.

"Yeah, you're so—gentle," Stella says, nodding.

The three women all look his way, smiling, surmising his worthiness as parent, as guardian. Harold, protector of the children. The grimness of it almost makes him laugh aloud.

Darlene laughs then, perhaps sensing his discomfort. "This is some great first date conversation, Leah. You really know how to lure them in."

Blushing again now, Leah laughs too. "Right."

"It's okay," Harold says and smiles at Leah, wanting to reassure her, not wanting her to feel awkward. He excuses himself to the restroom, gently touching Leah's shoulder as he rises.

In the bathroom, facing the urinal, Harold attempts to order his mind. Most of the time, it's possible to forget the parts of himself that make him feel disgusted, though dating has often been a strong trigger. As if the mere potential for human contact requires him to evaluate the risk he poses. Harold feels a tinge of rage echo in his chest. He clenches his jaw in response. Here's a why-God moment. Why trap me in this mind? Why make me a predator? How unlovable must I be in this life?

The cold space of the bathroom does not respond and Harold, always alone in his thoughts, moves to the sink to wash his hands. The soap smells like apples and reminds him briefly of his mother and the pies she would make on Sunday afternoons in the fall. He'll need to go on his drive tonight. After this date, after he says his goodbyes, pays his tab. Once Leah and Darlene and Stella are safely headed home; he will take the drive and it will calm him. Give him a chance to think about this girl, his plans, the possibility of being normal.

Back at the table the conversation has changed to Stella's new job at a nonprofit for immigrant rights, and Harold makes sure to look warmly at Leah to reaffirm his interest in her.

A final round is ordered and the evening winds down shortly after. Harold insists on paying for Leah. Stella and Darlene leave in Darlene's car and Leah and Harold linger in the parking lot to exchange numbers.

"I'd like to see you again," Harold says the words and feels their truth.

"I'd like that, too." She smiles and turns her almost golden head with its doll-like features his way. Her arm brushes his and so he leans in to hug her.

She feels bigger in his arms than he'd expected, like they're evenly matched, each able to lift the other off the ground if they so desired. Harold pulls back to kiss her, a peck, an affirmation. Her lips soft and her breath slightly tinged with the sweetness of bourbon. This candy of adulthood.

"I'll call you soon." Harold pulls away, sees himself before her, almost vulnerable, and his body tenses.

She smiles, moves in the direction of her car and he watches her, feels relieved when she's safe inside her vehicle.

Harold unlocks his own car, noticing that the warmth from the day's sun has worn off with the coming dusk. He waits, watching, as Leah makes her way out of the parking lot and into the neighborhood. He keeps waiting, sitting in his parked car, until she turns left and he can no longer see her dab of yellow hair through the distant window. It's early days, thinks Harold, we are both still unknowns. And yet, in his chest, a tremor, a hope.

At the 7–11 by his house, Harold stops to pick up peanut M&Ms and assorted Laffy Taffy, his usual provisions for his drive. The drive Harold anticipates is a ten-mile loop of the suburb, one he has charted and repeats on days when he needs to feel sober, be reminded of the consequences of his brain chemistry. Some-times, Harold thinks the loop forms the shape of a dinosaur, an imperfect, child's approximation of the reptile. Other days it's a loop of depravity. Of humans who lack control, of double-sided misery. A misshapen slug, undeserving of design or order.

Each of the five pins that form the loop represents the dwelling of a registered sex offender. The information blasted online, available for any curious or fearful individual to access. The worried and the lascivious, thought Harold as he himself pored over the findings when first creating his map. Housewives and neighborhood watches, anxious to know where danger lay. To quarantine it. To keep their loved ones safe.

The first house on the map belongs to an older gentleman, a neat home with a silver Pontiac always parked in the narrow, steep driveway. The house itself brick and shuttered. Harold parks across the street and watches the windows for any sign of movement. As expected, there is none. These marked homes tend to be quieter than most, as if the creatures inside were trapped captive in their shells, avoiding any unnecessary temptation or scrutiny.

Harold lingers for a few minutes, aware of his semi-conspicuousness as he pretends to check his phone, his eyes watching the home, studying its curtained windows and the neatly manicured hedges, two of them, twin and forest green, nearly waist high. A man jogs by and Harold hears the smack of his footsteps on the pavement through his open car window. The night air slowly settling like a sigh.

The next house is smaller with white vinyl siding and a birdbath in the front yard that seems always strewn with leaves and other detritus. The man who lives here is younger, only a few years older than Harold himself. According to the internet his act involved the sons of his then girlfriend, though even this small detail was too much for Harold at first. Harold, not needing the titillation that makes *Law and Order* so popular, the depravity that others might dwell in at leisure.

Once he'd seen this man, sitting on the stoop of his weath-
ered front porch, smoking a cigarette and scratching at his jeaned
ankle with a white, burly forearm. Harold, like an entomologist
who finally spies his own species beneath the magnifying glass.
But we're not the same species, thought Harold, because I have
not acted.

Today, the driveway's empty and there are no lights on in the
house. A soda can, partially crushed, decorates the front lawn, but
Harold cannot be sure the litter was an act of rebellion against
the man inside. An act of vengeance by the neighborhood children, high on sugar.

Harold pops a handful of M&Ms in his mouth and drives on.
The interior of his car silent except for the nearly muted radio
playing its classic rock, and outside the night having fallen, the
clouds denying the stars access to the land below.

The third dwelling is a garden apartment and Harold pauses
here only briefly. He hasn't yet developed the courage to figure
out which apartment belongs to the man on his list, and the parking lot itself is often a flurry of activity: kids, moms, dads, the
elderly, all coming and going as they live their lives. Any one of
them could be the predator, thinks Harold, though more than
likely they're just normal, healthy people.

The fourth house is a duplex of white-washed brick. Harold
pulls up across the street, parks beneath an oak tree and carefully unwraps a strawberry Laffy Taffy, sliding the candy into his
mouth. The porch light casts a weak glow on the concrete steps
that lead up to the house. The grass is short and the remnants of
a tree, a trunk with four branches sawn off, sits squat in the middle of the small yard. The quiet is nice, thinks Harold. Here is a
moment in which the unknown is known, thinks Harold. He rolls
his window down slightly to let the cool air come in. All across
the land, the children sleep, and here Harold keeps watch. The

sound of these words, warm and soothing in his mind. Perhaps there's security in knowing where the badness lives, perhaps he could be its keeper.

A few moments later, a red sedan pulls up to the stop sign at the end of the block, and Harold watches as the car slowly approaches the house and then stops directly adjacent to the tree in the front yard. The engine idles briefly before turning off. A man sits in the front seat of the car. Harold leans forward slightly to see him. He's read about this person, seen his mugshot, but never seen him in the flesh. He, like Harold, is attracted to young girls. Harold breathes in the neighborhood air as it enters through his partially cracked window and sees himself and this other sharing the same air, the same evil.

The man lingers in his car a moment longer, his hands resting idly on the steering wheel and then he opens the door and stands outside, his face shadowed by the starless night. Harold's mouth opens and closes. The man turns and slams his car door shut. He pauses and peers back in the direction of Harold's car. His body twisted, contorted like a dancer.

A shiver seems to run through the man's body, as the moment holds, but then he faces Harold's car and walks directly toward him. He comes to stand by Harold's window, peers down, what looks like a grimace smeared across his thin, angular face. Inside his body, Harold's organs rotate and squeeze.

"What are you doing?" The man's voice is low, calm, almost a whisper.

Harold cannot speak. He puts his tongue against his lower lip. Hesitates.

The man squats down so he and Harold are at eye level, but in the darkness, the man's face appears like a geographical survey, a map of shadowy gradation. "Why are you parked outside my house?"

"I'm sorry." Harold speaks now. The words forming more of a question than a declaration.

The man stares at him, silent, as if awaiting an answer.

"I'm sorry." Harold says again, a grotesque confusion growing in his veins.

The man shakes his head. "You people who do this—who come and watch me—you're perverts, too, you know." The man looks as if he might spit at Harold's window, might bash it in, but he sighs and rises. His head obscured now entirely in shadow. He stands. Stares at the car and Harold, its occupant.

Harold reaches for his door, the lock, but halts, unsure.

The man turns away and walks toward the house and Harold, grasping, rolls down his window farther. Wait, he thinks. Tell me what it's like. Don't leave me. Just, please.

The man turns back once more and pointing at Harold, shakes his pointed finger, shakes it. "Please," he says, "just leave me alone." Then he's gone inside the house, and Harold hurriedly turns on his engine, leaves the neighborhood, his headlights like twin lighthouses in search of safety. The feeling of it all, sick in his gut. His innocence a false idol not even he himself can worship. The drive home, a painful one.

Over the course of the following week, Harold manages to recover from his confrontation, and in the light of day his sense of his own moral rightness is restored. How could anyone question Harold's good fight? Who else could manage such an internal demon as he has for some twenty-odd years? This man, who in his lack of understanding of their common ground, has cast against Harold, and yet Harold, Harold is the one who abstains, whose ability to do so should warrant something, some applause if even in the quiet of his brain. Still, the encounter provokes ambivalence in his thinking, and each time he tries to find a way to feel, Harold becomes confused, unnerved, unhappier than before, but also, oddly, righteous?

But Leah. Leah is a good thing. Five days after the first date, on a Friday night, Harold takes Leah to dinner where they eat sushi with chopsticks, and later hold hands in the movie theater as images of sweaty, war-torn men flit before them. The following Sunday they eat eggs and sip champagne, and take a long walk around the town's lake, pointing out ducks and egrets and turtles to one another. They make out on a picnic blanket, Harold's hands venturing cautiously across the argyle terrain of her sweater.

Over the days and nights they spend together, Harold discovers that Leah is easy, kind, natural with him, and only rarely does she speak about the little children in her classes. Only rarely does Harold become aware of his body and its unconscious reactions to the stories she tells, the images she describes. On the fourth date, Harold cooks dinner for Leah, linguini with pesto and sautéed spinach, and then after a bottle and a half of red wine, they retire to Leah's bedroom where they have mild, curious, and only slightly awkward sex. Not a bad time, Harold thinks. Not for their first attempt. And Leah seems to like it too, or so she says, laughing, when they try again the following morning to, in her words, "greater success."

The weeks pass quickly and intensely, Harold willingly consumed in the idea that there might be a girl in whose arms he can seek refuge, and Leah, seemingly invested in his kindness, the bravado of her last partner something she says she's glad to have left behind. Meanwhile, the echoes of Darlene, excited for the connection and casually commenting that Harold, might finally be finding love.

\*

On the day before Halloween, Leah texts Harold and asks if he'll come over the following afternoon to hand out candy, the holiday this year falling on a Friday. Later, the two will hit Stella's party that she and her roommates host each year. Harold agrees and feels a pang of excitement, a note of pleasure in his chest that makes him realize that the prospect of seeing the girl is enough to whet his heart, to make him smile. It occurs to him that he might become a normal man, a man whose desires are boring in their wholesomeness.

I could be average, thinks Harold. Maybe it just takes the love of the right girl to be a normal guy. Maybe this Leah can make me good.

On Halloween, Harold dresses as a wolf to fit the fairy tale theme his coworkers at the bank have chosen. The costume is a plastic mask, and a tail which he pins to his suit pants. The suit itself, gray, so that the double-entendre of a wolf on Wall Street will make an easy transition to the party that evening. Leaving work just after four, he heads to Leah's small duplex where she lives alone, aside from her two fish whose tank is the principal feature of her small, carpeted living room.

She greets him at the door, wearing a pig snout and pig ears, "I'm a capitalist," she laughs, and they hug. He pulls back to kiss her on her snout. A moment later two very small children in witch outfits are led to the door by a mother. Harold settles himself beside Leah on the wide concrete steps that lead up to her front door. The day is still light and reasonably warm. Leah holds a large bowl of Twix, Butterfingers, and Starbursts and offers it to the children in their black cloaks. Harold watches as the small hands reach into the bowl and select a piece of candy, depositing it with determination into the plastic pumpkin-shaped pails they hold.

"Say, thank you," the mother prods and the little witches mumble thanks through their shy, smiling mouths.

The group moves on and Leah turns to Harold. "Did you want anything to drink? Beer or water?"

"I'm okay right now," he says and points to the next group of children approaching, two zombies and an evil doctor with blood splattered on his small, white lab coat.

"Tough day at work?" Leah asks the doctor, and he shrugs his shoulders in response. She laughs, a sweet note, and offers the kids the bowl.

When the children have moved along, she turns to Harold and leans her head gently against his shoulder.

"It's a strange holiday." Leah shakes her head. "Especially when you grow up and you're the one handing out the candy."

"Yeah." Harold nods. "It'd be a weird day to visit Earth if you were an alien."

"All these small people dressed all scary, and then this door-to-door collecting."

Harold laughs and Leah sits up, takes a Starburst from the bowl and opens it, offering one of the squares to Harold who accepts, taking the orange one and leaving her the pink.

Another group, this time the children slightly older, approaches the house, and Leah rises, smiling. Harold watches as she effortlessly comments on their costumes and offers them the candy. The confidence and ease in her actions, qualities Harold knows he lacks. He unwraps the orange candy and slips it into his mouth, playing with the wolf mask in his hands.

When the children are gone, Leah yawns. "God. I might need to make coffee."

"Long day?"

"Oh, yes. Halloween is never an easy day in second grade."

"I can imagine."

A dad comes forward then, pushing a baby in a stroller and holding the hand of a small girl in a princess dress from a Disney movie Harold cannot name. The exchange is made, and Harold finds himself watching the small brunette head with its plastic tiara moving down the path and into the neighbor's yard.

"I remember being scared of Halloween as a kid," Leah says, leaning back to place the bowl beside the lit jack-o-lantern on the stoop behind them.

"I think I loved it. What was scary about it?" Harold asks. The soft body of the orange Starburst rests on his tongue, just slightly impairing his speech.

"Not the costumes or anything. It was all the stuff you'd hear about, like poison candy or razor blades in chocolate bars or kidnappers." Leah squints and lifts off her pig nose, resting it on her forehead. "The real stuff. Not that any of it was actually real."

"Humans can be pretty scary."

Leah looks at Harold, reaches to take his wolf mask and places it over his face. "Yeah." She slips the elastic behind his head so the mask is attached. "Maybe it's our lack of fur."

"Hairier is scarier?" Harold peers through the eyes at Leah's face, the soft pink lips and round chin.

"Maybe so." She laughs. "Though maybe hairless is scariest?"

A quiet settles between them and Harold, self-consciously, swallows the candy still marinating in his mouth. Leah looks at her fingernails, and through the mask, Harold's breath feels hot and sticky. The air cooler as the sun begins to wane.

"A beer sounds nice actually, but I can get it." He begins to stand, but Leah touches his arm.

"I'll get it—no problem. I'll make some coffee, too."

"Thanks."

"You man the bowl?"

Harold nods, raises one hand like a wolf paw, and pounces on the bowl pulling it into his lap, making Leah laugh as she stands and turns to go inside.

Alone, on the steps, Harold appreciates this break from trick or treaters. With Leah beside him, the purity of the activity feels believable, feels right. But alone? He straightens the mask on his face, imagines wolf teeth inside his mouth. In another version of his life, he'd lure them in, terrify them, eat of their flesh, their sex.

Harold shakes his head, pulls down the mask, and sees two girls coming his way, a mother trailing behind as she holds the hand of a tiny boy dressed like a ninja turtle. The girls are dressed as ballerinas, the tulle of their tutus flaring out to form the shapes of exaggerated flowers. Tulips, young and lithe. They float toward him, attempting pirouettes and other moves their untrained bodies cannot quite perform.

"Trick or treat!" the one in purple shouts. Her friend or sister echoing the words as she spins once, then twice, the pink of her tutu still bright in the fading October light. They laugh, these trilling birds, these friends, and Harold smiles, holds out the bowl, his own heart, a hummingbird.

"Ballerinas?" he asks. The girls nod as they lean forward examining the contents of the bowl. The smell of their hair just perceivable as they reach forward to take a piece of candy.

"One piece?" asks the girl in purple and Harold nods.

"What're you?" The one in pink asks, reaching for a Twix then dropping it in lieu of a Butterfinger. She doesn't look at him directly, her eyes cast on the candy before her.

Harold laughs, shakes his head. "A wolf."

The girl nods, her eyes now on his mask and then catching her friend's hand, the two are turning, shouting, "Thank you!" and

Harold nods, waves to the mother who watches, smiling, from the background. They leave, their thin bodies skipping and the skirts like pale ghosts in the front yard.

The door behind him opens, and Leah, in her pink sweater and pink jeans and pig ears is beside him, handing him a bottle and he hears his own thoughts, the prayer for her return, the cooling of sweat at the nape of his neck.

"Looks like you survived," Leah says settling down beside him. The porch light above them now visible in the oncoming darkness.

Harold nods. "Thanks for the beer."

"They're not so scary."

"Who?" Harold turns to look at her face, the snout still settled on her forehead like a third eye.

"Children," says Leah.

Harold nods, but finds he cannot speak. Instead, he places his hand on her thigh and squeezes, lets the feeling of her girl flesh excite him, satiate him, make him feel, at once, and first, a human. This moment, he knows, is not the stuff of dreams. They are here, on this porch, the concrete step beneath their fleshmade selves. The grass shorn and earnest in the fall dark before them. And here, the body beside him, with heat and breasts and his own true longing, not now, this time, an unclean thing, but maybe, oh possibly, whole.

# The Pleasures of Television

We call it Watching TV. We say to each other, you want to watch some TV later? And the other one says sure, and then we both laugh because it's only us that knows what we're talking about. Me and Beau, we're the only ones who know what we mean. And that's what makes it funny, and also, I'd say, what makes it special.

I like that it's special. That it's something just for me and Beau to share. Like twins. Like two birds on a wire that fly off at the same second like they planned it or something, and you're just standing below, looking up, hoping they don't shit on you as you watch them rise into the sky.

Beau's real name is Landon, but we both think Landon doesn't fit. When Beau's boss at Krystal's calls him back to the office, it's like *Lan-dumb*, and he says it makes him feel like some kind of hick or dummy, so we decided Beau was a better fit because it's simple, but it's elegant.

I say, Beau, you want to Watch some TV later? And he says, Sandy, I thought you'd never ask, and we decide to meet at Ricky's which is a video store, but also, it's a tanning salon, and it's where we like to go sometimes to relax and to get us in the mood for our Watching.

Neither of us, not me or Beau, care for Ricky, but me and

Beau both like to tan on occasion, even though me, I can only tan my legs, and even though we have both figured it might give us cancer one of these days. We know this because of the signs on the walls, and because of what happened to Jadine, Ricky's wife, who was one of the most beautiful girls back twenty years ago, but now she's pretty much an old, shriveled carrot with only one boob.

Beau and I are not in sexual love, and I know it's because he's queer, but we haven't talked about it, and I think he'll say something when he wants to say something. Our favorite movie, both of ours, is *To Wong Foo*, and it's the one we rent most often from Ricky's when it's not checked out by someone else.

The first time me and Beau Watched TV it was on the Saturday after high school graduation, which was almost three years ago now. We had gone to take his Mom's Chevy to get its oil changed down at the AAmco, and when we were waiting in the bays, I looked over and saw a blonde lady I'd never seen before. I watched her sitting in her car, and for some reason, the position of the cars or how it was, she didn't see me, and so I watched her for a good five minutes. The way she smiled at Davis who was working her bay and this little sigh she gave when she thought no one was looking—the way it moved across her whole face down to her shoulders like a wave of sadness was passing right through her—and it was a grave and important feeling I had in knowing that I was seeing something honest. I told Beau about it right away, right there, and he said, Sandy, it's like you were watching reality TV, and I said, yeah, Beau, that's exactly like what it was. But here I was an audience of one and this lady, she was the real real thing.

At the time, I don't know that I thought about it like voyeurism, seeing folks in their so-called naked states, but that was what came out later when me and Beau made the mistake of telling his older brother one night over a case of Ice on Beau's dad's front porch.

By that point we'd Watched TV maybe five or six times, mostly sitting in the car in the Winn-Dixie parking lot and watching the little old ladies push their carts. The way their faces some of them look real determined and whereas others of them look mostly lost or confused. And then one time at the Sonic when we reclined back real far in our seats and watched Tiffany Moses and Andy Smith on what we decided had to be a date, even though Tiffany, last we knew, was dating Zack Mason of Mason Auto Repair. Beau said this was what in-love looked like, and I thought maybe or maybe it was just desire. All big lipped and uneven and desperate.

When we told Beau's brother about it, he said we were people watching, and it was disgusting, like we were a couple of voyeurs, and Beau told him to go to hell, but I realized he was maybe probably right. I have always respected the opinion of Beau's brother because he was one of the only men I'd met, besides Beau of course, who were kind to all the girls no matter how they looked on the outside.

From then on, me and Beau decided this was a secret thing we were doing, and because it was secret, we should not tell anybody. This was also good thinking because pretty soon on, Beau and I realized it wasn't so easy watching people without them knowing it. People are like animals in that way. Most of the time they don't have much sense, but then, when they're being watched, all of a sudden, their hair stands up and their nose gets cold and they know, even if they don't know it, that they're prey. That someone out there is ready to eat them up. That someone out there is ready to get them good.

*

Most people would not say that Beau and I are of the popular sort, and we would say to most people that for this we're glad. In this town, Beau jokes, popular seems to mean pregnant, and I laugh though I also feel a little badly because being pregnant seems like not the worst thing that could happen to a woman.

When I was little, I used to like to dream about a houseful of babies, all the rooms soft with that good, thick carpet and those little legs and feet everywhere just crawling around and being nosy and being loved and loving back.

If Beau liked ladies, I once thought I might ask him to give me a little baby, but chances are things are for the best in that regard. I love Beau, and I hate the thought that anything could come between us, even a little tiny person, all round-cheeked and rosy. And besides, not all babies are easy, some of them they mostly cry and fuss and grow up to be people who you can no longer put your finger on, even though once you rocked them in your arms the whole night through and you two were the only things that mattered to each other.

Beau and I think that Watching TV is a lot like being a scientist or a doctor because it lets us see how people really are when they think they're alone, and they think they can be their most honest self.

It's refreshing, I think, because it seems like so much of the time you're just seeing people acting how they think they're supposed to act and not like how they would really be acting if they weren't afraid of being judged or being hated or being found out for all the craziness they're hiding inside.

At first, me and Beau would Watch TV in public, in almost plain sight, and so we had the tricky idea of getting sunglasses to help us avoid being noticed. We got these big old sunglasses down at the Goodwill, and they must have belonged to some blind folks because they take up most of the face and they're dark as heck.

We would go to the park, and we'd sit with these big shades on, or else we'd go to the mall the next town over and sit at the food court and just sit there like a couple of blind kids, only we were actually seeing things as they were.

Once or twice someone would come up to us out at the park or by the Dairy Queen and say, Sandy and Lan-dumb, what are you losers doing, and on those occasions, Beau and I would just start to laugh until whoever was bothering us took their leave because it was secret after all and because who has time for people like that in the end.

Then Beau had the idea that because the people we were watching were still mostly in public, that maybe we weren't even really seeing the good stuff yet, the dark and the honest, he called it. And so that's when we started to get serious, and that's when we came up with the System.

The System involves a little bit of creeping and a little bit of luck. It came to Beau one time when he was driving to pick me up, and he got stopped at the four-way stop on Elm. He got stopped because Lucinda Jones was walking her pack of dogs, and those dogs are always getting all tangled up in each other's leashes.

As Beau was waiting for Lucinda to cross, he saw that he could see right inside the Matthews's house, right through their big old bay window, and he saw Mrs. Matthews at the piano by herself, and he said he could see so clear that he could see the muscles in her shoulders moving as she cranked out some song like the ones we used to hear her play in church.

Beau does exaggerate from time to time, so I don't know about the muscles and all, but it did tell us that hey, maybe people's own windows are the best way to see through to their lives, so that's the first part of the System.

The second part of the System has to do with my job at Maid

to Win which is a local maid service I work at. They have two cars that say the name of the service on them, and on my days that I work I show up there and get the car and then I drive to my houses that I clean. The business we do is only okay because mostly there's not enough people who can afford us, but my boss, Miss Emma, she likes to think big so that's how we got our start.

What my job does is it gives us some cover for being in these neighborhoods where we mostly probably do not belong, the two of us. What'll happen is I'll be cleaning a house and I'll be almost finished, and so I'll call Beau who will come and meet me, and he'll bring some of those little burgers which we'll eat out in the car. Then I'll say, Beau, you want to take a walk because of having eaten all those burgers? And he'll say, yeah, Sandy, I could use a stretch, and then we'll walk around the block pretending to be regular folk admiring the architectures, but really, we're looking for a good window. When we find a good one, something big and wide, we remember it, and the next time I'm out that way, we make a point to go by it again.

All of this has let us see some pretty interesting Television, and it has only led to us being seen once or maybe twice, if you believe according to Beau or according to me.

Beau's favorite piece of TV was when we saw Mr. Handler, who teaches math at the high school, training his dog, Princess Jasmine, without a shirt on. At first, we didn't realize that it was training a dog was what he was doing. He was standing and then clapping his hands and then he'd be walking out of the room and back into it. But eventually we worked it out that he was leaving the room to get a dog bone which he'd balance on his shoulder, and so he'd sort of squat down a little and say, Jasmine, in this real high voice, and then that dog would jump up there on that shoulder to get that bone. Beau and I did not have the right kind of words for this one at the time, but I will say it has given both of us something of a new type of respect for Mr. Handler, who always had seemed rather single-minded about the business of algebra up till then. People have got a specialness, says Beau, and I agree, but I say Beau, what's strange to me is how they seem to keep the good stuff, the most interesting stuff, all to themselves.

Beau will say to me, Sandy, you want to watch a re-run? And I'll say, Beau, let's get us down to Ricky's before they close, and what this means is that we're going to get a video and a tan and then talk on things we have seen that week whether we were together, or we were apart.

Sometimes it's the case that we've seen a lot of things, and other times it's the case that we haven't. Every once in a while, when we first started out, one or the other of us would say, what if it was that we saw something truly that we should not have seen? And then the one of us would pat the other one of us on the shoulder and say, maybe tonight is a night we watch that Swayze and that Snipes and that Julie Newmar and leave the real people to let themselves be.

*

Something to know about me is that when I was four years old, my momma was so tired she accidentally dropped boiling water all over my face and my neck and my chest. What this means is that I have scars, red patches, that some people think make me ugly or a freak but not Beau, he loves me for what matters, which is what's on the inside.

If a regular person sees me, someone I don't already know, I see how they look and then look away and then look back, and Beau calls it the trinity of seeing because it's three times that it takes for them to understand me and my beauty and my worth, according to Beau. This is a time when I don't know that Beau is being all the way honest, but I do know that it must mean he loves me, and I figure that is what matters most of all. Even in broad daylight, Beau can see what's real, what's underneath.

On television, the real kind with a plug, me and Beau's favorite show is *Friends*, and we like it because everyone on it, the ladies at least, are beautiful, and yet they are also finding life to be something complex and not just an easy place to be all of the time. My favorite is Phoebe and Beau says he's probably a Rachel, and then we laugh, and we feel like if we knew those ladies in real life, they might understand how it is that we Watch TV, and sometimes, Phoebe at least, she might want to join us.

On Thursday, I show up to Maid to Win and Miss Emma, the owner, tells me we've got a new client and I am to go over there ASAP because they are an emergency client, which means that they're having a party and so they need their place to be spick and span.

The Allens is the name of the family, and as I drive over, I try to think that I know of any Allens from school, but I can't think that I ever did so I figure they must be new to town. The house is on what Beau and I call Movie Star Row, which is to say there are only five houses on the block, and they're bigger and nicer than any of the other houses in town. This house is made of red brick, and it looks like a house from a Christmas card only it's June now so there's no snow or anything, just lots of flowers, and all kinds of roses, red and pink and yellow and some kind of purple thing creeping up the side of the brick.

When I ring the bell, at first there's just a lot of noise and scrambling sounds, and then finally the door creaks open, and it's a small, old-looking woman and she's wearing what looks to me like a black and white maid's uniform, and so I sort of step back and check that house number again because this might not be the right place after all.

"Are you from the maid service?" The woman's voice sounds real light like music, but also like it's got an accent, maybe Spanish.

I nod, and she steps back and looks at me real quick and cold, like she was expecting some other girl, and then she pulls me forward by the arm, and so I grab my equipment, my mop and buckets and my upright vacuum, and I go into that house.

To me, this house looks already pretty clean, which is often how these houses look the more money the people have got. She points me up a staircase and says there are two bathrooms up there, and I should clean each one and then come downstairs and clean the ones on the first floor and then the one in the basement.

Beau asks me sometimes if cleaning other people's houses isn't kind of like doing the sets for Watching TV because it's me somewhere most other people don't get to go and by myself and everything. I tell him I guess this is true, but most of the time there's no time to be gawking or snooping and you're never sure if they're somehow seeing you when you don't know it, and besides, I don't want to lose the job because Miss Emma has always been real kind to me, especially since I've been living on my own.

I find the first bathroom pretty easy, and I set up and start to clean first the counters and then the toilet and then the shower and the floor. As I'm wiping the mirror, I hear this sound like a little cough, and I look around, but I don't see anything, so I keep doing what I'm doing until I hear it again, and then I see that there's a door on the other side of the bathroom that's part of the way cracked.

"Hello?" I say it nice and friendly.

I don't hear anything back, so I start on the counters and then I hear another kind of sound sort of like a wet mouth breathing, and I feel the little hairs on my arm all tingly. I turn slowly, and I see through the door what looks like an eyeball, and as I watch, the door moves open and I see it's a kid, only this kid I can tell doesn't look all the way right, like her eyes are too far apart and her parts don't look even, like her arms don't match and her neck seems crooked. I can't help but wonder if maybe this child has been hidden away and on purpose, but I smile, and I turn back to what it is I'm doing.

On occasion, when I'm cleaning a home, I will see a child or sometimes a grandma or grandpa, someone who's home in the day same time as me and mostly we go our separate ways. They'll look at me a little and be surprised, but then they'll realize that we are not so different.

As I clean the counter, I try not to watch the girl in the mirror, but she's staring at me and it's hard not to feel like I should say hi or to let her know I see her.

I finish the counters, and I get out the shower scrubber, and I feel like as I turn my back to the mirror that I am leaving myself vulnerable to this child, but I tell myself that's craziness, and so instead I say something to stop the quiet.

"What's your name?"

I can hear the girl breathing, and it sounds like it's not the easiest thing for her to be doing, like all the spit in her mouth is getting in the way.

"What's your name, honey?" I ask it again, and it makes me wonder that if I'd baby-sat more or had any brothers or sisters, if I might be better at this.

I lean into the tub then because I've found a little stain in the enamel and so I try to scrub that sucker away but it's real resistant.

Then I feel something on the back of my head, and I turn real quick and it's the child, and she's patting my head with her little strange hands, her fingers are on my face, touching my cheeks and my nose, and I know in my heart that I should be sweet to this child, but I cannot stop my body from feeling like it's going to be sick.

"Marjorie!" The little old lady from downstairs is in the doorway from where the child came, and she's hustling into the bathroom and pulling the girl away from me. "I'm sorry, I thought she was napping."

I shake my head like it's nothing, and I watch as the lady pulls the girl back from where she came and slams the door behind her, and so the two of them are gone and I'm alone. The room smells clean like bleach and like cleaner, and I breathe it in, and I think about Beau and his handsome face, his teeth which are white from whitening strips and baking soda, and I smile even though what it is I'm feeling inside is not the happiest feeling I've ever felt.

Sometimes, when Beau has had a bad day, which is usually when someone has treated him unkind and called him a slur, he'll say, Sandy, you think we could change the channel? And what this means is that we are going to do something different that evening, but what it really means is that Beau does not want to live here anymore, that he's wanting to leave this town, and he is wanting to start a new life, and this is one of those times when I feel that little knot in my belly, and I take Beau's hand in mine, and I say, yes, Beau, but not yet. Please, Beau. Just not yet.

\*

There was only one time that me and Beau saw something Watching TV that I decided it might have been better if we hadn't of seen it, not only cause of what it was we saw, but because of how it made me and Beau have what I called later a misunderstanding. This was about six months ago, and it was one of the times Beau met me after cleaning a house, only this time it was later in the afternoon, close to five as I remember it.

I'd been cleaning the Jacksons' house who are a really nice family, where Mr. Jackson is a lawyer in town who always takes on cases for free when someone can't pay but has been wronged by something or other. I like to clean their house because it always feels so bright and safe inside, and it always smells like apples and cake even if the oven is what I'm cleaning, so I know there's nothing baking.

After I cleaned the house and Beau met me and we ate some burgers, me and Beau took a walk down the block as we do. Our plan was that we were going to check out the McGruders, as they have a great big window into their kitchen and once or twice before Beau and I have watched Mrs. McGruder and one time their son, Michael, make a smoothie or a milkshake, we couldn't tell which.

Me and Beau were standing by this big oak tree and looking in the window, which is easy to do because of the cover the oak gives when we're tucked up against it, and then we saw something strange happen. It was one of those things where at first you don't know if you're seeing something or not, but inside your stomach you feel a little uneasy like you've just eaten something not all the way cooked. Or like you've bit into a peach and it's just the slightest bit mealy.

All that we saw at first was Mr. McGruder and his daughter, Tammy, who we know not personally but because we know she sings in the church choir, and even though she's in middle school, they give her a solo almost once a month, so we've heard. The two of them were standing real close together, and what it looked like was that they were in a fight, only it looked like Tammy was the angry one, and Mr. McGruder was saying he was sorry or

that's how his face looked. Then Mr. McGruder put his hand
on Tammy's belly, only it was lower than that, it was like he was
touching her where he should not have been touching her, and
then he bent down, and he kissed her, only this was not the kind
of kiss that you see from a daddy to his daughter. It was a kiss that
had passion to it, the kind you see between two lovers, and it just
kept on going for what felt to us like the longest time. And afterwards when Mr. McGruder pulled away, so he wasn't touching
her anymore, Tammy's face looked sort of strange, like she was
angry and then she wasn't so angry, but she looked sad kind of,
like sick almost, and that's when Beau grabbed me and pulled me
away, so as we wouldn't get caught seeing what we'd seen.

When we were walking back to our cars, neither of us said
anything, which for us was something, and even though Beau and
I had sometimes talked about would we do something if we saw
something terrible, I think in seeing something, to me, it was hard
to know what to do. Then we were at the car, and Beau said,
Sandy, I think maybe it's time we write us a review, and what he
meant is that this is the kind of TV that cannot be just for us. We
have got to tell somebody.

Only I don't know that I felt the same way as him, and this is
how me and Beau got into the only real fight that we have ever
had. It lasted us almost a whole month, and in the end, I don't
know that either of us, me or Beau, came out just the way we
went in.

It started with neither of us knowing exactly what it was we
should do, but Beau saying maybe we should go to the police and
me saying I wasn't sure that that was the best of ideas.

And why not, Sandy, he asked me, and he was sucking at his
teeth like he does when he's worried and he doesn't know what
else it is to do.

And I said I didn't know but that would anyone believe us?

And he blinked at me, big eyed, and said, Sandy, who else do we tell? And I said to him, Beau, let's wait a day and see what makes sense tomorrow because we both know that sometimes time is the thing that heals, that makes things unright right.

And only the next day we still weren't sure what to do, so I said why don't we try and talk to him first that Mr. McGruder, and see if it was what we thought it was? And where would we talk to him? Beau asked me, and I could tell he was worried, and also he was a little scared, and so I said, why don't we do it at church? Because being in church might make him want to be honest? And besides Mrs. McGruder will be there too, and if we need to maybe we could talk to her also? And I could tell Beau still wasn't sure on account of how he knows how the church feels about people like him, which is most of why we stopped going a few years back, but he said, okay Sandy, and I could tell he trusted me then, and it wasn't that I ever wanted to let him down.

On Sunday morning we got there just before the service started and sat in the back row, and mostly I tried to ignore the sermon which was about sin and the blackness in our hearts, and other things I'd heard about before, things me and Beau used to roll our eyes about when we were little, but now we had to keep it hid because church is one place where you know everyone is watching someone else.

And then that's when we saw Mr. McGruder come in late to join his wife and son, and Tammy who was on the stage with the other choir folks, and Beau pushed his elbow into me, and we watched Mr. McGruder sit down next to his wife, her scooting over to make room and how he kissed her on the cheek, and squeezed Michael's shoulder, and how we could see this family, how they acted like a family, but we knew their ugliness, and it was up to me and Beau to set it right, to find out what was what and to help this child out if that's what needed doing and be the good and righteous ones in place of everyone else.

The service lasted what felt like forever, us not being used to it, and during it I just tried my best to keep my eye on Tammy who did sing so beautiful and even though I couldn't see Mr. McGruder's face, I could see his shoulders rise a little like he knew it was an angel's voice he was hearing, and how his wife would lean against him like all they were feeling was joy in what they'd been able to make.

After the service, me and Beau went outside to wait and I could feel a nervousness in my belly like being on the top of a rollercoaster, and Beau was tucked close beside me and smiling like he was just waiting for this to be over with, and meantime it was all these people we knew surrounding us, people we'd grown up with and their parents, and our neighbors, and everyone in their pastel best and stopping to say hello to me and Beau and how nice it was to see us after so long a time away and did this mean we were recommitting ourselves to Christ? And then Mr. McGruder slipped out, his wife smiling big beside him and Tammy and Michael trailing behind laughing with one another, and it made me sick to see it, but it also made me confused, if I'm honest. How happy they looked and how normal and maybe this was my first little bit of doubt.

But then Beau was pushing at me, because someone had pulled away Mrs. McGruder and left Mr. McGruder standing all alone and this was our chance. And then Beau was taking me by the arm, dragging me along, and we were in front of Mr. McGruder. Beau was shaking his hand and turning to me, and Mr. McGruder looked my way, but it was like he didn't see me or he didn't want to, the way his eyes went right over my face like I wasn't there, like I didn't even exist. And Beau was saying, sorry to bother you, and Mr. McGruder was looking over our heads at his wife and his daughter and his son, and Beau said, me and Sandy were hoping to talk to you, and Beau looked at me, and I opened my mouth like I was going to say something to this man, to put it right, and Mr. McGruder looked at me and this time he didn't look away, he stared at me, his eyes gawking, his lips turned down like he was disgusted at what he was seeing, and instead of saying something, I swallowed and I said nothing. I just shook my head, like there weren't any words in me, and there were always words, except for right then. And then Mr. McGruder was giving us a funny look, and shaking his head like we were losers and we were wasting his time, and he slapped Beau on the back, not friendly-like, but like he wanted it to sting, and he said to us, I need to get to my family, and I'll bet, said Beau, and Mr. McGruder frowned at him, but then shook his head again, like what do you know, you fag, and you freak, and then he was gone and it was me and Beau alone in front of the church we used to go to as kids.

And Sandy, what happened, Beau said to me, and his eyes were round and wet and white, like two saucers filled with milk. And I felt something like shame welling up in me, and I said, Beau, what if it isn't our place to say something after all, and what do you know that he would have even heard us, let us say it?

But we have to try, Beau said to me, if not with him, then with someone, and I looked down at my shoes, which were white sandals and all marked up with smudges, and I said, Beau, I don't know if there'd be any TV again, say the review were to come out, and they figure out what it is we've been doing.

And Beau gave me a look like I had never seen before, like a lovely thing made ugly, the way that frown took over his cheeks and his eyes and his big old mouth, and he said to me, he said, Sandy, if somebody had been watching you and your momma, back when you were little, don't you would have wished for them to say something? Don't you know what could have been stopped if somebody had been looking?

And what I thought was how could you, Beau? How dare you. But what I said was something else.

Maybe that was love, I said. Maybe that was love, and we are not people who can understand what a thing like that is to other people.

And even though I knew I was wrong, I could not help but feel the strangest, loneliest thing, like what if my own daddy had cared for me like that. What if anyone had? What would I be like then?

And that's when I realized that it's not too easy to understand other peoples' lives, even when you're seeing them honest and all. It's not so easy to know what to do. Beau, don't you see?

But Beau he just shook his head and he got that faraway look in his eye like he does when he's dreaming of anywhere but here, and he put his lips together like he was going to say, Sandy, but then he didn't, and he was quiet and we both were. And it was a month before Beau wanted to talk to me again, and then when he did, it was because he knew how sad I was to lose him, and it's important to have a friend like that, someone who is there for you no matter what because not everyone has that and I am the first to know it.

*

When I was little, just after my accident and back when my momma and my daddy were still in love, and we were a family and taking care of me and making me better was the most important thing, I remember thinking that if I could grow up to be anything, the thing I'd like most to be was a cartoon. One day I'd wake up, and I'd get out of bed and my hair and my hands and my nose and everything would be just like Disney or like Roger Rabbit, meaning I would be drawn but the real world would stay normal and like it is. Me as a cartoon would mean that anytime there was danger, I could just jump away at the last second and I could do anything, and everyone would love me because I was goofy and silly, but also I was kind and easy to know. Beau is the only one I ever told about this idea, and I think the reason we became such good friends is because when I did tell him, when he and his family moved to town and he was in my fifth-grade class, I told him and he said to me that he understood because he had always wanted to be a transformer, so that he could do anything and help anyone who ever needed help, and that if his mom needed to go to the store but she didn't have a car, he could transform and be the car that got her where she needed to go.

Sometimes I'll say, Beau, you know what the pleasure in Watching Television is? And he'll say, Sandy, what is the pleasure? And I'll say, Beau, the pleasure is knowing that all the time you're being you, there are all these other people being themselves, and they can't help it, so neither can we. And we'll nod at one another, like it's the truth, because it is. Sometimes, afterwards though, Beau will give me a look that says, Sandy, you know there are things we should have said we never did. Things we do that we could also not be doing. And so I'll say, Beau, you mind if we go ahead and unplug? And then we'll laugh, both of us, because it's true, sometimes you just don't want to know. Sometimes you just don't want to feel a thing.

*

On the Tuesday before the Fourth of July, me and Beau both have the day off from work, so we meet at Beau's to make to-go margaritas. Even though I'm the one that lives alone, we meet at

Beau's because that's where we can get the tequila because his daddy always has some extra lying around the house, and neither Beau nor I have yet turned twenty-one.

We make the drinks big and strong with lots of ice and triple sec, and then we take our walk downtown, and it's a secret that we're drinking them because you are not allowed to drink in public where we live or most places. This is a hot day, and we're wearing hats and shorts and our big blind folk sunglasses because it's been a while since we Watched TV in public like we used to do, on account of Beau's new schedule as assistant manager and him not having as much free time these days or that's what he says.

We find ourselves a good spot on the bench right between the playground where the kids go and the statue of Robert H. Hatton which right now is covered in a heck of a lot of bird shit. We sip our drinks and I feel the sweat drip down the backs of my knees, and I imagine it's a comfortable silence between the two of us. Sometimes Beau will say, Sandy, you want to press mute? And I'll say, yeah, Beau, and we'll just the two of us be quiet and think about what it is we have to be grateful for in this world.

Today, I watch as two little kids from the neighborhood take turns pushing each other on the merry-go-round. Then Beau nudges me, and I look over and there's a couple walking through the park. The guy is tall and skinny, and he's got red hair, and the girl he's with is real beautiful, I can tell even from far away, and she's wearing a sundress with tiny yellow flowers on it and the dress itself is purple and it's hazy or that's the sweetness of the drink.

The two of them, they're holding hands, and they're smiling in that way that it doesn't matter if someone is looking or isn't, if someone sees them in their private moment or doesn't, they're just the two of them and they know it and it's all that matters, it's all that's true and all that's good and right. And then as we keep looking at them, we see the man stop, and me and Beau watch as he puts his hand on the woman's back, the small of her back, and she just so barely leans into him, and it's nothing big and it's not like he's even thinking about it or what it means, but I can see it, Beau, and it just about breaks my heart, and I don't know why except for the fact that there is so much loveliness around us, Beau, despite anything else there is so much something to be felt, like a great big chandelier with each little light coming on. You know what I mean, Beau. Please tell me you know what I mean.

# Mouse

Mouse's bedroom is on the second floor, next to his sister's room and down the hall from his parents. The walls in Mouse's room are painted green. A pale green, almost lemony—or so it tastes in Mouse's mind at night when he lies in bed awake, thinking about the room. Lately, Mouse is not so good at sleeping. One time he got up and licked the wall to be sure. Yes, Mouse was right; lemon.

The taste has faded. The bedroom is far away. This new room is white. No, not white, it is dingy, if that's a color. Like a dingy igloo. Mouse wonders if mice live here in this dark, dingy igloo with its dingy walls. Mouse wonders about the other room, then forgets. He tries to picture these white walls as something other than white. He fails. There are no lemons here. None that Mouse has seen. Mouse needs to get rid of Horace, but Horace won't go away. Horace is sneaky. He's such a quiet guy most of the time. Most of the time when he isn't being loud. When he isn't cruel.

Mouse has done a bad thing. Four bad things. He would be sorry if he could remember what he did and why, but it is all blank. Still, Mouse says that he is sorry. Why, they ask him, why?

Mouse shrugs. He is here and he is sorry that he is here.

Here, they don't even know that his name is Mouse. Here, they call him Alan.

\*

"Mouse," his mother says his name. It's morning in the visiting room. Her face looks red and baggy. They sit at a little metal table in an empty room. The room is empty, except for the guard who pretends not to look at them.

His mother says his name again and he can tell that she's been crying. He wants to help her stop, but there's a buzzing sound, then a voice, and so he shrugs and puts his hand on hers. She cries even though he can tell crying is not what she wants to be doing.

"Dad's with Sam, Honey. He wanted to come but——" Her lips shake like a baby's, like a baby who won't stop crying and no one knows why.

"Am I coming home soon?" Mouse hears his voice and has almost forgotten its sound.

His mother takes his fingers in hers and he feels their warm fleshiness. She doesn't answer him, but her face grows even redder. The redness makes him think of berries, their sweet-sour taste.

"Oh, baby," she says.

I'm not a baby, thinks Mouse. I'm almost fifteen, thinks Mouse.

"Did you bring me anything to eat?" asks Mouse. The food here is not so good. He asks for macaroni and cheese and they, the men and women in the hallways, the guards, do not look him in the face.

"I can't," says his mother. "But I put some money in an account for you so you can buy candy and snacks. Does that make sense?"

Mouse shrugs. It sounds like his allowance. "When are you taking me home?"

He sees his mother look at him like he's an alien that she loves. "I don't know. I—" Her voice is high, strained. "I'm going to meet with the lawyer but, Honey—" she looks at him directly in the eyes. He wants to look away, but he doesn't. There is banging upstairs. He blinks. Stupid Horace. Mouse has company. "You need to help us understand this. Okay?"

Mouse nods. "Okay," he says. Okay? whispers Horace.

His mother smiles, she takes his hand again. She squeezes his fingers so tight he can feel her bones. "It'll be okay, honey."

Mama's boy, says Horace. Stupid bitch, says Horace.

Mouse swallows his spit. "Okay," says Mouse.

She'll die, says Horace. She won't believe a word you say.

\*

Inside Mouse's head there is a little place, some kind of pocket, a damp sucking hold. When he puts his fingertips to his skull and presses he cannot find the door. Then later, it opens on its own. Inside the place is where Horace hides out. Shhh. Quiet, Mouse. I am here.

This place is a new thing. For thirteen years there was just Mouse and his little sister, Sam, and his Mom and his Dad and Bruno, the Dalmatian, and Maxine, the tabby cat. And they were happy, and Mouse was happy and they lived in a house with a room for Mom and Dad and a room for Sam and a room for Mouse with green, lemony walls. Then, that Horace came around. Horace doesn't have his own room; he tells Mouse that they can share. Mouse does not trust Horace. How can someone invisible be so loud?

In this new room with the little sink and the metal bed, Mouse wondered if maybe Horace would not follow. But that was silly. Horace is inside. Oh, please leave me alone, thinks Mouse. You're a murderer, says Horace. And Mouse does not know how to respond.

You're lucky you have me, says Horace. No one likes to be alone, says Horace.

Mouse taps against the back of his head. Where are you? Hello?

It is true that Mouse does not like feeling lonely.

You're lucky I told you my name, says Horace.

I'm watching out for you. They want to hurt you. Don't you get it? Horace laughs.

Still some days, Mouse has never felt more by himself.

*

"Alan." The man in the gray suit says his name, and Mouse smiles at him, confused but also not so confused because he has seen this man before. "Alan? Where are you?" The man snaps his fingers, annoyed seeming.

Mouse sits up straighter in his chair. The chair is metal. Aluminum. Lots of things here are metal.

"This is serious. You did a very serious thing, you know that?" The man looks at him, then rubs a hand against his eyebrows.

"I know," says Mouse. He doesn't know. But when he acts sleepy or forgetful, they get mad. They give him more things to swallow.

"Do you know?" The man looks at him again. It's just the two of them in the room. The man has given Mouse a tiny cup of juice. Apple juice, what used to be his favorite. "Who am I?" the man asks him.

Mouse bites his lip. There is a part of him that wants to cry because he cannot remember the man's name. "My lawyer," he says. Horace laughs and Mouse glances up toward the ceiling then closes his eyes.

"Yes. I'm one of your lawyers. I'm Mr. Bailey." The man smiles at Mouse and Mouse likes the smile, but he knows it is the kind of smile that is only pretend.

"We're going to have you meet with someone, Alan. Another psychologist, like last week, remember?"

Mouse pulls on his lower lip. The skin is dry and cracking. He hears a woman singing but the sound is faint, so faint it might be coming from underwater.

"She's a really nice lady who specializes in working with children. She's coming on Friday, so two days from now. Will you be honest with her, Alan?"

Mouse nods because it's what Mr. Bailey, the man, wants. He hears Horace breathing loudly. The singing stops. I'm going to kill your mother, whispers Horace. We'll do it together, says Horace.

Mouse opens and closes his mouth.

"Yes?" asks Mr. Bailey.

He's a bully, says Horace. He's a liar. They all are.

Mouse shrugs. He shakes his head. "I'll be honest."

*

The big guard with the curly brown hair lets Mouse out to watch TV. His mother has told him that when the folks there know him better, he might be allowed to go watch TV whenever he wants. But for now, she says, the guard will keep him safe.

Mouse walks next to the guard, and the man is like a giant. He does not smile. He is not friendly.

One time, this guard, or Mouse thinks it was this guard, called

him an evil fuck. Mouse did not tell anyone, not his mom or anyone, but Horace knows because Horace was listening. Horace
thought it was funny. Mouse did not.

In the TV room, Mouse is not the only boy and the curly-
headed guard is not the only guard. The guard points to a seat. A
yellow chair in the middle of the room and Mouse sits and stares
up at the TV in the corner. Two other boys who look older than
Mouse sit at a table on the far side of the room. They half watch
the TV, but Mouse feels them looking at him, too. He leans forward to make himself as small as possible.

The curly guard goes to the side of the room to chat with
another guard Mouse has seen before. A blonde woman who does
not look like his mother. She is more orange and her breasts are
larger.

Mouse watches *The Fresh Prince of Bel-Air* on the TV. Carl-
ton shimmies and Mouse smiles. There is something about TV
that makes Mouse feel normal. Feel like he did when he was lit-
tler. When things seemed to look like what they were and before
things had a haze where what you saw wasn't really like what
was there. Now, the way it happens sometimes, Mouse can smell
ketchup. But there's no ketchup anywhere that he can see. He
licks his lips. The smell remains.

The credits flash on the screen and Mouse is sad to have
missed so much of the episode. Horace is sleeping, and Mouse
knows these moments are important ones to enjoy. There is
another quieter voice he can hear, but it's just the singing woman
and she's still new to Mouse, so he is unsure whether she's like
Horace or maybe she is someone who will be kinder.

The six o'clock news begins. Two people sit behind a desk.
To Mouse they look like the cardboard cutouts of Luke and Leia
from his bedroom. He drops his eyes to the floor. The news is boring. It does not distract in the good way that TV does.

The boys at the table start to shout and point and a guard walks toward them. "That's him!" The taller boy with a thin mustache points from Mouse to the TV. Mouse moves his eyes slowly to see but they feel heavy now. Distant.

The TV shows a picture of children standing with candles. The children cry and touch one another. Hugging. Then the TV shows a boy who looks like Mouse.

Look at the screen, says Horace. They're telling your story, says Horace.

There is laughter and shrieking and a woman's voice he cannot recognize, and Mouse puts up his hands to his ears and shakes his head. Your story, thinks Mouse. Not mine.

"You're a fucking psycho!" The mustache boy stands a few feet away from Mouse. He points his finger wildly at Mouse, and Mouse sees the tip of his finger like it's a wand.

Mouse looks at his hands then at the face on the screen. Is it his face? No, this isn't his face. He tries to recognize the kids whose pictures are being shown but he cannot. It doesn't make sense. I told you, says Horace. It needed to be done, says Horace.

The lady guard stands between Mouse and the boys in the room. "Alan. We need to take you back to your room."

Mouse watches her lips move, but they don't make sense. Someone screams to the far left but he can't see them. He turns and turns. But he can't see them.

"What are you looking at?" The lady guard purses her lips at him in disgust. She looks at him the way his mother looked the first time he saw her in here. Before she remembered who he was. That he was Mouse.

On the TV, Mouse sees his father. A person with a camera sticks a microphone in his father's face and his father shields his eyes like the sun is too bright.

The lady guard touches his shoulder, prompting him to stand. Mouse stands.

On the TV, his father says how sorry he is. He apologizes. Mouse cannot remember his father sounding this way. Mouse shrugs and looks away. That man is not his father.

He allows himself to be led by the lady guard.

Whatever they feed you tonight, Mouse, don't eat it.

*

Not every day is the same. This is something Mouse has realized. One day, he and Horace wake up at the same time. The next, it is just Mouse. Or Mouse and someone else whose name he does not yet know. Horace had warned Mouse he would bring friends. They are coming, Mouse. Soon, they will be here.

The not knowing reminds Mouse of Sam, his little sister. She'd jump on him to wake him up on weekend mornings for pancakes. She was loud and sometimes she was funny. But she only woke him up sometimes. Not every day. He hasn't seen Sam since they moved him here. He misses her a lot. He wonders if she remembers that he's her brother.

It was Horace who told Mouse where to find the gun. It was Horace who told him to steal it from the neighbor's den. To break in when they were at church with the hidden key and take the gun and hide it under his bed. I'll rape your sister, Mouse. Don't think I won't.

Mouse used to cry when Horace was mean. Now Mouse understands that this is just Horace being Horace. Some people are cruel sometimes. They cannot help it. It is the only way they know how to be.

In this new room, at night, Mouse likes to lie on his back in the dark and think about igloos. He pulls the thin blanket tightly over his chest, but he leaves one arm out to feel cold. If he leaves the arm out of the blankets all night, maybe it will get frostbite and fall off.

If he had only one arm maybe everyone would leave him alone. Maybe no one would think he was a bad guy. He'd just have the one arm after all. He would be harmless.

Mouse is ready to go home. Please, thinks Mouse. His stomach rumbles.

I heard that, says Horace. I'm trying to sleep, says Horace.

Mouse squints his eyes as hard as he can till his eyes hurt with the pressure. Then opens them.

There is never any relief.

*

On Thursday, Horace tells Mouse that he's his best friend. I care about you, Mouse, says Horace. I don't want you to fail on your mission.

When Horace tells him this, Mouse feels a warm feeling in his chest, like ice melting. Mouse smiles, embarrassed. He thinks about his best friend, Thomas, from elementary school.

Mouse and Thomas's favorite thing was to dig in Thomas's backyard and one summer they dug a hole deep as a grave, six feet, and they took turns lying down in the dirt at the bottom and feeling the potato bugs crawl on their skin.

Sometimes at night Mouse can feel little feet walking on the back of his neck, tickling his hair with their weight. Horace tells Mouse this is how he shows his love. Can you feel that Mouse, asks Horace. A voice sings rockabye baby, and Mouse feels hot all over.

At lunch one day in seventh grade, at their new middle school, Mouse asked Thomas if he wanted to try digging an even deeper hole. That maybe they could reach the earth's core if they kept going. They sat with three other boys, boys that were new friends of Thomas's, who played with him on the basketball team.

At first Thomas didn't answer. Then he asked Mouse if he knew he was a baby cunt.

One of the new boys laughed and Mouse could feel something wet on his cheek, and then another boy told him maybe he should bury himself alive. Thomas looked embarrassed. Then he laughed.

Mouse could not remember what happened next, but he knew Thomas was no longer his best friend.

Sometimes Horace will tickle the back of Mouse's neck and Mouse knows that this is Horace being friendly, even if it makes Mouse feel nervous. Here comes the song, thinks Mouse.

I am the only one that loves you, says Horace.

What have I done, thinks Mouse.

Cradle and all, whispers Horace.

\*

"Tomorrow is important, sweetheart. Do you hear me?" His mother's lipsticked mouth gapes at him.

"Alan, answer your mother."

This time, Mouse is with his mother and father. This is the second time his father has come to visit. But this time, his father has started to call him Alan.

You're not a kid, his father said a moment before while his mother spoke to the guard outside in the hallway. He watched his mother through the thick glass. She looked so soft and foreign. No more nicknames, Alan. You do a grownup fucking thing, you're a grownup.

Mouse is dead, thinks Mouse.

"Tomorrow is important," Mouse says to his mother, to his father. He smiles and blinks and tries to sit up straight in his chair.

"And why is it important, Honey?" his mother asks.

They are in the room with the metal table. He sits across from them like at a restaurant. Only Sam isn't next to him. His father's chair is pushed away slightly. His father keeps glancing at the guard. At his own shoes. Like he might get sick just being here.

"I'm meeting with another psychologist," says Mouse. "A lady." He can hear himself sounding normal. All morning he has been alone. And he has been practicing sounding like himself.

"Good. Yes, that's right, Sweetie," his mother smiles at him. Nods.

Mouse smiles too. He folds his hands on the metal table. He wants to ask about going home but he hesitates. Then he shrugs. "After I talk to her—will we be going home?"

His mother frowns. She glances toward the guard then at his father shaking his head. His father puts his hands against his forehead. The shaking stops.

"I just—" his father looks at him. His lips curl back in pain or is it disgust. "I just. I don't understand this. What did we do?" He looks at Mouse's mother. Then he looks at Mouse. His eyes are black and angry. "How could you do this? What kind of person are you?" His father puts his hand to his face, his eyes. He starts to cry.

Mouse feels a thing. An electric spark in his groin that travels to his belly then his brain. He licks his lips to stop the feeling of electricity. To cool it.

"John, please." His mother puts an arm around his father then reaches her other hand to Mouse. To comfort him, he knows.

His father sits up and looks at him. His graying hair frames his face. He looks old. He jabs a finger at Mouse. "No," he pushes Mouse's mother's arm away. "If you're crazy, tell us you're crazy. I mean—you murder these kids, and you act like you have no idea what's going on. What is the matter with you?" His father stands up and the guard walks toward the table.

His father shakes his head and puts a hand up to his eyes. He turns to Mouse's mother. "I told you I shouldn't have come. I can't. I just can't."

Mouse feels himself turning invisible. He looks at his hands, but he cannot see the blood, but there is so much blood there. He knows it. The singing has started. The banging has started.

You fucking say my name—Horace makes the sound of throats being slit. The woman sings loud. So loud. Down down down. Now, she screams. It is nonsense. All of it. He cannot hear his mother.

His mother kneels beside him, puts her hands on his shoulders and he feels himself looking wildly from side to side. It is all so much. It is all too much.

He hears his father leave the room but he can't even see him now, everything is blurring and the screaming is all around him. It is high-pitched and ugly and sad.

His mother hugs him. Her arms, so fleshy, she tries to suffocate him. He cannot see her eyes, but he knows they're black, too. Who is this woman?

He pushes her away. If he could kill her too, he would. Horace laughs and laughs.

"Leave me alone," Mouse shouts. "Leave me the fuck alone." He closes his eyes. He closes them tighter and tighter and tighter.

*

First, Mouse, you will get the guns. Pretend you are sick and stay home from church. Your parents will believe you, Mouse. They love you. But if you do not listen, they will stop loving you. It is what people do.

Your neighbor keeps the guns in his den. The bullets are in the kitchen in the junk drawer. They are gone on Sundays from 9:30 in the morning to 1:30 in the afternoon. Find the key in the fake rock. Do not let anyone see you. Put the guns in a backpack and put them under your bed. Do not tell anyone anything or they will have to die also. Be a good kid, Mouse. Don't be a rat.

When your parents get home pretend to feel better. Act normal. Don't be a fucking loser, Mouse. Act like you are someone worthy of love.

On Monday, you will go to school early. Walk there. Tell your parents you are getting a ride. But walk there. Go to the bathroom nearest the cafeteria where most people have their lockers. Load the bullets into the gun the way your grandad showed you last Thanksgiving. The way we've seen on TV. Don't make any extra noise. If you make any extra noise, I will know and I will run your father's car off the road. He'll die, Mouse. That is the price you'll pay.

Tell fucking no one.

Wait till four minutes before the first bell. Walk out with the gun loaded. Begin firing as soon as you reach the first bank of lockers. Hit as many of them as you can. Remember how they treated you, Mouse. These are not innocents. They get what they deserve, same as you.

Aim for the middle of the bodies. Ignore the screams, Mouse. Ignore the blood, Mouse. This is God's work, Mouse. This is what you have to do to stop from dying.

But why, asks Mouse. But why. But why but why but why—I already told you, Baby cunt. Because I say so. Because they don't deserve you. Because you must prove yourself worthy. Because how else will you get me to go away.

*

The walls of this room are not as dingy as Mouse first thought. This is because what Mouse thought was dinginess are messages on the walls. Mouse cannot read them, but they are there. There are no vents in his room, but still somehow, the wall has found a way to show these messages. If only Mouse could speak their language. If only Mouse could turn off the cameras.

Mouse lies asleep at night and tries to freeze off his left arm. Then his right arm.

Mouse chews the pillow till it is wet with his spit and then the wetness makes his cheeks cold and he wants to ask his mom for another pillow but she is not there.

Sometimes, when Mouse does sleep and he does dream he wakes up and he sees blood and he sees faces and he sees mouths with braces and the teeth are bleeding and the eyes are bleeding and Thomas is there looking so sad and Mouse has to wrap his arms around his body to not explode into tiny pieces of Mouse because he deserves to die so badly and he is evil and he knows it's true. Everyone does.

Sometimes in these moments, Horace is there and he's laughing and he's telling Mouse about the practical joke he pulled. About this hilarious prank where he got this stupid kid to kill four people at his school. To steal some guns and then shoot up some other kids. And then he laughs and laughs and Mouse feels vomit in his throat. In these moments Mouse wants to cut out the part of his brain where Horace lives. One of these days, Mouse will steal a knife from the cafeteria. Even though they are plastic. With enough tries, it might work.

Horace, I'm coming for you, thinks Mouse. Down down down, the lady sings.

*

"Hello, Alan. My name is Ms. Hodges. I'm the doctor that Mr. Bailey, your lawyer, told you about."

Mouse smiles and nods and shakes the woman's hand. She has black hair that is tightly curled and big glasses and she smells good, like cookies and flowery hand soap.

"How are you feeling today, Alan?"

"I feel okay." Mouse smiles and rubs at an itchy spot on his nose.

"That's great, Alan." The doctor smiles like his grandmother used to before she died. "So, what's it been like since you've been living here? Has that been hard?"

Today, Mouse is not in the empty room with the metal table. He is in another room, one with yellow walls and a couch and a big chair. Mouse sits on the couch. The doctor sits in the big chair. She holds a notebook and a pencil, but she holds them in a way that shows they are not that important. Mouse is important.

"It's been okay. I miss my room and stuff." Mouse hasn't heard from Horace or the singing lady or anyone else the whole morning. It is like they are hiding because they're afraid of this lady. But the lady is so nice. Why would they be afraid.

"It's definitely hard to live in a new place without your mom and your family. I bet you miss them a lot."

Mouse nods. He does miss them a lot.

"Do you understand why you're here, Alan?"

Mouse begins to shake his head then shrugs. "It's because of what I did."

The doctor nods. "And what is that? Is it okay if I ask you to tell me? In your own words?" She smiles. Her mouth opens slightly.

Go ahead, Mouse. Tell her.

Mouse shuts his eyes. He has come.

"It's okay, Honey. You can tell me anything."

"I—" Mouse puts his hand over his left eye. "I hurt some people."

Liar. Liar. Dog's on fire.

The doctor nods. Mouse watches her through his right eye. Then he switches hands and watches her through his left eye, covering the right.

"Do you know why you hurt them, Alan?" The doctor looks at Mouse and he can feel her looking at him like he is a person and not like he is a monster.

He puts his hands in his lap.

"I don't know."

The doctor nods and smooths out the material of her slacks. The room is quiet. He can feel the doctor waiting for him. Giving him time.

Well, Mouse. Are you going to tell them?

"Do you remember what you were feeling before it happened?" Mouse sees the doctor's glasses and how the light from above shines through them. Like lasers.

"Yeah," says Mouse.

"What was it like?"

Mouse closes his eyes again. Not like when he is trying to disappear but like when he is trying to remember.

You little cunt. You think you can tell them about me?

"I felt scared."

"Why did you feel scared?"

Mouse digs his fingernails into the meat of his palm. "Because of what I had to do."

I'll tear your throat out. I'll burn your mother's face off.

"Had to do?" The doctor's voice is even, calm, like a lullaby almost.

Mouse pushes his nails down farther, harder. He can imagine

blood on his palm but it might not be there. He can't know if he doesn't look.

"I had to do it."

I thought you cared about me, Mouse. I thought we were friends.

"Who told you you had to do it, Alan? Did someone or something tell you to do this?"

I'll rip Sam's body open. I'll make you do it. They already know what kind of scum you are. You don't deserve to live.

Mouse opens his eyes, relaxes his fingers. He looks at his palms. There is no blood, only half moon marks.

Mouse nods. He looks at the doctor and she looks at him in the eye. His eyes are black.

"Yes."

The doctor leans forward. She looks at Mouse, she nods. "Who, Alan? Who made you do it?"

Mouse leans back. Shrugs.

"His name is Mouse."

*

In bed at night, Mouse imagines a world where he is safe. Here is a place where Horace is not allowed. Here is a place where songs are only sung by people he can see. Here is a place where all of the candy and the corn dogs and the macaroni are safe to eat and Mouse eats and eats and he and Sam hold hands and watch the killer whales swim overhead and the sun doesn't set, it is always bright and there is always someone, his mother, waiting with open arms.

In his bed, at night, Mouse knows that time has ceased to pass. Mouse knows that he has ended lives.

He knows that Horace is there, waiting, hiding, but always there.

Mouse must keep the secret. He's the only one who can keep them safe. He will wait and wait and wait till this is over.

Goodnight, Mouse, thinks Mouse.

In his bed, Mouse closes his eyes. He waits. The dark room gets darker.

Knock knock.

The bed creaks. The walls move. The cold air gets colder.

Mouse opens his eyes. "Who's there," says Mouse.

Knock knock, says the voice.

Mouse touches his forehead. He makes a fist and then relaxes it.

There is no use.

Knock knock. Knock knock.

Hello, says Mouse. "Hello."

# Our Daughters Whose Blood

On weekdays, at the lunching hour, the skate park is often my home. I sit, a quiet passenger, the contents of my pastrami sandwich rest gently on my lap. My dark hair slicked back with pomade and the dint of sun flashing bright upon my polished loafers. The children who skate do not see me in my trappings of middle age, for they are thigh deep in their own slick youth, blinded by the innocence they inhabit. The acts these adolescents inflict into the air make me breathless as their knee bones bend and the arcs of their young, lithe bodies will them into a god space.

I cannot speak when I am here; it is my church. These children who ransom their bodies against the bite of asphalt, their invincibility, a truth, a promise, a gift, until the fall, its own truth inevitable with time. I hold my breath, I pray. The vision of my daughter as she was eclipses my sight and, briefly, my salvation appears. With the skater's spilled blood, I see our shared failure, and then, only then, can I return to work.

I man the counter. The clothes whir past overhead, and I and they are made clean. In our community, Gregor Cleaners is a household name and for good reason. We take the stains of others and purge the filth. Three stores within a ten-mile radius means that much of the business of cleaning is done by us. Our franchise is the most lucrative and for this I feel some pride. The children of the park do not know, but I know. We are mostly unexceptional beings. We are mostly nothing in this life.

At six, I tell Rodrigo that I'm leaving and ask him to close the store. I originally had dinner plans with Veronica, my girlfriend, but she has had to cancel them on account of her daughter, Annie, who claims to be ill with symptoms of the flu. Instead we have agreed that I will come over once the child is asleep. Veronica is my girlfriend, a curvaceous woman with dyed black hair and wide, red lips whose weight sits prettily on her frame. We met online. I, a former doctoral candidate in classics cum franchisee and she, an emergency room nurse. She is a delightful woman, smart and empathetic, and so I date her despite the daughter: a spiteful teenager, nothing like my Aileen would have been had she had the chance.

When I arrive at Veronica's home, just after ten in the evening, the daughter is fast asleep, drugged with Benadryl, laughs Veronica as she opens the door to my quiet knock. On the blue couch in the family room, we sip glasses of merlot and Veronica nestles beside me. We watch the local news and Veronica laughs at the repartee between the weatherman and the anchor. During a commercial for Lysol spray, my Veronica sighs, and in the sigh I read the history of what has been lost. The other lives once begun, now abandoned and this here, her truth. This sigh, familiar, as its company I myself have known.

I place my arm around her to demonstrate security and soon we are both readying for our move to the bedroom. Our lovemaking is pleasurable if not subdued. We each know the orgasm to be reached, the journey a direct one.

Postcoitally, I allow myself to be submerged, lulled by her soft flesh, or so I imagine it. My own rather knobby frame engulfed in the warmth of her being and the animal power of the body which can create. I sleep best when she is by my side. This night is no exception; my dreams come easy.

The call arrives in early morning when Veronica is still asleep, her flesh emitting a gentle hum of heat. I do not recognize the sound at first, but slowly the ring pierces into the dream that I am having, a good dream where I lay splayed on an orange beach towel licking barbeque sauce from my fingers.

I answer the mobile phone, slipping into boxers and navigating my way out of Veronica's room and into the kitchen. The house does not stir; her child is still asleep.

The voice on the other line is gruff, a permanent smoker's hack and it's my turn to sigh.

"Hello, Marilyn."

"Well, you answered. I'm impressed."

"And?"

"It's Aileen."

"Right."

"Remember her?"

"Marilyn."

"It's worth asking."

"So, what is it?" In the background of the call I hear the sound of slurping like a wet smacking of oversized lips.

"I need you to watch her tomorrow." The slurping lets up and now I hear the inhale of Marilyn's breath, perhaps filtered through a Marlboro Ultra-Light.

"Right."

"Can you do it? I need this. I got to go out of town—just for the night."

My left hand draws a letter "A" on the Formica countertop. In the far room, I hear the sounds of Veronica waking, a shifting of floorboards beneath a body's weight. I don't speak.

"Malcolm. I swear. She's still yours, too."

"Where are you going?"

"My mother's. She's not doing so good." I can picture this mother. A small, grim woman with unnaturally large, doughy hands and the smell of canned green beans lingering in her wake.

"Huh. Why not take her with you?"

"Just please help me out here."

"And this is why I argue for the Home." I hear movement again. A flushing toilet and the subsequent water coming from the sink. The daughter's room is silent, but in moments Veronica will appear, flush with the day's promise before her.

"So you'll get her? I wouldn't ask if there was any other person, but I can't just drop her anywhere you know that. The aides won't do an overnight this short notice."

I hear Marilyn's voice and its once sexy rasp now a rattle of impending cancers. Our infrequent conversations focusing solely on Aileen, the ongoing tether that is our daughter.

"I'll come by tomorrow. When?"

"It's got to be before 8 a.m. I got to leave on time."

I acquiesce and the call is dead on the line. Veronica enters the kitchen, and she looks to me with raised eyebrows.

I shake my head. "Marilyn."

My Veronica purses her lips knowingly and comes forward to give me a half embrace. Her thin, yellow robe is parted just barely and the warmth of her stomach and breasts almost eclipse the dread blooming in my veins.

"What'd she want?" she asks, her head cradled against my chest.

"Money. Something about a house repair."

Veronica emits a low grunt, her animal sound of protection

for me. Her own husband, an absentee figure whose seeming aim in marrying her was to break her spirit and ruin her interest in live music, was at first, for us, a point of mutual psychic unburdening. My Marilyn and her Hamilton ("Hammy" to his friends) were the scourges who in their neglect enabled Veronica and I to find solace with one another.

Veronica shakes her head and pulls away to begin brewing a pot of Folgers coffee. While the coffeepot percolates, she begins the process of knocking on the daughter's door to awaken her, and I take this moment to shower and ready myself for the hours to come. I have not told Veronica the full story of Aileen, though I want to, I do.

The shower water is warm and the soap slips between my hands as I lather my frame. Aileen. The word tastes almost alien in my mouth and rightfully so. It's been six months since I opted out of her regular care. Five years since she was herself. Aileen.

Despite the water's heat, a shudder runs through my innards, and I finish my shower quicker than normal. Shrouded in my towel, I enter Veronica's bedroom with its thick carpet and abundant decorative pillows.

At Gregor Cleaners, the uniform I've chosen for myself and my employees is a white polo shirt and green, khaki pants. I feel there's something vaguely militaristic about the combination of colors, and yet the crisp white polo connotes a sense of class.

As of late, I've taken to keeping an extra set of clothes at Veronica's and it is into these vestments that I change. I am careful to keep the door fully closed as two weeks ago an ajar door led to an awkwardly close call between the daughter and my naked backside.

What Veronica knows is only that Aileen exists. That my once baby girl is now vegetative, living in a facility in another city near her mother. The facility and the distance, small white lies. I do not speak of her, and Veronica, in sensing my pain, does not ask questions. It is easy to elide that which lurks at the periphery of our daily doings. It has become easier for me to pretend Aileen is gone.

Dressed, I head into the kitchen to drink coffee and bid my Veronica goodbye for the shop waits as does the day. Veronica's child, newly risen sits gruffly at the table, her mouth sloshing cereal and her cellphone grasped tightly in her left hand. I nod her way, say "Feeling better?" and she rolls her eyes in response. Veronica busies herself with Tupperware, preparing her lunch and the lunch of her child. I kiss Veronica's forehead, the tenderest part of a woman, and tell her that I will ring later on. We had plans to spend the weekend together, but now they must be interrupted, a reason for which I will need to supply this afternoon. She squeezes my hand, the Morse code of her love for me and hands me a granola bar. I depart the house.

Arriving at Gregor's just after seven-thirty, I find Claire greeting a regular, Ms. Newman, whose collection of embroidered jackets alone allows our business to thrive. Ordinarily I would linger at the counter to gossip and flirt, but today I feel the egg of tomorrow hatching in my belly. I head back to my office to look at paperwork and peruse the faded Virgil who lingers still in this new monied life. The work I do a sacrifice for the child I must provide for—the cost of which, unlike her mind, is ongoing.

I am told that Aileen is a miracle of science. A child who should be dead, whose once waterlogged brain should require the use of breathing tubes and stomach pumps, and yet she exists as a standalone. A human whose physical body functions independently but whose mind is an erasure of being. If she speaks it is nonsensical. She will not eat or clothe herself without guidance. There are fits like a seizure of rage against the life she leads and sometimes a stream of drool will flow like she is a machine left on by accident. And yet her face looks like that of a normal girl, a teenager of seventeen with thin, brown hair and eyebrows perfectly curated by her mother's hand. The photos of her I see online, the offshoot of a reckless perusal of her mother's Facebook, are enough to keep me distant. She is the specter of the child I once loved; she is not her.

A bell interrupts my thoughts and I leave the back office to see who has entered the shop. Claire helps a series of customers and I step in to offer my assistance. The register clangs its happy noise and the clothes in their plastic sheaths rustle and sway, and I am transported to a better place.

At noon I dial Veronica, anxious to set the lie in motion that will free me for the following day's trial. I explain the tickle in my throat, the heat beginning to lick my forehead and her murmurs of compassion let me know the illness I have feigned is satisfactory. I agree to call her the following day with a report of my hopeful good health that will allow us to resume our time together.

I leave the shop shortly after the call with plans to pick up some lunch, a burrito today's calling. As I drive, I find myself led to the familiar destination of my lunchtime hours, the Hoobernath Skate Park. I pull into the parking lot. The park itself is adjacent to a green space featuring a manmade pond with a bridge that crosses over and a gazebo where women with small infants seem to congregate on sunny days. The usual rush of anticipation doesn't meet me, and I cannot will myself to leave the car. Instead, I watch through my rearview mirror as a young father leads a small child on a tiny bike down in the direction of the park. I watch them, the father walking behind as the boy, helmeted and decked in pads, cycles before him. They disappear

beyond my view, and I continue to stare at the blank pavement
where their bodies were moments before.

I put the car in reverse and head to Hector's where I order
a chicken burrito to go and subsequently consume the meal in
eight large bites in the sanctuary of my office. The afternoon pat-
ters onward. Clothes are made clean. Phones are answered. But-
tons are sewn and mended. The day is as any other.

In the evening, I return to my condo, a two-bedroom garden
apartment with views of a small patch of trees and a field where
dogs are led to run. Veronica calls to check on my well-being,
and we speak for several minutes about our days and the daughter's latest episode in cruelty. I admire this Veronica who can take
the grief given her and meet it with a wet salve of kindness and
love.

"Be sure to get lots of sleep—I'd love to have you healthy by
tomorrow. The flea market will be open, and I was thinking of
looking for a new piece to restore."

"I'm hopeful it's just a passing bug."

"Well I hope so. I'm sure it's us that got you sick."

"It was worth it if that's true." We laugh and make plans to
speak the following day. I say goodnight, willing her presence to
stay beside me still.

In the emptiness of my bachelor home, I recline. The couch's
pillow beneath my head and a warm aperol in my left hand. The
television, on silent, an easy companion for this night. And yet,
my mind, active in its unrest. When I was a younger man, how
could I not have basked always in the privilege of my suburban
glow?

Mine was the life made from fish sticks and duvet covers, rides to green places and lakesides where hot dogs sizzle and children run splashing from the gooey feeling beneath their feet, a life of porch swings and sheets rumpled from use and deposited in the laundry hamper made from woven twine purchased on sale from a discount store. All of it the stuff of envy, the quotidian beauty that only an ingrate would not yearn for daily. A life flat-lining on a suburban street is not the wreckage that a youth might paint it, rather the secure harness we vest ourselves in when leaping from a plane. The risk exists inevitable so we must wrap ourselves in normalcy when we might. Our daughters whose blood could just as easily not spill might and so we are led to believe that this is what we augured when we asked for a life of highs and lows. We who asked for a life of passion and feeling and instead we find this, the lows unspeakably far below the surface. Our depth a place of no return. The boring stuff of suburbs a wet dream.

In the waning light that passes through my sliding doors, I make a Stouffers lasagna and fall asleep watching reruns of *Cheers*, my dreams punctuated by the semifrequent greetings of "Norm!" Tonight, my sleep is not quite sound, yet dreamless.

The morning comes earlier than most and rising at six-thirty I brew coffee and sit in my boxer shorts on the couch waiting for the time that I should shave, shower, and head to Marilyn's. At this moment I picture Veronica, the soft clinging fabric of her nightgown and the mouth partially ajar in sleep, perhaps a single bubble of saliva glistening on her full lower lip.

I leave the house at seven-thirty, anxious to be on time but hesitant to arrive too early thus prolonging the forthcoming episode. The drive is a decent one, and I cannot ignore the loveliness of the streets, sun-dusted at this early hour. Marilyn lives in

a small, shotgun house on the far edges of town, yet near to the
home we once dwelled in together. I park on the street in front of
the house. The grass, a few inches too tall for comfort, and the
front porch empty, but for the wooden swing and the pail of cigarette butts, the evidence of Aileen's mark on Marilyn's psyche.

I knock twice and Marilyn answers the door, a stuffed sea lion
clenched in her left hand. Her face is thin, the nose an angular
hook and the familiar smoker's lines form a morbid halo around
her mouth.

"Malcolm. Thank you for coming."

I nod, stepping into the house, its living room filled with haz-
ily remembered furniture and thrift store art. "Where is she?"

Marilyn points toward the sofa in the far corner of the room.
A figure I hadn't noticed is positioned with its head facing the
closest wall. The body has the appearance of an action figure,
placed and then forgotten, left behind for a more inviting or
immediate thrill.

"She's been good today so far. No fits or anything, so I'm
hopeful the transition won't be too jarring for her."

"Right."

"Lately Teresa, the aide, watches her during the week and
then I got her on the weekends and evenings. It's been a little
while, I know, but you remember the basics, yeah?"

"I do."

"Well. It's like riding a bike." Marilyn laughs once, a staccato
beat.

"Has there been any change? In ability, I mean."

"It's hard to say. You know me, I see her in there. So I see her
growing up, but, I don't know. You tell me. I'm around her so
much it's hard to tell what's new."

"Right."

"Listen. Don't just camp her out at your place all day. She

likes to ride around. Sometimes we just go for long drives and I think it calms her."

I watch Aileen as she sits there, almost mannequin-like in her stillness. The room smells faintly of lipstick and baby powder.

"And Malcolm. She likes it when you talk to her, so please, treat her like she's there."

"What time do I drop her back tomorrow?"

"I'll give you a call when I'm on the road but by early afternoon at the latest I'd say." Marilyn sighs, and I watch as she walks over toward Aileen, holds out her hand, prompting the girl to stand. She leads the child toward me and I am struck by the new thinness of her face. The baby fat dissolved and this vacant young woman left in its place. Her lips press together and from them emerges a drop of liquid that rests briefly before dripping down her chin. The eyes do not meet mine and appear fixed on a spot within a dimension that I and her mother are not privy to. If she were to have been born this way, the facial disfigurement would be God's clue toward her insides, but here the horrible joke lies in the distance between this teenage beauty and the emptiness within.

Marilyn squeezes the girl in a tight hug and hands me a large diaper bag filled with things related to her care. Though it's been months since we had any regular contact, the contents of the bag are still familiar and still invoke the same feeling of retching disassociation in my bones. I take the girl's shoulder and with Marilyn beside me, we lead her to my car and buckle her securely in the front seat.

"Call me if you need anything. I love you, sweet baby." She leans in kissing the girl's brow to which the child does not react, and as we pull away, I see Marilyn shudder and pull a cigarette from a pack on the porch railing. We leave her in her cloud of smoke.

\*

It happened on a Sunday afternoon in late summer. The sort of day that colors itself sepia in its promise of fragility and melancholy. The good kind of sad as Marilyn and I used to refer to it, back in the days when we had the privilege of romanticizing sorrow. The events themselves are slippery, an eleven-year-old girl, a lake, a swimming contest, several cases of beer, and the girl, a good swimmer by any account. She must have gotten tired is all—that's all we have. When we knew she was drowning, it was our neighbor Frank who was the first to go after her, his own days as a competitive swimmer only a decade lapsed. Her body dragged to shore then resuscitated, then an ambulance, hospital, and the rest, slippery. The thing I remember most is Frank's wife, Jackie, shaking her head and holding my arm and saying, "For how long she was out—you all should be careful with your hope." And then Marilyn spitting on the ground at her feet, not speaking, but pulling me with her to protect and save our little girl.

I turn the radio on to an Oldies station which is what Aileen often requested as a child. Her placid face now turned to the window, accepting the intermittent strips of sunlight and shadow without reaction. I find myself driving up and down neighborhood streets, each house a refuge for some individual, a place to be entombed in platitudes and thus made safe. Runners jog with dogs on leashes. Strollers are pushed. The radio sings and the child beside me quietly gurgles.

"Aileen."

There is no response.

"This is your father, Aileen."

The teenaged child remains silent, her hands limp and open-faced on her lap as if she were awaiting a coin or heavenly bestowal.

"You and I used to be close."

The statement is not untrue, but the chasmic distance between then and now renders it a falsehood in my ears.

I turn the radio louder and Little Richard enters the car between us. May we lose ourselves in this familiar noise with its mention of beguiling girls. The road lined with strip malls. The signs like so many individual attempts at being.

I pull into a parking lot and let the car idle in front of a Wings to Go. Though the store is not yet open, the smell of fried meat leeches into the late April air. I turn to look at the being beside me. Her green eyes belie the missing sentience in their glassy pallor. "Your mother really loves you." The quiet like an animal, a waiting beast. "Do you know what that means?"

"Can you describe the shape of your mother's love?" Square? Triangle? Heart?

I turn down the radio and let silence fill the car, listening for any sound of life. None is produced, so I roll down her window and turn off the car.

"I need to make a phone call."

Leaving the car, I stand ten feet away, watching the girl carefully for signs of movement.

"You feeling any better?" Veronica's voice an immediate kindness registered in my reptile center.

"A bit, though sleep is pretty much all that sounds good. This one really knocked me out."

"I'm sorry sweetheart, I hate that I gave it to you."

"I'll survive. How are you and Annie getting along?" I kick a fast-food wrapper that blows past in the breeze.

"Oh, all right. She swore she was better so I let her sleep over at a friend's last night."

"There's some relief."

Veronica laughs and I dwell in that sweet chord. We talk a

moment more. I provide a cough for authenticity and the call ends with her well wishes.

Reentering the car, I find myself slick with sweat and with no idea of where I might head for relief. The girl must be fed and changed, and the threat of this reality splinters the day before me. The car like a vacuum, like a black hole of her needs. I place the car in drive and leave the parking lot and so, without purpose, we head on.

An hour later I find us at my park, the skaters to our left and we securely tucked in a spot diagonal from the gazebo, beneath a shade tree. This day a drain on the limits of my imagination, and so I have come home.

The one-sided nature of the day bores into my being and it is this which I seek solace from. Would I were a ventriloquist that I could make this child speak.

"What's on your mind, Aileen?"

I picture this mind: static. The soft tissue of brain matter, once carefully lined and now smeared like a finger painting.

"Do you like to hear my voice?" Its language and its timbre fading from memory.

"What does your mother say to you?"

Of memories. Fairy tales. Oh, magical prince of science, save our little girl?

"Does she pretend you're a real person?"

A car pulls into the spot beside us and a mother pulls out a stroller, then a tiny child. She places the child in the stroller and the two roll away. "Does she read to you? Does she tell you about me?" Am I tall? Evil? Kind? Dead?

I turn off the car's engine. The sun's warmth through my window cloys the air between us.

"Did you know lots of girls suffer abandonment? Have you heard?"

Our stroller was red with white rubber wheels. Once Marilyn had me fix the right front wheel when it came loose.

"Oh, Aileen. Lots of girls get left behind or worse."

And what is worse. Raped? Kidnapped? Plain old dead? Which is the worse that I describe here. "Aileen. You'll never be left at prom." Your beauty might have saved you regardless.

"Without consciousness, what do you have?"

A sound emits from her mouth like a small whine and then a few spastic movements of her head. There is a wild animal beside me, a creature ensconced solely in biologic momentum. She is alive so she continues to be so. Perhaps I am no better.

"Leenie, do you wish you'd died then, too?"

The body beside me begins to shake slightly and then bows forward so that the seatbelt across her chest is all that restrains her from buckling in half. I reach to straighten her and her body flinches under my touch. I hold tighter pressing my fingers firmly into the flesh of her shoulders. I keep pressing until I can feel the bone beneath her flesh and then I press farther. I do not stop until she emits a cry of pain and then, drunk, I release her, straightening her body so she is sitting. I wipe the foul drip from her mouth. She slumps again to the side and I leave her this way, her forehead pressed against the window where vacant animal eyes peer toward a better place. "Where is this place?" I ask and no one answers.

There is no voice besides my own, rife with its hate. With its longing.

"Are you hungry? Thirsty?" I grab a water bottle from the bag at her feet and attempt to spray it in her mouth, tilting her head back to swallow. The water drips down her face. She coughs, sputters, involuntarily. I open the lid fully, ready to pour it down her face and then a muscle memory ignites in me and I am cradling her toward me, wiping back her hair from her face as I attempt to get her to drink. Her eyes open and focused on a spot above my eyes, her lips chapped and parted.

When she was a small child, we played laundromat. Aileen, forever the proprietor and I the pest who brought her objects to wash. A dinosaur. A Barbie. Several bags of potato chips. And each time, she, hands on hips, correcting me and informing me what a laundromat was for and where I might deposit these objects splayed before her. The gossamer quality of her child laugh, an imprint on all noise to come after—a sound hungrily desired now and each night whose absence has spanned since.

I put down the water bottle, breathing. I open my car door, moving around to Aileen's side to open hers and helping her to stand beside me. I grab a blanket and pillow from my trunk and slowly we make our way to the manmade lake and its grassy shore. Her body, as an automaton, moves forward in the direction of my urging.

By the lake, near a family of ducks, I lay our blanket down and then, now gently, I guide Aileen to lie. I settle her head atop the pillow, her face turned to the limpid blue above us, the clouds, a series of incoherent shapes before her. Their mass, a passing beauty, nonetheless.

The sun on our bodies like a tremendous weight, we lie. I beside her and she with her hands folded across her stomach where I have folded them. And so, the wail begins.

A waver at first, the loss of life in her, a voice sprung from the depths of her still functioning entrails.

"Here is the sky," I say. "Here is the sky. This is the sky."

The sound continues higher and louder. "And this is you, Aileen. Leenie. This is you."

There is grass beneath her head beneath the pillow beneath

the blanket. The sound, a whine, a shrill note flags, then strengthens. The water before us ripples. The ducks swim. Blue waves come toward the shore, but they're not really blue, they're clear. The children know this and so do I.

A single note erupting from my child, grows louder now. A flute-like beacon, the light of noise, the prehistoric channeling of loss, Aileen. They hear it. It is so loud, how could they not?

From all around the park, they all come toward. The mothers, the youth on their skateboards, the infants in their swaddled armor.

Your sound continues, this whistle from your depths. The piercing note of all our great unhappiness.

They are all now looking at me, as I at them. I see their faces, young, unhappy, wise. I see the evil things they've done and now the good. Can you hear that sound, Aileen?

Aileen, it is the loudest thing. I will not hear it again. It will not end.

# A Most Pathetic and Confused Creature

In Maggie's kitchen, the cat food is kept in a tall plastic storage bin to the left of the refrigerator. A hum emits from the automatic waterer. Her cat, Markus, gets thirsty and he drinks. On the refrigerator door, there's a Photo Booth photo of Maggie and Sadie and Dan from a recent wedding. Maggie wears enormous sunglasses and her lips are pursed as if to kiss the eye of the camera. Sadie pretends to lick Dan's face and Dan wears a feather boa wrapped python style around his neck. Dan belongs to Sadie. Or so Maggie jokes to Sadie, her closest friend since college. On the phone on the way home from work, Maggie and Sadie make plans for happy hour, either Babe's or the Blue Bar. Dan, Sadie's husband, has to work late at the firm, so it will be Maggie and Sadie alone.

"I have to feed Markie, so I'm going to stop home but then want to meet at Babe's?" Maggie speaks into the car's Bluetooth. Her hands are on the steering wheel, the tips of her fingers recently manicured. The shade is pale blue and there are small white flowers on her thumbs. She thinks about the texture of the steering wheel underneath her fingers, the way it responds to her pressure. Almost like a human body.

"Good by me." Sadie's voice sounds raspier than normal

through the car's speakers and Maggie thinks about telling her she sounds like a lounge singer, but then she doesn't say anything.

They chat for a few minutes more and then Maggie hangs up. Her car is stopped at a traffic light and she pulls to adjust the seatbelt which feels slightly too tight across the already too-tight bust of her button-down. She'd meant to do laundry the night before to have something better to wear to work, but then she hadn't and now it's Friday, so it doesn't really matter.

Maggie feels eyes on her and glances to the car in the lane beside her. A middle-aged man with a visible belly and baseball cap watches her through the window but looks away when she catches his eye. "Gross," says Maggie to the empty car. She raises a hand to touch her throat, moving her tongue across her lips. She glances back at the man, but he's looking away. The light changes. Maggie drives on.

*

Back at her condo, Maggie can hear the cat's hungry mews before she even opens the door. She has tried to put Markus on a diet after the vet told her he was overweight, but he always seems so pitiful, the crying and the way he'll lick the empty food bowl, that Maggie can't help feeding him like normal, and slipping him a little extra now and then. And anyhow, at least let one of them be fulfilled, Maggie likes to joke to Sadie and to Dan.

As she enters, Markus wends his way around her legs almost causing her to trip, but she catches herself on the small table in her foyer. She bends down to pet his gray head and he accepts her affection for a moment before mewing and moving toward the kitchen as if to lead her there. Sadie kids with her that *she* belongs to Markus, and Maggie agrees that it's probably true. He is the most consistent, and certainly the most demanding presence in her life.

After feeding the cat, Maggie steps into her bathroom to look at her face and reapply what needs reapplying. She takes off the button-down, exchanging it for a looser flannel shirt and slips out of her black pumps and slacks into a pair of worn flats and pale jeans ripped at the knee. In the mirror, she doesn't study her face too long. She's learned to ignore the parts she doesn't like. The swell of a second chin and the small wrinkles gradually appearing near the corners of her eyes. Her hair feels extra coarse today, so she puts it back in a loose ponytail and puts on some dark red lipstick to make herself feel prettier.

In the kitchen, she eats a handful of peanuts then peels and eats a clementine making sure to get the skin off in one single effort. She pulls out her phone to check the time, then texts Sadie that's she heading out and shouting a goodbye to Markus, she leaves the condo.

*

Maggie is thirty-five and has never been in love. Though really, that's not true, she thinks. She has been in love at least three times, but the love has never been returned. So, Maggie is thirty-five and has never been loved. That's the way she ought to phrase it, but of course this is more painful and definitely more pathetic. And again, it's not really true. Maggie has been loved by lots of people: her friends, her parents, Aaron, Sadie, Markus, Dan. And maybe there was unrequited love, someone who had been there, loving her, who was simply too shy to make his move, though of course, even in her mind, that sounds like wishful thinking, like the Hallmark version of reality. But there *was* the tall guy in her organic chemistry class who she always caught staring at her, or at least in her direction. Or Paul, the other programmer from her last office, the one she used to do impressions of world leaders with and then made out with drunk at the holiday party. But then he'd grown distant. Stopped laughing at her jokes. So maybe not Paul, unless, like Sadie suggested, he was afraid of rejection? But Maggie figured this couldn't be the case as she had made her own feelings very clear, through text and later through email.

As Maggie pulls into the small parking lot of Babe's, she feels herself consciously brightening. Her lips bending into a smile to reveal her whitened teeth and her shoulders relaxing back to better her posture. Spending time with Sadie is the easiest because she knows not to bring up dating. She knows not to suggest the latest online site or to quote from something she read about how successful women are intimidating to men or to tell Maggie she's better-looking than she is. Maggie isn't ugly; she's successful, and she's smart, and she's funny, or can be funny, and she's not a complete weirdo. And sure, she has her quirks, her undying love for Buffy and her inability to sit through an entire movie, but she feels certain that most everyone has at least one or two things about them that other people would find strange. So Maggie wonders if what's really at fault is her loneliness, those sometimes bitter, often desperate, feelings that she does everything in her power to hide. And yet, does the loneliness somehow taint her in a way she cannot conceal? So that anyone who looks at her intuits her lack of love. Can sense her brokenness—or is it unworthiness? A woman destined to be achingly and painfully alone. Except, of course, for Markus.

Yes, Sadie knows better than to say all of this. Sadie loves Maggie, and what's best, Sadie understands Maggie. At least as much as one human is able to know another. At least as far as someone who is loved unconditionally can understand the lack that another might feel. Sadie, believer in fate, in timing, in ghosts, though she denies it. Sadie who tells Maggie she could easily be in her position, if not for Dan, and Maggie swallows, smiles, and nods. It's true, says Sadie, running her fingers through her blonde pixie-cut hair. If it weren't for Dan, who knows if I'd be like you.

At the bar, Maggie orders a whisky and soda then changes it to a whisky and ginger at the last moment. She takes her drink and goes to find an empty booth to wait for Sadie. Sadie is usually late to things, which used to irritate Maggie early on, but which now Maggie understands is just part of Sadie's worldview. Sadie thinks or knows the world will still be there. Maggie is never quite sure.

As she sips the sweet drink, Maggie watches a youngish woman, maybe in her early twenties, swivel back and forth in her seat at the bar. The woman is thin, but her features are too sharp in Maggie's mind, like a woodpecker. The girl sips a clear drink and stares off into space. Her lips open and close like she's singing to herself, but from this distance, Maggie can't be sure. Then, there's a change in the girl's expression. Her lips pout and her cheeks rise and it's like a light, some great big sun has been cast on the plains of her face, and she's lovely. The sharpness is still there but now it's golden. It's fierce. But then Maggie can't see her anymore. The girl's face is eclipsed by a dark haircut, a man's head.

Embarrassed, Maggie looks away and sees Sadie arriving and waving to her, giving her a look that makes her feel like she too has been watched. Then Sadie points at the bar. She watches as her friend orders a drink and tilts her head back to laugh at something the bartender has said, and Maggie smiles, as if she too is in on the joke.

*

"Well, today was a lot," says Sadie done with her first glass of pinot noir and onto the second.

"What happened?" Maggie asks. Her tongue feels warm as she maneuvers an ice cube into her mouth from her almost empty drink. She and Dan used to jokingly call this part of the conversation Sadie's litany.

"I mean it's fine. Just more of the same ego from Richard. And now Marlene's starting to realize that if she sides with him, he'll lay off of her, so, you know. It's just a mess." Sadie rolls her eyes and smiles at Maggie. Maggie nods warmly, encouraging her to go on.

Sadie continues. "Anyhow, Dan keeps telling me that if I hate it so much, I just need to find another agency to work for because what's the point of dealing with this shit, you know? Life's too short." Sadie takes another sip and shakes her head as if in frustration. "I mean, if it weren't for how good the benefits are, I'd be long gone."

Maggie nods, half listening. She thinks about getting up to order another drink and maybe some fries, but she likes this feeling of being Sadie's sounding board, of being needed this way.

"Anyways, I'm talking too much. It's just. Part of me, and this is something Dan and I have been talking about this past week, part of me thinks what if I just get pregnant and take my leave while the benefits are good, and then be done with that place when it's over. You know?" Sadie takes a long swallow and looks at Maggie, as if waiting for her response.

The ice cube in Maggie's mouth is just a tadpole now, then it's entirely melted. "Yeah?" Maggie's tongue feels thick.

"I mean I know we'd talked about how we didn't think we wanted kids, but I don't know. Lately Dan's been talking about it again. I mean, remember when we used to tease him about it senior year, his dad vibes?" The wine has given Sadie a slight moustache, but Maggie doesn't say anything.

"Well, I mean, that's exciting." Maggie smiles brightly and reaches a hand out to touch Sadie's shoulder in its pale-yellow cashmere. The fabric feels so soft under her fingers. "I mean, wow, that's big, right?" Maggie looks at Sadie, then at her hand on her friend's shoulder.

"Thanks," Sadie laughs. "I mean, nothing has happened yet, but I wanted you to know first. You'll be an amazing aunt." Sadie reaches out to smooth the flyaway hairs that have escaped Maggie's ponytail.

Under the touch, Maggie feels ashamed. She picks up a napkin and motions to Sadie's lips. "Here." Then she takes her hand from Sadie's shoulder and places it on her own belly above her flannel shirt. "I can't wait."

*

An hour later, sitting in her car in the parking lot, Maggie feels more sober than she'd like. She and Sadie had continued the discussion of pregnancy and babies and then talked about Maggie and Maggie's job and then Dan and his new haircut, and she had done her best to bury herself in the chatter and to help Sadie process her excitement, even if inside her own stomach she felt a familiar pang of worry. How the world keeps seeming to move forward without her, and how this anxiety, this self-pity, is the exact kind of ugly feeling she hates having.

The way that her loneliness distorts her, makes her feel mean and bitter and jealous so that the happiness of others, at times, can feel like a sharp rod jammed right into the emptiest parts of herself. And what can she do but try to tell herself that maybe this is the life she's meant to live, that not everyone gets reciprocal love, that she's simply the product of bad timing, and imperfect choices of partners, and what's so wrong with being alone if she loves herself? If she has great friends, like Sadie, and like Dan.

Maggie feels the wave of self-pity leading to a wave of tears, so she pulls out of the parking lot to head toward home. As she drives, she concentrates on the road, ignoring her desire to critique her behavior at the bar and whether Sadie could pick up on her hesitation, her selfishness. Her phone beeps and at the light before the Kroger she checks it and sees a series of hearts and baby emojis from Sadie. She smiles and holds the phone to her chest. She knows she is still capable of great love.

*

Back in her condo, Maggie pours a large glass of merlot and takes a bag of sour cream and onion chips and Greek yogurt dip and goes into the living room to watch TV. Markus has been following her since she got in the door and now, settled on the couch, she takes him into her arms to snuggle, but this is not what he wants, so he hisses once and then nestles on a pillow at the far edge of the couch.

"The least you could do is cuddle me," says Maggie. She grunts and takes a gulp of wine then opens Netflix to scroll, trying not to think about her love life, but doing it just the same.

Aaron had been Maggie's first love. Aaron of the gentle voice and blond, curly hair. Aaron, from her freshman dorm, who told her she had great cheekbones, who kissed her a few times when he was drunk, who was her unequivocal best friend until she met Sadie at the beginning of sophomore year. Aaron with whom she shared her extra-long twin bed when he was too tired to find his room upstairs. And they would spoon each other, his skin smelling like coffee beans from the café where he worked, and he would tell her about being forced to go fishing with his grandfather, the creak of the rowboat and the hooks jutted in the mouths of the fish, and they would shudder together, and she could feel the hiccups of his breath through his chest, so close to her own. The way he looked at her, his eyes, clear and engaged, though sometimes looking past her, to a place she couldn't see. And, even though sex was absent, Maggie felt that this was love, it had to be, and she would close her eyes and feel small and warm beside him, his bony arms holding her until he drifted into sleep. Aaron who sometimes let her believe he could love her, too, until finally he came out their junior year. Aaron, who she pretended could still love her even after she knew, even after he rejected her and told her she had to move on. To let him go. To let him breathe already. And all the cruel things she wanted to do to him, to say to him, but instead she sucked in her breath and frowned. Ugly.

Sadie, of course, had been there to make her feel better. It was so not your fault, Maggie. He definitely liked you at least a little. The signals had not been clear. And maybe, if only Aaron had been willing, Maggie, he could have chosen to love you, too. But he hadn't. So that was that.

Maggie downs her glass then refills it from the bottle. Markus watches her and something in his whiskered face irritates her, so she snaps her fingers at him, and he looks away.

Sadie has always moved through life easily. The jobs, the boyfriends, it's all just always seemed to work out. But that's not true. Maggie smacks her cheek, making it sting. She hates that these shitty thoughts have access to her mind. We're all so gross, thinks Maggie. So selfish. And it hasn't been easy for Sadie. She's had her heart broken, at least once, which Maggie thinks she understands but sometimes is unsure. If no one ever loves you, is that pain worse than having love and losing it? And besides, maybe there's something depressing in how normal Sadie's life is. The college sweetheart. The husband. Now the baby. Eventually a picket fence and blouses stained with spit-up food. An already lapsing sex life.

Markus has joined Maggie in the kitchen and now he stands crying next to the bin of cat food. Maggie earns enough money now that she can buy Markus the highest quality food. Organic and everything. Sometimes she and Sadie joke that Markus eats tuna grade sushi while Maggie stills uses the canned stuff for her sandwiches. But it's not that funny. Cat lady jokes are Maggie's least favorite, though she herself is the first to make one when she starts to see a look of pity. A self-important smile. A hand reaching out to pat her shoulder.

Maggie hears her phone beep from the other room and goes to check the message. It's another text from Sadie, but Maggie doesn't feel like answering so she opens Tinder instead. It's been maybe four months since she opened the app and the faces that greet her are unwelcome. Somehow expected despite their randomness. She swipes left a few times then pauses. Here is a face that looks more familiar than the others. The hair is dark brown, nearly black, but she can tell it's turning gray in places. His eyes are also gray or look gray in the image. She swipes through the pictures. Here's one of him on a mountaintop, here's another at a party laughing, his mouth open, his head angled back. Another photo of him kneeling, petting a Dalmatian. It's uncanny how much this person looks like Gabe, but it's not Gabe. The caption says this man is named Sam. He's handsome. Late thirties. She swipes right. It's a match.

A pang of embarrassment hits Maggie's cheeks when she finds herself smiling, and without thinking she reaches to stroke

Markus's head. He obliges for a moment then play-bites her finger and she pulls her hand away. The oven timer beeps, and she bends to get her frozen pizza out of the oven.

The cheese has burned in places, but Maggie feels distracted and doesn't care. She slices the pizza and then takes a bite of a slice, burning the roof of her mouth. In the living room, her phone beeps.

The man, Sam, has messaged her.

*

What made Maggie fall for Gabe six years back was his directness. He was at least a decade older than her, his hair graying, his face just barely lined. They'd met at a gallery, someplace Sadie had dragged Maggie, and he'd approached her, asked if she'd like to get a drink, and the forwardness of this gesture confused Maggie, made her wonder if she'd always been more desirable than she knew, and blushing, she agreed. Gabe would take her out on dates to see the ballet or to eat tapas, and when they made love it was clear to Maggie that he liked women's bodies and all of their curves and idiosyncrasies. He would kiss her belly and he would tell her stories about traveling to Lyon and walking in the ruins at the top of the city, and about the houses in Sausalito that scared him as a child because they had little skinny elevators to get from the street to the front door, the hills they sat on were so steep. And he would tell her that all these things, the minutia of his life, it bored his wife, and Maggie felt young and she felt sexy as she straddled him, wide-eyed and listening.

And for a while, at least the four months when things were good, Maggie could convince herself that the intimacy they had was the early stages of love, and it wasn't just that Maggie was once again falling for someone who would not or could not love her back. That when he told her he cared about her, it was not because of her own drunken admissions of love and the moonlike nature of her wide-cheeked face, tear-stained and lips wet with a silent begging. That when she finally confronted him sober and asked him whether he loved her, too, whether they had a future together, he touched her back so gently, like she was a child, a lost bird, a most pathetic and confused creature. And she could tell in the way he disappeared from her life, that the ways she had agonized over his infidelity had been for him nothing but a series of orgasms and her the empty vessel which he'd filled. Because if he had loved her, too, how could he have let her go from his life so completely.

So far, Sam seems nothing like Gabe, apart from his looks. They spent the better part of Friday night, after the burning of her mouth, messaging back and forth. Now late Saturday afternoon, Maggie is still in her sweats not even having bothered to brush her teeth.

When they make plans to have a beer the following afternoon, Maggie feels a mixture of hope and confusion. How promising it all seems and yet how she's been down this road before. So many false starts. So many times when she'd been willing to try, and yet the man had already decided against her or decided that he could do better or that all he'd really been looking for was sex. And then other times she was forced to navigate her way out of a gross situation, the rare circumstances when someone else's loneliness managed to overwhelm her own. But then it was like she wasn't even a person, she was a human body pillow being grabbed at for its soothing potential. Well, at least this time it seemed like he was human. And like Sadie said, if you never put yourself out there, you'll never have a chance to find someone. The least she could do is try.

*

They meet at Frank's bar, and though in the moments before getting out of her car, Maggie feels a strange retroactive sense of panic, one that she had become inured to over the years of first dates with strangers, the feeling returns this Sunday. There's the concern over her looks, of course, and the anxiety about her lack of romantic history, but there is the equally troubling feeling that she might end up liking him, and then what does one do with all that feeling?

But it all goes fine. The initial hello is awkward, a tentative hug into handshake, but this itself feels charming and later they agree, over their second drink and shared order of onion rings, that as far as greetings go, theirs is not the worst they've each encountered. Whether it's the alcohol or the sunlight streaming in through the bar's windows, Maggie senses the conversation between them is easy, warm.

"So, you travel much?" asks Maggie.

"Mostly for work, but I do try and get to at least one of the national parks every year. My dog, Will, and I love to camp. You?"

"Camping? Oh, wow. Not since Girl Scouts, but I recall being pretty good at the finding sticks thing. You know, to make a fire."

As they talk, she finds herself thinking how less and less he's reminding her of Gabe. That the way his eyes—brown it turns out, not gray—look at her, it feels like he's trying to understand her, to really listen to her, to learn who she is, and Maggie, she's falling, she's trying her best to be herself, to be whatever it is he wants.

When they've finished the third drink, Maggie surprises herself and suggests they go for a walk at a park nearby, not wanting to get too drunk and not wanting the moment to end. Sam agrees, and it's at this moment that he leans in and kisses her ear. Then he shrugs and laughs, and she, blushing, touches her cheek.

"It's okay," says Maggie. And she means it. And she takes his hand and kisses the open palm. He laughs and looks at her, and then he pulls his hand away.

\*

Only once in their friendship have Maggie and Sadie ever gotten truly upset with one another to the point that Maggie wondered if they would continue being friends. It was shortly after Gabe stopped seeing her, and Sadie was trying to make Maggie feel better by telling her she dodged a bullet, really, because anyone who engaged in cheating had to be pathological on some level. That even if Gabe had left his wife, Maggie could never really trust him. And that Maggie, she believed, deserved real, honest love. And then, for the first time, something in Maggie snapped.

No, Sadie, she'd said. What if I actually deserve to be alone the rest of my life? What if I'm not meant for love? What if I just stop trying because it doesn't matter, it never has?

And Sadie, sighing, rolling her eyes saying, Maggie, if you weren't so goddamn negative maybe by now, you'd have found someone to love you. They'd gone three weeks without speaking, and then finally Sadie called, and they made up.

The park is nearby enough that Maggie and Sam decide to take one car to get there. Sam offers his car and Maggie consents, curious to learn as much about this person as she can. The car is a black compact SUV, relatively clean with the occasional white dog hair visible on the seats and floor. A coconut La Croix can sits open in the middle console. There's a brief wave of awkwardness being out of the environment of the bar, but Maggie decides the silence is a comfortable one and replays the feel of his hand in hers. Sam breaks the quiet once, asking for directions and Maggie tells him when to turn right, to turn left, and then points out the parking lot, empty, but for a scattering of cars. The park is small, a planned loop with still-young trees and a duck pond absent of ducks.

It's early March and the air has something of a sting to it, a wetness. As they start to walk, Maggie finds herself struggling slightly to keep up with Sam, whose gait is just a bit quicker than her own. There's another brief period of silence, not altogether uncomfortable in which Maggie thinks about commenting on the water, how blue it looks, or on the single Canadian goose that's nesting by the sapling closest to the water's edge. But then, she doesn't say anything.

After another moment of silence, Sam reaches for her hand but instead of holding it, he squeezes it and lets go.

"This is nice," says Sam. He doesn't look at her but raises a hand to shield his eyes from the sun.

Maggie smiles almost against her will. "Yeah. I think so." She can feel the heat from the sun on the back of her hair, almost like a warm hand.

"A lot of the time, you know, it isn't this easy."

Maggie nods. It isn't ever this easy. Not really.

As they approach the middle of the mile-loop, Sam points to a bench. "You want to sit for a minute?" He looks at her now, and in the sunlight, she can see the lines in his face from where he must have been a smoker at some point in his life. Maggie nods and lets him lead her to the little bench.

"In memory of Susan Susanson," says Sam. He points to the plaque on the bench's back and Maggie leans over to read.

She smiles and pushes lightly at his arm, and he uses the touch to pull her into an embrace. They kiss for a long moment, his tongue groping her mouth and the scruff of his beard rubbing against her chin. It's a rhythmic kind of kissing, but Maggie feels unsure of what to do with her tongue, and she can feel her chapped lips under the lipstick now worn off. He puts his hand near her breast, and she gets the sense that he's trying to swallow her. Then, before she wants it to end, they pull apart.

Maggie puts a hand up to her throat and then looks out at the lake. It's a small lake, manmade but with cattails planted along the shore.

"You know," Maggie shakes her head.

"Yes?" Sam asks. He looks at her a long moment and then squints his eyes and looks out at the lake.

"It's just so fragile, you know?"

"What is?" Sam rubs his hands back and forth along his jeans, then yawns and puts his hands in his pockets.

"Just. I don't know. Just this." Maggie feels herself blushing. She points at the lake, the single goose. Her hand lingers in the air, not pointing anymore but without a place to be. Then she wraps her arms around herself.

Overhead, a pair of pigeons fly by and Maggie thinks about saying something else, anything else, but then she doesn't. The sun is just beginning to sink and the light it casts is too bright, rude almost, thinks Maggie, and despite the light's violence, the air is getting colder. And, why?

Sam yawns again and then makes a slow show of standing up. "It's getting late, maybe we should head?"

Maggie nods and follows him as he starts to walk, to finish the loop. He doesn't look back at her, but she is right there beside him, or rather a step behind, doing her best to keep up.

When they get to the car, Maggie hesitates at her door, wants to ask him to kiss her again, to push her up against the hood, but her mouth is thick. When he opens her door for her, she laughs, and the sound is too high-pitched. Strained somehow. "How chivalrous," she says.

Sam nods and shakes his head. "Sorry about that." Then he goes to his side of the car. Maggie opens her mouth to explain she was kidding, she appreciated the gesture, but instead she says nothing.

At the bar, he pulls up alongside her car, and Maggie waits for him to put the car in park, to let it idle or to turn it off. But the engine stays on, and he looks out the windshield for a long beat before he turns to her and smiles. "This was nice." There's a kindness in his face, something about the brown eyes and how light they are or the way his skin wrinkles from maybe too much sun, or maybe it's the bit of gray in his beard. The beard that rubbed against her face and now or in a few hours will give her a rash. There's something in all of this that makes Maggie close her eyes, and then bring her hands up to her eyes to cover them. She can hear his silence, his confusion at what she's doing, why she isn't leaving the car and she bites her lip, feeling the shame of what she's created.

She drops her hands and smiles as big as she can. "Maybe I'll see you again?" she asks, and she doesn't want to hear the answer. But she forces herself to smile even brighter and to look at him, to lean forward slightly so he can kiss her. But he doesn't.

"Of course," he says. And then there's a moment when she believes him. When she has to believe that people say what they mean.

"I had a nice time," she says again, then she squeezes her lips together until they hurt and puts her hand on the door handle. He does not stop her, and so she opens the door and a moment later, waves, as he pulls out of the parking lot and heads onto the road.

*

On the drive home, Maggie thinks about stopping to pick up something to eat but decides instead to treat herself to delivery. Her phone beeps, and she looks at the message. It's from Sadie asking if she wants to get lunch the next day. Maggie closes her eyes for a moment longer than she normally would while driving.

When she opens them, the road is there. The streetlights are there, blinking on. Nothing has changed. She's still alive. Still alone. And Maggie lets herself do something she rarely allows herself these days. She thinks about Mark.

Mark of the long hair and imperfect teeth and nearly hollow chest. Mark of the skinny arms and the warm breath and the pale blue baseball cap faded out of recognition. They'd met on her thirtieth birthday while she was out celebrating with Sadie and Dan and a few other friends at Babe's.

"So, you're like that girl from the Rod Stewart song?" he had asked her, standing beside her at the bar.

"Are you an idiot?" she'd said, smiling coyly, for once feeling coy.

Later, against the pool table, he kissed her, and it was wet and consuming and perfect, and that night and for the next four weeks they spent every possible moment together. It got to be that he knew the constellation of her freckles, would trace them making up stories about the astrology of her skin, and that she could recite the story of each and every one of his scars, that she could be naked with him in a way she'd never been able to before. He told her about his mother, the thinness of her fingers and how it had helped her play piano, and then the neglect, the emptiness of his childhood home after her death, the sounds that it made. She told him about the times she wanted to scream at herself for being alone, about the times she wanted to yell at Sadie for her inability to imagine her life. And then she would braid his hair and sing to him the songs she made up in the shower and touch his teeth with her fingers to count them and ask about every cavity, every filling, every mistake. It was love.

And Sadie would call Maggie and say that it seemed fast, and that Mark seemed nice, but what did he do for work, and why did he still smoke cigarettes when they give you cancer, everyone knows? And she and Mark would eat frozen burritos, and he would say, Maggie, I love you, and she would ask him to pass the hot sauce and tell him that as dumb as it sounded, she didn't know that this had been a way that she could feel. And then, at the end of the four weeks, he was gone. Disappeared. And Maggie never heard from him again.

Sadie guessed that he was crazy or something like it. Dan said he was just using her for her apartment or for sex. That guys like him were everywhere. That she shouldn't be so stupid. And frowning, holding Maggie's hair back while she vomited, blind drunk, Sadie told Maggie that, see? Love isn't always so great. Sometimes it makes you feel more lonely in the end. And Dan and Sadie both agreed that Maggie deserved better. And maybe she did, but Maggie, dumb Maggie, maybe she also didn't.

Outside her condo door, Maggie hesitates, puts her fingers against her temples. She can hear Markus inside first mewing, now slamming his body against the frame. All twenty-five pounds of his Maine Coon body doing its best to get her attention. And when she opens the door, there he is, the cries and the mews somehow more pitiful in this moment, more lonesome than she's heard them before.

She steps inside and kicks off her left boot. Then she kicks off her right boot. It hits the cat, brushes against his tail, and he arches his back in anger, then comes toward her.

"Sorry, friend." Maggie kneels down, putting out her hand to touch the cat, to apologize. Markus rubs his face into her knuckled fist, then rubs his body against her outstretched arm.

"That's all you needed. Just a little bit of affection." Maggie lets her head hang, her eyes closed. Markus meows, purring. His tail flicks back and forth.

As he starts to move toward the kitchen, to lead her there, Maggie reaches out and grabs for his body. Startled, the cat snaps its head back in her direction and hisses. Maggie takes her other hand and cups it around his backside. She rises, holding the cat's body in her arms like an infant's, adjusting him so the claws can't scratch her. She moves with Markus into the living room.

"I like that we're here for each other, you know that?" Maggie pulls the animal toward her chest, holds him tightly against her sweatered breast, so tightly he cannot struggle.

"I love feeding you and caring for you. Being there for you." She lifts the animal above her, holds him out so she can see his angry face, the slitted eyes, his swiping claws. Her arms strain from the bulk, the weight of carrying him, but it's a good pain, isn't it.

"You know I'll always be here." She feels the muscles in his body writhing, the heat of his desire for release. "You have to love me." Her hair is in her eyes, her face is hot, the fur, she can feel it in tufts in her fingers coming loose. It's part of her.

She pulls the cat close again, up to her face, their hearts so immediate, their bodies and their faces side by side, like mother and son, like two lovers, like dear friends. "I love you," says Maggie.

Markus frees his paw, he scratches her, a thin line against her throat. The blood beads out. The pain vivid and sharp.

She drops the animal. She doesn't mean to, but she drops him.

Maggie crumples to the floor, is on her knees. She doesn't mean to be but she's on the floor, she's on the floor, and this is what she deserves.

It's all you've ever deserved, isn't that right, she thinks. You get what you deserve.

"I don't," she kicks out at nothing. The empty room. The coffee table. The mewling cat. She closes her eyes. The world behind her eyes is dark, but not black, never empty, even if she wishes it were.

By the front door, from within her purse, Maggie's phone beeps.

"I know you love me," says Maggie. She says it to the empty room.

# Our Sister Who Will Not Die

We wait for her to die. The room we're in is small, white, and clean. I stand behind the others, my siblings, a witness to our family's story. Andrew, our eldest brother, forces his hands in his pockets, leans against the wall by the machines. He wears a pale blue suit—a withering carnation tucked into the breast pocket. Melanie, the middle child, our leader, grips the sterile bedpost. She squats down, pulls at her trouser sock which has slid down into her loafer, its useless elastic a focus for her frustration. Arlene, the youngest of us, sits in the chair nearest the body. Arlene's head stays downcast, dyed brown hair falls over her face. She mumbles a prayer, the faith in her still audible, a pact between herself and what comes next. Pamela and Frank, the twins, they flank the sides of the bed, their mouths open dumbly, their jawlines slack, their arms hang like deadweight by their sides.

We are siblings. The six of us, now aging and gray, and her, Ellen, the one who lies pale and inanimate on the bed before us, our oldest sister. We all once lived in mother's womb; the hot, shared space intimate and now distant. The cancer sucks at Ellen's bones, the slurp nearly palpable in the confined space. The body loses its humanity here before us. We agree to wait. The hours long and the boredom rank. We will leave, one by one, but she our sister, she will leave first, yanked up into God's mighty fist or sublimated into light into ether into nothingness. She does not love us, cannot, though some of us pretend she does. See how we wait for her to die. Thank god, I think. It's come.

The machines beep a melody of invention. Outside the room, doctors and nurses shuffle past, other families murmur, slip past the door, glance shyly toward us, their existence a quiet background to our scene. It's a slow, hot thing this dying. A dream unfurling into day. And here we gather, through Melanie's beckoning, swept from across neighboring states to congregate and say some truth. To share, in the privacy of family, the pains that a life may give.

The room is hot and small, yet private. We stand around in varying degrees of closeness to the body, for some of us, our grief, a source of great confusion. Then Melanie, whose slender neck and long, narrow nose most resemble the dying one, asks for the first reckoning. "Andrew, do you have something you want to say?" He's the eldest. He sighs, moves toward the bed, the dull silver of his hair enhanced by the pale colors of the room, of his suit. His hands, large and calloused, grasped together.

His mouth opens and closes. He takes the empty seat beside the bed, the one that Arlene frees as she slips back by Frank to make space for our oldest brother. We, who can step back, step back. Then Andrew, settles himself, and speaks.

"We were little together. She was born second and so we were children together, I mean, toddlers. We shared a room, and I remember she used to cry at night, and I would think about taking my blanket to cover her crib. Like we covered the canary in the kitchen, remember? Mom would say, goodnight, Sally, and the bird would sleep in the dark? I remember thinking, why not her, too. She had the sharpest cry, and they never came to comfort her. Sometimes I couldn't fall asleep because of it. We were living on

Bloom Street in the two-bedroom. I was so glad to have a sibling, but it was so loud. Sometimes I wanted her to disappear."

His hands clasp and unclasp. The fluorescents hum gently.

"I think I said it out loud sometimes, too. I yelled at her to shut up. I was only four, I mean. I know a baby can't remember, but sometimes I wondered, is it possible I hurt her when I thought I was dreaming? Is there something I don't remember?"

We don't look at Andrew as he speaks. Our eyes shift about the room. Arlene looks to Frank. I watch as he takes her hand and squeezes. Melanie closes her eyes and shakes her head. Pamela leans toward Melanie. Their bodies touch just slightly at the hips. These siblings of mine, paired and divided.

"I haven't seen her since she came to the lake house three years ago. When we all got together for Arlene's fiftieth. Elle used to call our house and Marie always happened to be the one who answered, and she would tell Marie I was an evil man. That I'd tried to kill her when we were children. I told Marie to stop answering, to check the caller ID. I didn't know what to say. It made Marie so upset. I didn't know what to tell her. It's nothing. It's just her. It's Ellen. What else was I supposed to say?"

The body of our sister moves under the white sheets before us. A moan escapes the lips, the eyes stay closed. The morphine drip more vivid than our words, we hope. Andrew pulls at the flower in his lapel, the petals stiff and dying. None of us are guilty, I think to say, but I stay quiet.

From the right side of the room, a voice comes forth, Pamela, her hair held back in a ponytail, her body leaning against Melanie, and her lips wet with spit. In her hand, a tissue, wet and clotted. "I like to remember her from when we were young before anything you know? When she was away at school, I mean. I would have been sixteen, so she would have been about twenty-one?" She glances across the room to Frank who nods confirmation, drops his eyes to the floor, his faded, white sneakers.

"You all know this story, I know, but remember the time she invited me to visit her at school? I don't think Mom knew, or if she did, I didn't tell her and Elle made it seem like I shouldn't, like it was our secret. She was a senior in college then, I think. Or almost done with school at least. I took the Greyhound bus into Cleveland and she met me at the station.

"We got so drunk. It was my first time drinking that much, and I don't even know what happened. At one point we were at this party, some guy's, I'm not even sure Elle knew him—the people there looked old to me then, like they were all wearing ripped up clothes and the music was so loud. We were sitting on the floor, people were stepping over us, and we were laughing about no idea what and I remember thinking, this is who I want to be. I want to be her. Her hair was so long then, and she wore it in those braids down her back. Her skirt she was wearing was leather, I remember, and had fringe on the ends and I kept trying to braid the fringe. She told me she felt like an animal, and I thought it was the funniest thing. I remember thinking, I needed to keep this memory. That I needed to keep it so I could be her later, when I grew up."

The room is quiet. The beeps staccato reminders of the place. A muffled call comes over the outside pager. We cannot understand its message.

"But what about what happened after?" Frank, his eyes, yellow and watery, fix without focus on his twin.

Pamela wipes the soggy tissue across her lips, blows her nose, then squeezes it in her dimpled fist. She raises her eyes to Frank and shakes her head.

"Because I remember how you were when you got home. What Mom said, remember?"

Melanie's arm cradles Pamela's shoulders, secures itself around her waist. She whispers something in Pamela's ear, glares at Frank. He stares back down at the floor.

"Tell us what happened," I say, and the five of them look my way, startled, as if they've forgotten me, alone at the edge of the room.

Pamela blows her nose into the crumpled Kleenex. "Fine. So, I made it back to her apartment somehow—I think she gave me money for a cab—and when I get in the door, I immediately felt very sick—I mean that much to drink with my tolerance. Eventually, I passed out on the sleeping bag on the floor of her room. She had a twin bed, I remember. And then at some point she came home with someone. I woke up because they were having sex in her bed in the same room as me. I was so embarrassed. I tried to shut it out, put my pillow over my head and everything. But then—and this is what I wish I didn't remember—she just started screaming. Something from deep down, like she was being tortured. A sound I had just never heard before, and I don't know if it was anything the guy was doing but he pulled away and then it was three of us standing there in the bedroom.

"I didn't do anything, I just stood there. And she starts begging him not to leave, practically ripping at his hair, but he left. And it was like she noticed I was there for the first time. I didn't move, I just stood there. And she got in bed and started sobbing, and I didn't do anything. I mean eventually I got in the sleeping bag and tried to sleep, and I think eventually I did, I mean eventually I fell asleep. Then in the morning she acted like nothing had happened. But when she dropped me at the bus station, she said, 'Don't you ever do that to me again.' I never got her to tell me what I'd done. But I think she hated me ever since."

A knock comes at the door and we turn to see a nurse, a woman our age, enter the tight space. Those of us in the way, apologize and step aside. Pamela moves to the back and sits down in an empty chair beside me. The nurse checks the machines and Melanie apologizes for the size of our family. The nurse laughs, "The bigger the family, the bigger the love."

We laugh, murmur our agreement, and in the bed before us our sister's foot kicks beneath the sheet like a dog caught dreaming of an open field.

When the nurse leaves the room, the silence reemerges. We face the bed. Andrew moves back toward the machines. Arlene and Frank huddle together. Melanie joins Pamela, stands loyally by her side. I lean against the back wall beside the door, our only exit to the outside world. The chair beside the bed sits empty now. The body covered in white sheets like a pristine landscape of fresh snow. We wait for someone to speak.

"I always thought you two had a closeness. I'd heard that story before, but I thought you were still close at times after." Arlene's voice breaks the quiet. She doesn't look at Pamela as she speaks, her small mouse face made smaller by the long, thick hair surrounding it.

"We were close at times. I'd visit her or she'd come stay with George and I. But then she'd end up getting so drunk and wanting me to get drunk, and George didn't like it. He told me I acted like I hated myself when I was around her. And then at the lake, well. She told me she and George had made love every time she'd visited over the last ten years. I know it didn't happen but—. Why would she say a thing like that? What was the point?"

Melanie rubs Pamela's back. She gestures to Arlene. "Come say something, Arlie." She points to the open chair beside the bed. "Go ahead."

Arlene, the youngest of us, rises. She, the coddled child, the one most protected from our sister's wrath. She settles herself before the bed, clasps our sister's hand. Ellen's nails are chipped, the cherry red polish unpretty on her slender, dying fingers. With her free hand, Arlene fingers the thin cross around her neck and speaks.

"Ellen was always kind to me when I was growing up. She was eight years older but she made me feel included, even when I'd be told I was too little to join in.

"When mother made her give up the baby in high school, she was fifteen and I was only seven at the time, but I knew it was a secret when she went away and came back. She told me to pray for her, I remember. When she came back, she said I was the only one who understood her, and I was her favorite. She needed that kind of love from someone, I guess."

Melanie rubs Pamela's back; her hand slows as Arlene speaks.

"I know she loved all of us, it was just harder for her to love us the same. She needed to be understood first before she could trust you. I think that's why she and I always kept in touch. She knew she could trust me. She could tell me about the cancer and her treatment. I never judged her for who she was."

The room an ocean stripped of life. The we of us disintegrates bit by bit. Arlene hums. The waiver of her voice, like a faded prayer flag strung along a chain-link fence.

"I loved her, too, Arlie." Frank's yellow eyes stare at the back of Arlene's head, until she turns, her smile thin and tight, attempting kindness.

"Of course. I know you did." Arlene turns back to the body before her. The prostrate form, unmoving in drugged slumber.

"I tried my best, Amy and I both. We took her in for a few months after John died, you remember?" Frank folds his arms over his stomach. "But it was hard. And she was cruel to Amy, always pestering her about how she couldn't have children. I felt like I had to protect Amy from Ellen all the time. I know you had the same experience." Franks looks at Andrew, who nods his agreement.

"And the spending. She used to take my bank card right out of my wallet. You remember when she bought the damn car? We returned it—but what is that? If we'd had kids around, I don't know if they'd have been safe. What do you do with a person who won't get help? Who won't admit they're mentally ill?"

We watch our brother, the redness of his face, his searching, yellow eyes. The guilt we reject or recognize in our own mirrored expressions.

"I know she loved you, Arlene. But it wasn't always so easy for the rest of us." Frank moves toward our youngest to squeeze her shoulder.

Arlene's eyes are closed, her head shakes back and forth. "We didn't help her. We could have done much more. Mom could have done much more. You all were scared of her. Or felt put upon."

Frank's hand tightens on Arlene's shoulder then relaxes, drops away. I see the muscles of Melanie's throat tighten, her lips move apart to speak, to answer.

A sob disrupts the still air. Pamela, her pink face shrouded by white knuckled hands cries, a shuddering child's sob.

"Why don't you speak next?" I say to Melanie who flinches when she hears my voice.

"All right," she says, lips pursed.

"You all know how close Ellen and I were as children. She was three years older, but she felt like my twin. We always shared a room, and we'd stay up late, especially in high school talking about books and then music, the way we saw ourselves, the way you could be one person one place and then someone completely different with your parents. We used to prank you two, remember?" Melanie glances at Andrew, at myself, puts her fingers on her temples, pushing up the skin around her eyebrows, deeper furrowing the wrinkles carved across her forehead.

"Arlene, I was there the first time Mom had her hospitalized. She'd been awake for almost four days straight, and I got this call from her roommate, who she lived with after school, who said Ellen was scaring her, bringing home random people and talking about hurting herself and waking her up in the middle of the night asking to hang out. I remember she said that the night before she'd woken up and Elle was in her room, going through her CDs in the pitch black. I didn't know what to think, so I called Mom and we drove up together to get her. She acted like she didn't know who I was. I mean, up till then we'd still been talking on the phone at least once every couple weeks, and sometimes she'd sounded a little different—but I'd just figured she was tired or maybe depressed? We had to force her into the car—it was awful."

Melanie moves toward the bed, the body. She stands opposite of Arlene whose head is bowed as if in prayer.

The room is silent. The beeps of the machines a lullaby no longer powerful enough to fill the stillness. "Arlene." Melanie repeats her name. "Arlene."

"You all don't need to talk about her like this. She's dying." Arlene's words directed toward the bed. Frank touches Arlene's hair, rests his open palm on the crown of her head. I imagine the weight of his hand like our sister's presence, patient, unmoving, the gentlest crushing force.

"This is the way it was, Arlene," says Andrew. "There was good and bad like with anyone. But she didn't make it easy for us."

Melanie nods. "Right after Dad died, before she married John, she went off her medication and she drove all night to see me. You all remember this? She brought those two giant German shepherd dogs she'd found somewhere? She said she needed to stay with us for a bit. I didn't really want her around the boys—they were only six and four at the time, but I thought it would be okay for a little while at least. While I was at work, she came and picked up Tommy at preschool, told them she was his aunt, and it was my order and they didn't call me to check. She took him. I mean—she took him and was driving to who knows where. They got almost 200 miles away before I got John to call her and convince her to turn around. You all know this story, I know. But just—crazy."

Melanie stops speaking. She shakes her head. Everyone averts their eyes, our mutual shame, our guilt on display. But I don't look away.

"Tell them about the note, Mel," I say.

Frank looks up. "Mel? What note?"

"Claire, what do you mean?" says Andrew.

Melanie looks at me, raises her eyebrows. "Claire?"

"Is it my turn?"

I glance at my sisters and brothers, then I begin. "You all know that Ellen and I were never close. Even though we were only born eleven months apart, she used to tell me I was a mistake. I don't even know how she knew to say that, but she did, all the time. She called me ugly, and she used to whisper to me at night when the three of us shared a room that I had a different father from everyone else."

Frank laughs and I nod. The story absurd. Its truth like a gargoyle perched upon our family.

"I mean, we were just never close. I know she was kind to all of you at times. But she and I never got along except for the summer I was twenty-two and she was twenty-three, and even then, well. We were both living in the city, so I think that's the only reason we spent time together. We mostly drank a lot together. I'd been dating Hank then about a year and we were living together. And so the three of us went out a lot. You all know this summer."

"It was the summer she was raped," says Arlene.

I nod. "It was."

The body before us moves just barely. The eyelids flutter but remain closed. My siblings, they stare at me, except for Melanie whose eyes water slightly. Her fists clenched together.

"There was one night where she was drunker than normal. We all were, and, of course, she was hitting on Hank. You all know what she would get like. Just like in high school whenever someone liked me. So we all came back to my apartment, and there were these guys having a party down the hall. Hank goes and passes out in our bed, and Ellen and I go to the party. She gets more drunk, and she starts telling me how worthless she thinks I am, and how Hank must be under some kind of spell to be with me. I was so angry at her. We didn't know then what was wrong with her—this was before that. So when she went to the bathroom, I told the guy who lived there that she liked it rough, that she was a slut, and that she told me she wanted him. Then I left. I don't think I told her I was leaving. I woke up early in the morning to get a drink of water and she was crying on the sofa in our living room. We didn't talk. I didn't know how to explain what I'd done, and I was still angry at her. That was the worst part. I hated how she was the victim again."

I breathe in. I close my eyes. The noise from the hallway is too faint to be a comfort. "But you all know this story. Don't you?" I look around the room, but they don't look at me. I'm alone, we all are.

The room an empty aquarium. We're not together. We, in this tight space, are miles and years apart. The body before us steeped full of chemicals, the shape beneath the sheet angelic, perfect in its misery. Outside in the hall, we hear the noise of the everyday, its quiet chatter and wholesome pain, love, anger, loss.

Pamela doesn't cry. Arlene doesn't pray. Andrew and Frank don't protect or scold. And Melanie, she holds the note, drawn from her pocket, our sister's only chance to speak.

"One of the nurses gave me this note, said that Elle had asked her to give it to me when she was first admitted two weeks ago. I'll read it now, okay."

Into the silence, our sister reads, her voice clear and unfaltering. Some of us close our eyes, and we can imagine it is her, Ellen, speaking before us.

"Melanie, this letter is for all of you so I can remark on the betrayals that exist in a family such as ours. I know that you will say I'm mentally ill, but that does not mean my mind is wrong. With my suffering, I have also seen truth. Andrew will say that I was a burden as a child, but it was he who kept mother and father so busy as to neglect me. Despite this, I know he's tried hard to do good, and I hope he feels happy in his success, even though it's all material. Frank and Pamela are both good people, I believe, though we all know they're unaware of much that goes on around them. Their lives, like mine, were childless and therefore worthless. In this, I think they lie to themselves. Frank, who would peep at us when we were changing, remember, Mel? And Pamela, who wanted to be my friend only for my looks to rub off on her, to help define her shapeless personality. Arlene, she's the one that saved me when mother made me give up Owen. She's my child, in my heart, though she herself doesn't know how to love others. I've made her my own and spoiled her with too much tenderness. The one I feel most sorry for is Claire. She wanted to hurt me for all the hurt she thinks I caused her. I hope she's happy. Ask her to tell you what I mean. Her soul, unlike mine, is heavy. I've seen God. I am able to love you all because of this. Even you, Melanie. Who wanted to keep me from myself, gut out the illness, who betrayed me to mom when I confided about Owen, about the times I wanted to disappear. But still, we're family. We're deserving of at least each other's forgiveness. To each of you, I offer mine."

In this small, warm room, we breathe in and taste each other's breath. One blood, one strand runs through each of our disparate bodies. The hurt we wield, the family we embody, the joy we give to one another, here dismembered before us today. The hospital lights flicker overhead; the liquid drops from its bag through the IV into the body of our sister, to keep her alive, to ease her pain.

It's Frank who laughs first, quietly and then loud, louder, raucous, an absurdity to his shaking paunch and hot, red face. The laughter like a tremor, like a disease of joy spreading from his mouth to his throat to his shaking ribs.

Pamela is next. She blows her nose, an elephant like guffaw, and then holds up the disintegrating tissue for us all to see. "We're all so terrible," she says, laughing loud, awkwardly. Her eyes glassy with tears.

Melanie raises the note in the air and drops it. As it flutters to the hospital floor, she too, begins to laugh, soft, then higher, tears come from the edges of her eyes, she turns to our youngest sister. "Arlene, do you ever smile?" To which Arlene shakes her head, and then as if by the will of God, smiles before us all. She crosses herself and begins to laugh, this miracle of divine emotion painted across her upturned lips and now light eyes.

Pamela rises from her chair, comes to stand by Melanie, offers her the crumpled tissue, "You're crying," she says. And at this, even Andrew softens, shakes his head.

"We're all evil." I say, glad at last to speak this truth, and Andrew nods, points at the body before us, our sister who will not die, whose eyes just now are open, their blueness still stunning in this, her throes of death. She doesn't gasp, but stares up blankly, at God, at us, in peace? We wonder if she feels the love, the hate, our own forgiveness granted and received.

We all move forward to surround the bed. Andrew, Frank, and Arlene on one side. Myself, Pamela, and Melanie on the other.

We're imperfect, yes, this truth is known. Her illness something cruel but somehow weaving us together, our own weaknesses perhaps just now coming to light. We wait for her to die, but now, in this room, we stand together living. It's what we have; it's all that we have left for one another. We all lived once as children, as adults, but now in this small, white room we come, at last, to honesty, to ugliness, together.

# We Have Disappeared

Sammy and Mack were friends in middle school, then not really in high school, then found each other again at Lake View Community College in Dr. Magellan's Statistics I course. They were both pre-business, whatever that means, Sammy would say and laugh, sucking at the Merit Ultra-Light he'd taken from his mom's secret pack in her dresser drawer.

"You want one?" he asked Mack and Mack shook his head because those things gave him the worst taste in his mouth, like someone's grandmother's basement, mothballs, and faded yearbooks. And besides, Mack was trying not to smoke anymore. He was trying to be decent.

"You do any of the homework for today," Mack asked Sammy, his hand raised to his forehead like a visor against the blighted February sun.

Sammy exhaled through his nostrils. "You see that, the French exhale?"

Mack nodded and shrugged. "I didn't know they called it that."

Sammy smiled and showed a row of almost white teeth.

Teeth all straight in a line like some kind of teenage dental model. Like he might have been something, an actor or something, if he wasn't so short. Mack shrugged again, and looked away from Sammy, from his mouth. "Shit, I did like half if you need to see it or whatever."

Sammy stamped out the butt on the concrete. They were in the parking lot at Lake View, at the farthest end from the entrance. Sammy liked to park far away so that they'd have the walk to sober up, or so he told Mack the first time he offered to give Mack a lift. Sammy drove a Charger, and it made Mack wonder where he got the money, but then he remembered Sammy's house from middle school, and it made sense. Sammy didn't much worry about things, even though Mack figured sometimes, it was okay to worry.

"That'd be sweet, dude," said Sammy.

Mack swung his backpack off his shoulder and unzipped it, pulling out the folder labeled math. But the folder was empty.

"Fuck."

"Yeah?"

"I didn't bring it."

"Should we bail?"

Mack closed his eyes and counted to three, trying to picture where the paper was and if there was time to get it, and maybe there was time, but—. He could smell whatever deodorant Sammy was wearing, even above the smell of the cigarette. A smell like aftershave, only louder, more in your face.

"Emily's home today so we could go to her spot and smoke or something. Or we could go to your place?"

"Yeah," Mack blinked. Sammy leaned against the car, his face tilted toward the sun. With his eyes half closed, Sammy looked younger than nineteen, he looked innocent.

"Fuck it." Mack zipped his backpack. "Let's go."

*

Back in September, two weeks into his first semester at Lake View, Mack had moved out of his dad's place and into his first apartment. The reason he gave was to be close to work, the O'Charley's by the mall, but it was also true he liked the idea of living alone. He would only have himself to think about, he could concentrate on school, on getting somewhere with his life, and it wasn't like he didn't see his sister and his dad. They were always at the back of his mind.

Even though he was working full time, what with tuition and books and rent, Mack couldn't afford a car, so he'd take the bus to get to Lake View twice a week for his classes. He didn't really mind taking the bus that fall semester, it gave him time to think and watch people out the window. The older women with their hair wrapped up in scarves and their little push carts with their big, checkered bags of laundry, or sometimes there'd be a group of kids, his age maybe or younger, doing tricks right there on the street, old school breakdance moves, spinning on their heads or bending their bodies in ways Mack couldn't believe. He liked seeing these people he might never see again, wondering about their lives for a few blocks, and then forgetting them, trusting they'd be all right.

Mack wasn't lonely, exactly, during that fall before he ran into Sammy, but looking back, there was a kind of quiet that would happen, a stillness he would find himself inside, like he was in a music video, only the song had just ended, faded out, so there was a trapped quality, a swimming feeling, like he was standing in white space, watching Kurt Cobain move his guitar toward the ground in slow motion getting ready to smash it, and Mack could feel the sensation, but he couldn't hear it.

He'd get off work around eleven-thirty on Friday and Saturday nights and he'd walk back the three blocks to his apartment, his apron crusty in his hands wrapped tight to hold what he'd made and the pens he was always losing making sharp points he liked to jam against his palms. The only sound would be the squeak of his ugly black sneakers on the asphalt, shoes with soles made not to slip on the kitchen floor, nothing he would choose to wear on his own, and he'd study the apartments he was passing, the dark buildings, all their lights off, and he'd feel things that didn't make sense, that he couldn't put into words, like somehow he was stuck in the opening credits of a movie, and one day soon it would be like his life was finally beginning.

Sometimes on these walks home, Mack would feel himself not wanting to be home yet, so he'd go a block or two out of his way to make it a little longer, and that's how he came to find the old hospital, a small L shaped building, one story, that was vacant and had been for at least a few years, it looked like. A chain-link fence surrounded the place, but it was busted in places, the grass all overgrown and wild looking. There was a swing set where some-one had tossed one of the swings over, so it hung down too high for anyone to reach. The swing set something for the teenagers to hang out on maybe, if he asked his sister, she might remember because although he hadn't recognized it at first, this was where they'd taken her at least once for a few days' stay, right at the beginning of things.

The building was on a downhill slope, and when Mack started making it part of his routine to walk by the place, he noticed that when it rained, the runoff would flood the pathways, so it was like the whole place went underwater. And that some mornings, when he'd be going to his 11 a.m. class, he'd see people, grown men and women, sneaking through the windows, disappearing inside and not coming out, at least as far as Mack could tell, though he never had the time to wait.

The place gave him a funny, empty feeling, like it was a mystery, even though it wasn't.

Then it was January, start of the new semester at Lake View, and there was Sammy, excited to see Mack even after all these years, offering to drive him home, and wanting to hang out, and even though Mack felt surprised by all this at first, he was more glad than anything else. He had been lonely, maybe, even if he hadn't realized it.

*

In the third week of the semester Mack invited Sammy over to his place for the first time. It was a rare Thursday where he hadn't been scheduled, and on the walk to Sammy's car after class, Mack coughed and said hey they could chill at his place if Sammy wanted. He'd just gotten a fake ID from someone at work, and he'd bought some wine coolers the night before on his way home, so there were drinks and all if that sounded good. He hadn't known what to buy really, so when he saw the Zima, what his mom used to drink, he figured it couldn't be that bad. He thought Sammy might make fun of him, but he didn't.

"Dude, these taste like fruit snacks." Sammy lay on the brown carpet with his head on the yellow beanbag chair. They both faced the TV which was propped up on two milk crates. The apartment was shitty, but Mack only thought it was shitty because he figured that's what someone else would say about it. Someone who didn't know how many shifts he worked to pay for it every month. It was shitty, maybe, but not so shitty when it came down to it.

They listened to music off of Mack's boombox, a tape his sister had made him of throwback '90s stuff, mostly Nirvana, shit that was almost a decade old but still seemed pretty important to Mack.

Mack liked this music, liked Cobain's voice because of the pain he thought he heard in it. I mean this guy killed himself, he was a real person, like really real, and Mack would think this, and then think about if he could ever feel that real or if he had already felt that real or if he ever would. It was stuff he wanted to talk about with someone, with Sammy, but it was also stuff that seemed hard to say out loud, even when he'd drank enough to get comfortable. It was still on the tip of the tongue.

"Do you ever feel, like, wooden?" Mack sat on the other piece of furniture in the room, a loveseat stitched with images of a fox hunt that had been his granddad's.

"Like my dick?" Sammy looked up at Mack from the floor and laughed, tilting the glass bottle with its clear drink into his mouth.

Mack felt his face turning red. A part of him wanted to be annoyed at Sammy even though he looked so skinny on the floor in his too-big clothes. But instead, Mack laughed. "Shit dude, I must be drunk."

Sammy sat up, his hands resting on his knees. "Naw, I probably know what you mean." He went to take a sip, then he shrugged. "I like feeling nothing sometimes."

Mack nodded. The tape clicked to turn itself over. He thought about saying something else, but he didn't know what to say. They were on the last of the coolers, and then what.

Mack leaned over and pressed the stop button on the deck. "You want to check out a place?"

"Yeah?"

"This spot up the street. It's like abandoned or something." Mack felt a film of sugar or something like sugar covering his teeth. When he and Sammy first hung out, back when they were in sixth grade, Sammy's parents always had Capri Sun and Yoo-hoo in the basement fridge. It had seemed like a luxury at the time, a choice that meant not having to choose.

"Yeah?" Sammy looked at Mack, looked him right in the eyes and Mack could see the unevenness of his facial hair, the places where hair hadn't started growing yet.

"I think they kept crazy people there, teenagers or something, I don't know." There was a nervous feeling in Mack's stomach, and he swallowed the rest of his Zima to cover it.

"Tight." Sammy burped loudly. "The asylum."

Mack set down the bottle and reached for his hoodie. "There's a hole in the fence, I saw it last time I passed by."

\*

Even though he lived by himself, Mack still went and saw his dad about once every three weeks, and the reason he gave was to get his hair cut. The truth was Mack would probably have liked to have long hair, but he'd had a crew cut for so many years that he didn't know if his hair could even grow past the half-inch mark. So he let his dad keep cutting it every three weeks when he went home to do his laundry, and to see his sister, to make sure she was still okay, that she was getting along. It was the kind of thing where if he asked his dad to stop cutting it, he knew it would make his dad feel bad. So he didn't ask. And besides, sometimes Mack liked how it felt to rub his hand back and forth along the back of his head, right after Dad cut it, even though other times he saw his face and imagined the way he'd look if he wasn't an almost hairless alien fuckwad. But at least he was finally starting to lose his baby fat. There was that.

When he and Sammy were friends in middle school, Mack still had a mom, and he wondered if that made him a different kind of person to other people. He still had a mom, technically, but she was living somewhere else, either Arizona or New Mexico, Mack couldn't remember, and honestly, he was pretty sure it didn't matter. Or at least that's what he'd say if anyone asked, meaning if his dad asked, which he didn't.

When Mack listened to the Velvet Underground, when he first bought their CD because he liked the banana on its cover, and it was used, only three bucks, he liked how much space he could hear in the lyrics. It made him feel like he was in a coma or a hammock, and then he heard the song "Heroin," and he couldn't help wondering if he was missing something, if there was more stuff out there than there seemed to be. Like if he moved his hand quickly enough or punched hard enough the air would open up and there'd be something else, another place or another feeling or another color. It was something he felt sometimes when he was with Sammy, it was like he was on the periphery of another world and when he was with Sammy, he had an in. A window.

Back in middle school, Sammy had been the one who wasn't afraid of anything. The one who acted like he knew something about sex and drugs, even though Mack had his doubts. Sammy seemed to like to pretend things, and it was something Mack liked about him even though it didn't make much sense. Like how Sammy pretended to know something about hip-hop, or women, or even US history. When he claimed that Taft was his favorite president or that the Louisiana Purchase had been part of a conspiracy to eliminate escargot. Mack thought there was something about the way that Sammy postured that was sweet, that showed something about who he wanted to be and who he really was and the gap that existed in between.

Now at Emily's house, mid-February with the air still pretty chill, class abandoned for the day, he sat with Sammy in Emily's backyard by the gazebo her dad built for her mom for some anniversary. Emily was Sammy's neighbor, a senior in high school whose parents were rarely home, so she often cut school after lunch. Sammy was the one who sold her weed.

"This shit is deviant," Sammy exhaled and coughed and then coughed again, his skinny chest shaking underneath his No Fear hoodie.

Mack watched the smoke spurting from his friend's lips. He glanced at Emily who seemed to be watching Sammy, but Mack could tell was actually looking at a spot above Sammy's head.

"Yeah, it's all right," Emily said, turning to Mack. "You want?" She gestured at the pipe that Sammy was still holding in his hands.

Mack hesitated, but shook his head. "I'm good for now."

Emily squinted and shrugged, reaching to take the pipe from Sammy who was still coughing slightly but trying to hide it. Emily put the pipe to her lips. Exhaling slowly, she pointed to the spot above Sammy's head where Mack had seen her looking. "It's a bird's nest. You see that?"

Mack looked where her hand pointed and saw a small brown bird alight on a branch close to the tree's trunk. It had something in its mouth, maybe a stick. "It's got something in its mouth."

"I don't see it." Sammy craned his neck to see the bird.

Mack watched the bird hopping back and forth, like it was thinking, like it was making a decision about where to put the stick or if the stick was even the right thing to be holding.

In high school, Mack had been on the football team, and so that's who he'd hung out with, even though he never really knew if he liked football. He'd been an average player, and his teachers had told him he was an average student, an average thinker. Mack used to wonder if this was a bad thing or a good thing. His sister was special, or had been special, and how had that worked out for her? So maybe it was okay to just be a regular person with regular ideas and feelings.

"Isn't Sammy like a girl's name?" Emily had moved over and laid down so that her head rested on Sammy's thigh. This was only the third time that Mack had hung with Emily, and he'd thought she and Sammy were like brother and sister, but he wasn't sure.

"Isn't Emily a girl's name?" Sammy said and laughed which made him cough again just slightly.

"You're stupid," Emily said.

In the tree above Sammy's head, Mack watched a squirrel as it jumped from one branch to another. Then it stopped, and its nose twitched, and its tail bobbed in the air.

"You're stupider," said Sammy. He put his hand near Emily's head as if to touch her hair, then he flicked her in the forehead instead.

"What the fuck?" Emily said. Mack leaned back to listen to the two of them fight or play-fight or whatever they were doing.

It was getting toward the end of winter and the sun was getting stronger. Mack could feel it against his face, how it made him want to close his eyes. He could still make up the homework, he was pretty sure, turn it in the next class for some credit. It was all right to do the wrong thing sometimes if it meant you got to be with friends. He imagined his sister's face, her hands making shadow puppets to entertain him when he was a little kid, a bird alight then flying. Emily's voice was high-pitched in the background, telling Sammy to stop it, but not like she really wanted him to. Only saying it to mean the opposite. But there was Sammy saying sorry, not getting it, Mack knew, leaving her alone when it's not what she wanted. Then Sammy punched Mack, saying hey dude what are you asleep? And Mack opened his eyes, smiling without meaning to, squinting because of the sun, its light.

\*

Mack's dad said that what happened to his sister was no one's fault, but it was hard for either of them to believe that the drugs—mostly LSD and mushrooms—and that his mom's leaving—abandoning as his dad called it—had nothing to do with her break. It was schizophrenia, the doctors said. It was early onset, they said. It was probably the result of trauma and exacerbated by stress, but in all likelihood, it was going to happen at some point, so really no one was to blame. This kind of thing was genetic.

Mack's favorite thing about his apartment was when he woke up in the middle of the night and he could see a tiny piece of the moon from his bedroom window, and how it made him feel like he was in on some kind of a secret. How the moon had been there that whole time and how he could be awake or asleep and things would be the same no matter what. The moon was inside his room, its reflection lit on the old clock radio by his bed.

Sometimes, Mack thought that the reason he loved Sammy was because Sammy didn't let stuff bother him, and Sammy didn't care because he didn't have to care. Sammy wore his jeans extra low because he wanted to. He said idiot things, and he had eyes that were so blue, like a pool where all the chlorine had worn away, so it was just good and clear and natural. Sammy didn't care what other people thought because most of the time he didn't even notice. He just lived, and it was something inspiring, in a way.

Maybe one day, Mack and Sammy could get a place together, maybe once Mack got enough credits and transferred to a real college, and they both transferred, and they had a spot where everyone came and hung out and everything was good. And there'd be girls there, hot girls, and other guys, but at the end of the day what would matter was that Sammy was there, and Mack was there. And when one of them had a bad day, the other one would be there, like his sister had been there. And sometimes, they'd sleep together in the same bed, like brothers or like something else, but they'd be close, and honestly, that's all that Mack has ever wanted.

*

That first time Mack had Sammy over, after they'd finished the wine coolers, Mack walked Sammy over to the abandoned hospital, and they both agreed it was the kind of place they'd have been obsessed with back in middle school. They slipped through a hole in the fence, and Sammy swung on the one good swing. They talked a little about the future and about Emily and about Mack's coworkers. And Sammy wanted to try and get inside the building, but all the windows were boarded up by whoever still owned the place, so they gave up and watched TV at Mack's instead.

Then it was the middle of March. Mack had been pretty good at convincing Sammy not to ditch class, but this was a beautiful day, the first warmish day there'd been, and Sammy wanted to blow it off, but Mack said what if they didn't but afterwards, they could get some beers or something and hang out? He'd noticed the windows at the hospital weren't boarded up anymore, they'd been pried loose. And Sammy said okay, this one time, he'd be a good boy, for Mack.

Now they were through the hole in the fence and outside a window that had been boarded up two weeks before but wasn't anymore.

Sammy squatted down to look inside the window. Mack was behind him, a little nervous but not as nervous as he might have been.

"So, you said this place was for crazy people?"

Mack shrugged, "I think like teens who had psychiatric problems or something. I mean that's what I heard is all."

Through the window they could see what looked like a receiving room for a patient with metal cabinets along one side and a narrow hospital cot floating like an island. On the floor was a wadded-up T-shirt and an empty forty of Colt 45. Random sheets of paper with the ink stained and running were strewn across the floor.

"Shit, how long has this place been like this?" Sammy straightened up and turned to look at Mack. Mack shrugged again because he didn't know the answer.

"A while. I guess?" Mack sensed that Sammy wanted him to take the lead, to initiate going in.

"You think there's anyone in there?" Sammy leaned forward, bracing himself against the window frame. The glass had been cleared away and the plywood square used to cover the window had been pushed to the side.

Mack shrugged, peering into the space. He half closed his eyes, putting one foot through the window and carefully easing himself into the room.

"Fuck, dude. Okay."

Mack felt Sammy behind him, felt his hand on his shoulder using him as a support. The room was small and dim at the corners, but the window was big enough that the space ended up being pretty well lit. It smelled like medicine mixed with stale beer. Mack figured if he tried hard enough, he could smell urine, too, so he didn't try.

In high school, Coach always told Mack that if he was afraid of getting hurt, of getting tackled or thrown down or broken, that he would never amount to shit. That he had to get ahead of the fear. That he had to run toward it instead of away. That he might as well do the thing that could cause him pain because otherwise, he might just get caught off guard anyways.

"Dude," Sammy shook his head. He opened and closed the cabinets lining one side of the small room. Most of them were empty, but one still held tissues, and another had an unopened bag of tongue depressors. Sammy picked up a small glass beaker and put it to his ear like a seashell. He put it in his pocket.

The door to the little room was open, and they could see a darker hallway that seemed to act as a corridor leading to a series of similar looking rooms, ones with other windows that had been knocked down and subsequently boarded up by whoever owned the place or the police or whatever.

"We keep going?" Sammy asked. Mack could hear in his voice a hesitation, a sound that reminded Mack of middle school Sammy, when they'd dared each other to look at porn on Sammy's dad's computer and could have so easily been caught, but they hadn't been caught and everything had turned out fine.

Mack peered into the hallway. It smelled earthier here, like sweat and mold. He felt Sammy behind him again, stopping when he was as close to Mack as he could be without it being weird.

In the hallway, more trash appeared in little piles. Clothes and empty cigarette packs and crushed cans and trash bags that it was hard to see the contents of. On the wall, there was the remains of what must have been a bulletin board. On the floor under it there were photos, mostly torn or ripped. Mack bent down and picked up a couple of the least soiled looking ones. A woman, older, maybe a doctor? He put the pictures in his pocket. There was light coming from down the hallway, and Mack started to move toward it.

"Do you think there's anyone here?" Sammy's voice wasn't a whisper, but it was close.

"Maybe," said Mack. He moved slowly, feeling like he was inside an aquarium where the fish were all dead, the way everything felt sunken toward the floor, the air empty like it had once held so much life, and then someone had lifted the lid, broken the filter, and now everything was dried up and gone. Then he saw the source of the light. A string of Christmas lights plugged into the wall, and somehow, strangely, they were lit up. More light came through a hole in the exterior, another boarded up window knocked down. This was at the end of the hallway, a big open area that must have been an operating room or where they sedated people or something. Tons of cabinets lined the walls. The floor was tile and there was a metal chair, like a dentist chair that had been pushed to the side of the room. This room, like the rest of the place, was littered with trash. Mack wanted to imagine what they did here, the pain they inflicted or maybe the suffering they'd tried to remove. All of the patients, like his sister, writhing, moaning, gone.

In the corner, a man sat, leaning against the wall watching them. In his lap was a plaid blanket, duct taped in patches where it was ripped. His face was mostly covered by a reddish beard. Mack thought he could smell the man, but he wasn't sure because there was also a strong scent of spilled beer and what must have been vomit. The man grunted.

It was hard to tell how old he was, but he didn't look so old, maybe in his early forties. It looked like he'd been sitting against the wall a long time. Maybe all his life. As Mack watched him, Sammy come up behind Mack, then he heard Sammy talking out loud and it sounded like a dream.

"Hey, man."

The man against the wall turned his face slightly to look at

Sammy. He closed his eyes and seemed to fall asleep or at least not care that they were there.

"Are you okay?" Sammy moved so he was next to Mack, directly in front of the man. "What's your name, dude?"

Mack opened his mouth, held his lips an inch apart, but he didn't say anything. He didn't know what he was supposed to say. He thought about elbowing Sammy, but he couldn't do this either. Sammy knelt down in front of the man, a cruel smirk lingering on his friend's lips.

The man opened his eyes and stared at Sammy, then raised his eyes to Mack. "What?"

"Sorry, dude. We just came in to see what was up." Sammy half turned to look at Mack and Mack could see a kind of excitement in Sammy's eyes. A widening of the whites so that his eyes were like those of a child.

"Fuck off." The man closed his eyes again and Mack felt suddenly embarrassed. He wanted to see this man as someone's brother, someone's son, but he couldn't. There was too much distance.

"Sorry, dude." Sammy looked from the man to Mack. He spoke, not looking at the man, but looking at Mack. "I was just looking to buy."

The man grunted and made a show of pulling the blanket to his chest. "I got nothing." On the ground next to him was a bent metal spoon. The man looked at Mack, then shifted his body, like he was feeling for something in his pocket.

"I got a lot of money to spend," said Sammy.

"Fuck." The man heaved up again. He pulled his hand out from under the blanket and there was something in it, but Mack couldn't see.

Mack put a hand on Sammy's shoulder. "We should get out of here." His words recovered. Sammy shook off the arm.

"Hold up."

Mack wondered if he should run home, call someone, tell them about the man. He pictured his father, the way he looked when he made dinner for him and his sister, the way he mixed the spaghetti with the sauce, so it was all coated, all of it. The way he made his sister eat, knowing she was hungry even if she said she wasn't. Just one more bite. Like a little kid.

The man in front of them mumbled something to himself. His head slumped forward and then back against the wall. His fingers were grimy and balled into fists like an infant's, but slowly one hand moved toward Sammy then pulled back and thumped against the man's chest. "Show me." A thin line of drool eased out of the mouth down into the maze of crusted beard.

"I'm leaving," and as soon as he said it, Mack was at the open window, stepping outside into the light. Only when he was outside, calling back for Sammy to join him, did he peer back inside, but he wasn't able to see anything with the now blinding sun.

A few moments later, Sammy climbed out also. Mack started walking home, not looking back to see if Sammy was following him but knowing somehow that he was. Neither of them spoke as they walked through the grassy yard to the fence, slipping through the hole, one by one. It wasn't until they were at Mack's in the parking lot by Sammy's car that Sammy started to laugh.

"Dude, that was so fucked."

"Yeah." Mack could feel something on his skin, under his flannel shirt. Like sweat or like water. Like illness.

"What do you think his deal was?" Sammy pulled out his keys, opened the car door to search the console for a cigarette.

"I don't know." Mack looked at Sammy as he cupped his hands around the lighter trying to light the cigarette.

"I swear he looked like my uncle." Sammy laughed again and shook himself like he was shaking off a spider. He reached into his pocket and pulled out the beaker, showing it to Mack. Inside was something small and white. "Check it out, souvenirs."

Mack nodded, feeling inside his own pocket for the photographs he'd taken, but not taking them out. Keeping them tucked away.

Sammy exhaled a long plume of smoke. "He doesn't give a fuck."

Mack closed his eyes and rubbed his hands together. He could smell the smoke from the newly lit cigarette. The way its smell coated everything like a stain.

"Maybe not," said Mack. "Maybe not."

\*

When Mack and Sammy first became friends in the sixth grade, they spent most of their free time playing Ecco the Dolphin. Mack liked the game because he loved animals, especially sea animals, and even though he hated the panic that came from running out of air, the game mostly made him feel happy.

One time when they were playing, and it was Sammy's turn, Sammy asked Mack if he wanted to hear a story. Mack said yes, and Sammy licked his braces. Mack had thought it was impressive the way that Sammy could talk and play at the same time.

The story was something Sammy's uncle had told him, his mom's side of the family, when they were out visiting them in California for summer vacation back when he was maybe seven or eight. His uncle and his family lived in Berkeley, and one afternoon, Sammy's uncle took Sammy and his cousin Pete for a hike on Mount Tam. It was a hot day, sunny, and the hike was long and steep. They'd brought water, but they hadn't brought any snacks, and Sammy was hungry most of the way up.

"I remember thinking how boring it was going up, and how

it was going to feel twice as boring going down, and that Pete, he was like a year or two older than me, was being a real dick. So, basically, it sucked."

Then, when they were almost at the top, they heard a sound, like a rustling sound in the trees, and Sammy's uncle stopped the boys and told them to be quiet, to stop moving, and they stood like that for almost a whole minute, which was a pretty long time. At one point, Pete started to say something, and Sammy's uncle grabbed his shoulder in a way that Sammy had never seen an adult grab a child. And then another minute later, his uncle apologized and told them the story.

On Mount Tam, hikers are known to disappear. Some people think it's because of bears or the heat or even suicide, but that's not the reason. On Mount Tam, there exists a secret society of people, but they're not quite people, they're half human and half fish, and they live in a secret colony inside the center of the mountain.

Legend has it that these are people who never finished evolving. They were once fully fish and slowly they began to turn human, but they never completed the change. They couldn't live as people and they weren't good at being fish, either, so they were stuck, and they were outsiders, and so one night, they all came together and decided to drill inside the mountain and make a home where they could be together and live in peace. It was warm inside the mountain, and stalactites dripped water that they would catch in their mouths and on their skins to stay wet enough.

"My uncle said it was like the womb of the earth, and that's why they went there. To try and get reborn."

Only, humans aren't supposed to know about them, and if a human sees one, the fish person is supposed to kill them because the only way they'll survive is in secret. They can't let anyone know they exist, that they're different.

Mack remembered the way Sammy's face had looked, like he was recalling something deep and buried. He remembered the way it felt inside to hear it, how it was scary and yet somehow comforting. The way that hearing it meant he and Sammy had something special. Were something special.

"So, did you see one?" Mack asked.

Sammy shook his head. "I only saw some scales. My uncle took me off the trail to pee, and that's where we saw it. All these scales in a pile, like shiny and everything, and they smelled terrible. My Uncle said not to tell anyone because it was our secret. We didn't want the fish people to suffer."

"What do you mean?"

Sammy shrugged, didn't look at Mack, but kept staring at the TV, was quiet for a moment until he spoke. "I mean, it was bullshit. There's no such thing as fish people." On the screen, Ecco was running out of air. Mack watched as Sammy moved the dolphin to the surface. "He was just trying to scare me. He was just being a fag."

\*

Mack's sister, Janie, was only three years older than him, and this meant that once he went through puberty, they became friends and not just co-occupiers of their parents' home. Mack's sister had stringy, brown hair, and she was on the skinny side. Mack thought she was beautiful, that she looked like their mom from the pictures of their parents' wedding, all gauze and lace and lipstick. When Mack was fourteen and Janie was seventeen and a senior in high school, Mack would knock on her door, and if she was home and she was alone, she would let him in, and he'd lie on her floor and she'd play him CDs. Let him ask questions about the music. She'd ask him about school, but not the boring stuff, the people stuff, the stuff that was interesting. Who he liked and who was nice to him and who was cruel, and why people were like that and what it meant to have friends who you could really count on and love and would love you back.

Janie was a post-hippie she'd say, and laugh, and then make Mack listen to Janis Joplin and Jimmy Hendrix and Bradley Nowell and Nick Drake, and all the members of what she called the "felt good" club because they felt too good, and what that really meant was that they felt so bad that they ended up dying. They were the disappeareds she joked, because even before they were really gone, they were disappearing little by little.

Janie would tell Mack he had a good soul and a good heart, and that she knew he was going to grow up to be something worthwhile, a person worthy of great love, and so what if he wasn't a genius—he was kind and that meant a lot to the right people.

With Janie, Mack was able to be himself, or whoever he thought he was at the time, and it meant a lot to Mack to be able to just be a regular person.

Sometimes, all these years later, when he's alone, Mack will take out the photos he took from the hospital and study the faces. One photo is of a doctor, a therapist, which he knows because there's a typed name at the bottom, Laurie Jones, LCSW. She has brown hair down to her shoulders, and a skinny face with a skinny nose. She looks kind, Mack thinks. She looks like someone who might have really cared. The other picture is of a boy who Mack assumes must have been a patient or a former patient. He has red hair, and he's smiling, but his eyes look empty. Sometimes, Mack will hold the picture against his chest, and he'll whisper that he's sorry, and that wherever the boy is, he hopes he has found peace. Wherever he is, let him be in peace.

Then Mack will take the photos and put them back into the notebook and turn out the lights and go to sleep.

*

By the beginning of April, Mack had managed to maintain what he calculated as a B+ in Dr. Magellan's course, and even Sammy had managed to scrape together a C–, which was pretty much his average throughout high school. Mack and Sammy hung out most days that Mack wasn't working, and now Emily usually hung out with them, too. So, when Sammy asked Mack if they could scoop Emily and head to his place one Thursday after class, Mack felt sure it was because Sammy wanted to find a way to be alone with Emily, and so Mack said, yeah, of course, because there wasn't much else for him to say.

Sometimes it struck Mack as odd that Emily seemed to like Sammy, because Sammy wasn't particularly cool, and Emily was pretty popular from what he remembered. She could afford the right clothes and she was pretty and played field hockey, but then he just figured it had something to do with weed or the Adderall that Sammy gave Emily sometimes, or with the fact that they were neighbors, so they knew what it was like to live how they lived.

This was also why Mack felt initially shy when Emily came up to his apartment, but Emily didn't say much of anything, just, yes, she'd like a hard lemonade, and, yeah, she would sit on the loveseat. Thanks.

Mack and Sammy and Emily had been hanging out together, but now that they were together at Mack's place, Mack realized that Emily being here meant something more than it had meant when they'd drop by her house to smoke her up, or when she'd stop by Sammy's basement for a minute to say hey. Because Emily was here, but Mack didn't feel like Emily was his friend, no, she was Sammy's friend, and he was Sammy's friend and maybe that meant that Sammy was split between them.

So when Sammy asked Emily if she wanted to see where the junkies hung out, Mack knew it'd be better if he stayed back and let Sammy and Emily go on their own.

"You think our friend will be there?" Sammy asked Mack. And Mack knew Sammy was trying to impress Emily, to make her see him a certain way. Whatever that way might be.

Mack forced himself to smile, "Maybe, man."

Emily looked curious, but not that curious, Mack thought. Sort of, bored. Or maybe she was already stoned.

"Be careful, yeah?" Mack said as he walked them to the door and watched as they headed up the street.

When they were fifty feet away, Sammy turned back and shouted at Mack, "If we're not back in an hour, don't call the police." He made a gesture like pretending to hump and pointed to Emily, who seeing him, gave him a push that made Sammy falter in his balance and cling to her to stay upright.

*

The day that Sammy and Mack had seen the man, afterwards, when they were back inside Mack's apartment drinking beer, Mack asked whether they should call an ambulance, or maybe even the police, asked whether Sammy thought the guy was going to be okay, and Sammy laughed.

"The guy was just getting fucked," Sammy said. He patted his pocket and Mack stared at him, confused.

"What is it?" Mack asked, feeling stupid.

Sammy moved toward Mack, got so close that Mack could smell his sweat, the oniony flavor of his breath, the fading hint of Old Spice. He whispered in Mack's ear, the warm heat of his words, something Mack could feel against his skin. "Something even better than fucking, I bet."

Then Sammy pulled away just as quickly and kicked his feet out, his body splayed across the yellow beanbag chair. Mack could still feel his heart thumping as the space between their bodies grew. A longing like a tidal wave. A contract of intimacy tenuous as spider's thread.

*

If he'd wanted to know, from the beginning, Mack could have asked Sammy where he got his weed, his Adderall, the occasional Percocet he'd offer to Mack and Mack would decline. If it was the kind of connect that could get you anything you wanted, if you had the desire, and the money.

Mack could have told Sammy he used to smoke, a lot, with his sister, but that he'd stopped after she had her break, and now it just didn't do the same thing for him. He could have asked Sammy what it felt like to imagine yourself invincible. To live without fear. To let go and trust that you'll be caught.

Mack could have told Sammy not to fuck with whatever was in the baggie, to toss it, could have stopped him and gotten him help when he first suspected, instead of what he did do. Telling Sammy if he was going to do this shit, to do it here, so Mack could help him, take care of him if that's what he needed. Wanted.

Later, Mack could have asked himself whether he liked holding his friend's body, watching it fade, feeling his skinny chest in his arms, limp, underwater. Mack might have asked Sammy what it felt like to have Emily choose to rest her head against his thigh, or to sleep in a house with two parents and a little sister who ate dinner each night at a table, saying grace, and never wanting for anything. What did it feel like to have too much and still want more? What did it feel like to hate your uncle and to keep a secret?

Later, later that summer and into the fall, and up until Mack moved away for school, he could have asked Sammy about when you ground down the pills, when you had the spoon sizzling, did your blood already know what was about to happen? When you felt the prick did you even remember where you were? That you were with Mack. That he was rubbing your back, wiping at your face with a warm washcloth, breathing in your skin, keeping your secrets, putting his lips against your neck.

If Mack had wanted to know, he could have known. But he never did. It was as easy as that.

Once, nodding off in Mack's arms, sometime in early September at Mack's apartment, Sammy turned to Mack, his lips wet, his pupils like small, perfect beads, and he said, "You love me," and then he laughed, his neck slumped against Mack, and later, Mack could have asked Sammy if he remembered what he said. But he didn't.

*

About a week after Sammy and Mack had gone inside, Mack went through the fence by himself. It was in the early morning, sometime just after dawn and Mack felt like he'd been awake the whole night waiting for something terrible to happen. A phone call. A knock at the door. A rock pinging against his window. He kept having the feeling that something wasn't right, so finally he got dressed and went for a walk, didn't plan to go to the hospital but ended up there just the same, slipped through the fence, his hands tucked into the pockets of his hoodie. It was eerie so early. Lonelier than in the late afternoon, and Mack could feel his vulnerability like something he was trying to crush between his teeth.

Inside, Mack took his time, looking into each room with an

open door and any amount of light, and that's when he saw the couple passed out in one of the rooms. They were young look-ing, maybe in their mid-twenties, fully dressed. Mack figured they weren't asleep so much as passed out, or at the least they prob-ably weren't there just to fuck. The woman's mouth hung open partially, like a sleeping child's, but her dress looked dirty from where Mack could see. The man lay with an elbow over his face, like he was protecting himself from the sun, but there wasn't any sun in the room, just a slit of dawn light from the edge of the plywood's imperfect cover. There was a bizarre innocence to the way their bodies touched as they lay together on one of the small hospital mattresses on the dirty tile floor. What was more strange was what Mack felt in response. The pang of jealousy that despite all rationality stung him. It was Sammy and Emily. It was Sammy and anyone else.

Mack never said anything to Sammy about what he saw, or that he'd gone through the fence by himself.

Many months later, during the end of his second fall semester at Lake View, as Mack headed to his English class, he saw Emily outside the main doors, smoking a cigarette, one leg tucked behind her, leaning against the side of the building. He waved, but when she didn't seem to see him, he walked up to her and said hello.

"What do you want?" she asked him, and he felt taken aback, confused.

"Nothing," he said. And then she stared at him for a long moment.

"You knew, didn't you?" she said, her eyes, green, impaling him, and Mack, his mouth open dumbly, had not been able to give her an answer.

*

Sometimes Mack would think about all the bad things that could happen to someone or the bad things that a person could do to another person. Like what if it turned out Mack had killed that man from the hospital and he didn't know it, or what if Mack fell over the second story railing and broke his neck, or what if Mack was crazy, too, or what if Mack was like his mom, and it turned out he didn't give a shit, or else he cared so much he couldn't stand to see the people he loved being so imperfect. And Mack would think about Coach and about leaning into the fear, and he would wonder if he just did this stuff before it could happen on its own, would that make it better? Or whether this was all crazy thinking and if only he'd tried to talk about it with Janie before she became impermanent, a shell.

One of the last times that Sammy and Mack had hung out before they drifted apart, before high school started, they'd had a sleepover in a tent in Sammy's backyard. At the time, they both knew it was a little kid thing to do, but they'd decided it was okay because no one knew what they were doing, and they were going to be in high school soon and this kind of kiddie stuff definitely couldn't happen then.

Mack remembered they'd stayed up most of the night joking around and then talking, which was something they hadn't really done much before. They talked about kids from their school, and Sammy talked about Amanda, his crush, and Mack told Sammy about how his dad was an ex-Marine and how this made him seem both scary and cool sometimes, like just knowing that he'd been to war and seen people die. And then just as they were drifting off to sleep, Mack told Sammy that he loved him. And Sammy, to his credit, never said anything in response.

Later on, Mack realized he could have said it differently, could have said, I love you, brother, and it might not have made things feel how they felt, but at the time, Mack said it the way he felt it. Like there was no other choice. Like if he could have, he'd have taken this other person inside of his skin, clung to him, never let him go.

When Sammy and Emily came back from the abandoned lot and Emily went to the bathroom at Mack's, Sammy pulled Mack aside and whispered in his ear. "We basically got to third base, dude." His lips were wet with spit. His pupils were tiny pinpoints.

And as the toilet flushed, Sammy mimed making out and Mack smiled at his friend, but inside, it felt like something had come loose in his brain.

"What'd you think?" Mack asked when Emily was out of the bathroom.

Sammy looked to Emily, her face pale, her lips a thin line. She shook her head. "It's a shithole. What else am I supposed to think?"

*

In the years to come, Mack would think about these types of abandoned places and the people who found their way inside. If they were lonely people like how he'd seen himself back then, or if they were something else, alive, in the bittersweet way that he felt alive, taking care of Sammy in those days after he began to disappear. When Mack made the decision that he was willing to let Sammy feel joy. When he rubbed his friend's forehead, held him in his arms as he passed out so his head wouldn't hit the floor, inhaling the faint odor of Sammy's sweat as he lay on the ground, head sunk into the bean bag, eyes adrift, Sammy's small pink tongue visible through his partially open mouth. The spit bubbling up. The enabling that offered him his love requited, however meanly.

Now that Mack knew something about statistics, he wondered if this was a way to understand the world, by likelihood or by rarity or some combination of the two. For example, if Mack met a merman, what were the odds he would even get the chance to know its legs were fins? If Mack let Sammy crush oxy every other day for five months, how many more months would it need to continue? How high would Sammy climb? When would he run out of air? If Sammy and Emily and Mack made love without a condom, how many times until Emily was likely to get pregnant? How tall would the child be? How old? Where would they build their nest?

On the last day of the semester, Sammy picked up Mack from his apartment earlier than normal because that was the day of their statistics final. Mack had spent the last week studying as much as possible, which had been a little hard to do since Emily and Sammy had had a falling out, about what Sammy wouldn't say. They were done, he said. And that was all that Mack could get out of him, and so now, Sammy had nothing but time.

After the exam, Sammy suggested they go to the mall parking lot and smoke, but then Sammy realized that since it was earlier than normal, not everything would be open yet.

"Want to head to my place then?" Mack asked, and Sammy said all right yeah. That would be good.

At Mack's, they drank a celebratory High Life. After, Sammy said maybe they could go sit in the swings, smoke a cigarette, since it was such a nice day and there was nothing else to do.

"What made you notice this place?" Sammy asked Mack as they ducked under the fence, first Sammy, then Mack.

It was the beginning of May and wildflowers sprouted all over the unkempt lot. Some of the windows were re-boarded up since the last time Mack walked by. A blue sleeping bag drowned in a puddle left over from the last rain, nearly a week before.

Mack shrugged. "I'd see people go in. It made me wonder, I guess." Sammy wore a T-shirt that looked even looser than normal. His hair was slightly longer, too, and it looked a bit greasier than it did sometimes. "My sister stayed here for a little bit before it closed."

Mack looked at Sammy, and Sammy nodded, like he knew, like he understood.

Sammy kicked a piece of wet cardboard with his shoe. It got stuck on the toe, and Mack watched his friend try to shake it loose. "People just do what they need to." He looked up at Mack and put his hand in his pocket. "I'll be right back, yo."

Sammy went through the window. Mack watched the space where his friend had been, like a portal to some other world.

Instead of following, Mack went and sat on the only good swing that remained. He swung back and forth, and he kept thinking that any minute he would hear Sammy cursing or burping or making a fart sound with his armpit, but he didn't hear anything at all.

After a few minutes, Mack slowed the swing to a stop. He rose and moved toward the window. He looked inside, but he didn't see anything. Just another hospital cot and a shattered beer bottle and an empty plastic flask of Skol.

Years later, after Mack moved away and got himself through college. After he studied social work and figured out some things about the kind of man he wanted to be with, Mack came home for a long weekend to visit his dad and to see his sister who had recently gotten her own apartment. On the way to the house, he decided to stop and get some beer to bring his dad, and in the liquor store he ran into Sammy's mom. She recognized Mack right away, and she smiled, taking both his hands in her own. When he asked how Sammy was doing, his mom laughed, and said, Oh wow, I haven't heard him called that in years. She said he was doing good, okay, better at least. And Mack nodded, I'm sorry, he thought. And then he gave her a hug and it felt really nice to hold someone who loved Sammy as much as he had.

Mack never ended up going inside the building that day, and forty minutes later, when Sammy came out and walked over to Mack and vomited at the base of the swings, Mack didn't move his feet away, he didn't recoil. No, it was as if he'd been expecting it to happen. Here, finally, was his place. Someone's need, for the first time, so clear, so fully fleshed. Mack, smiled, leaned over his friend's body and rubbed his back, feeling the spine and the ribs and everything that was holding his love together.

# Gardening

I have organized my garden in the following manner. The carrots grow beside the sweet potatoes. The basil, the rosemary, and the thyme nest in pots beside the fishless pond. The heads of bib lettuce, the scaffolds of tomatoes and peppers, these grow to the left of everything else. They overflow when the weather and the rainfall are just right, but I do not allow them to extend beyond what is sensible. The kale and the cauliflower ferment in warm beds by the stone path. Wild asparagus grows against the shed.

For the past few months, my husband, Jason, likes to stand by the doorway and watch me when he believes I am unaware of his presence. He is desperate for the curve of my back. He imagines the spine beneath my white T-shirt, its bony perfection rising against the still-soft skin. I let him stare. I fold my body closer to the earth, and then I turn toward him in time to catch his shame. His desire hovers in the air like mist.

Today I smile and wave, beckoning him toward me. As he approaches, I rise up to face him and when he reaches me, I drop back down to my knees.

"Will you help me with this?" My fingers dig into the soil, the area beneath my nails blackening with the soft loam.

He is clumsy beside me as he eases to a squat. He's worried that his shoes will get muddy, that the cuffs of his tailored pants will touch the weeds I've been pulling out. Bending now, I wonder if he can smell my sweat. The absence of deodorant under the July sun. The sour herb of my body. The sun blasting at my cheekbones and his concern that I should wear a hat, something wide-brimmed and matronly.

"I can't get this cluster. It's the grass—the roots are too deep." I ease back to give him space, to help him understand the situation in the flowerbed.

He's wordless beside me as he rocks on his heels, one large dark-haired hand braced against the side of the planter. I point toward the weed I am trying to unearth, the trowel loose in my fingers. The roots of this wild grass desperate to remain where they have encroached.

"Just this one?" His voice cracks slightly as he speaks, but then he steadies himself and pulls at the stubborn weed.

I shrug and rise to my feet. The muscles in his forearms tense as he tries to rip the grass from the earth. His salmon-colored shirt looks newly ironed, but I can see the creases left from his inexpert hand. The fabric bunches as he exerts himself.

Then, the weed is freed. Jason catches himself from falling backward with his free hand. His balance has always been good.

He rises up from his squat, holding the trail of roots for me to admire. "If you catch it early, then these won't have the chance to take root."

Nodding, a smile forms on my lips, the strain of it forces my cheeks to dimple. "Sorry."

His cheeks flush slightly as he hears himself, but I come toward him and place my sun-chapped lips against the flank of his face. His body presses toward me, turning so that he might face me, rub against me, and I can feel his lips hesitating, readying to say something, so I place my soil-rich fingers across his mouth. I tense my pose. His movement stops, and I feel his body relax. I release my lips and step back, rubbing my hands together, loosening the remaining dirt.

"Not yet," I say. And Jason nods his head, unable to meet my eyes, or, unwilling.

*

The public library where I work employs four full-time librarians of which I am one. In addition, there are two part-time assistants, two janitors, and a summer intern from the local college, William, who I call Billy. I am the second youngest of the full-time librarians. I have worked at this library for seven years, the same number of years that Jason and I have been married. I am thirty-two years old as of this past March. It is now the middle of July, and my life is divided between the dense, central Texas heat and the air-conditioned chambers of this tomb. Once, I loved to read. Lately, the sentences, the words, even the letters feel like insects crawling over the soft lobes of my brain.

The summer is our busiest time of year, most likely because of the respite we offer from the heat. When our doors open each morning at 8 a.m., the mothers and the nannies and the occasional father come barreling through with infants and children in tow, anxious to read aloud in a circle or to find some relief from the empty hours of vacation. Glad to be in the sterile, sticky calm of our oasis.

Last year, Jason carried on a five-month affair with his colleague at the medical testing facility where he works. Her name was Erin and, strangely, we look quite similar. We're both slender, though her breasts are larger than mine. We both have dark hair and imperfect noses. She wears glasses, but I only wear glasses on occasion. When I want to look like a certain kind of librarian. When my contacts act up.

I did not discover the affair. I might have if I'd felt more than a general concern for my marriage, but at the time I was attempting to grow an award-winning tomato and with this hobby in mind, little else struck me as important. Jason and I had the sort of marriage where we were good friends, and we were lovers. A certain level of comfortability. And although at first in our courtship, it plagued me that I couldn't venture inside his brain to see his blue or his yellow or his understanding of what it meant to taste a banana, this had subsided into the gentle hum of living. Monthly or weekly, there were small tokens of our mutual and enduring affection: a shiny trowel, a pair of yellow gardening gloves, a book from me on the history of lab rats and mice. We were in love, and although on occasion he believed himself smarter than me, and though sometimes my orgasm was neglected, I had the strong belief that this was as good as it gets. I do not think I was wrong.

Our other most reliable set of library patrons are the elderly and the homeless, both groups of which trickle in throughout the day from their respective shelters. The rarest patron is the bored teenager or the lone researcher who has wandered in to find some information they feel will aid their existence. Oftentimes, the teenagers and the researchers leave disappointed. Their expectations exceeding our slight offerings. Our stacks not so well stacked for their needs. Scant knowledge here of plight, of the Arctic Circle, of human growth hormones.

On my first date with Jason, at Patricio's Italian bistro, I got very drunk and butted my head against his head in an attempt to enter his skull. I'm not sure he understood what I was doing, but at the time he found it funny. We laughed about it the next morning. I wonder now what I was thinking. What closeness I had desired. How still, years later, his animal scent feels borne into my skin and hair, unconscious. Three months later, Jason and I were married at the courthouse. We both wore white. His

suit was ivory, and my dress—short, lacey—was eggshell. When
I learned of the affair, it was through Jason and his swollen, tear-
stained face. I was in the kitchen, dicing sweet onions from the
garden when he came to me to relieve his guilt.

This was a wounding. I was surprised by the savagery of the
pain, like an avalanche of loss somewhere from the throat to the
groin. My mouth filled with saliva as he spoke, and I swallowed
the warm liquid of my making. He'd ended the affair of his own
accord, or so he told me. I suspect the guilt had purged all joy
from the feeling of being wanted by a stranger. Or maybe he was
lonely, and I hadn't noticed, and this was an act of desperation.
Or else she'd ended things and everything Jason said to me was a
lie. It's difficult to trust someone who fucks outside the marriage.
See how I should have known the importance of words and their
pitch, their hue. The impressions they make, like bullets or like
stones.

"What are you doing?" Billy, the intern, stands a few feet
away, staring at me. His hands placed awkwardly on his hips as
if directed there by some inner mechanism that wants to appear
casual.

"I'm making a grocery list." I point to the empty notepad
before me and write "eggs" in large, clear letters.

Billy has found me hiding in the stacks again. Though reshelving is work meant for the interns and assistants, I have a cart of
books ready at my side. In another life, I used the ruse of reshelving as a means to discover new gardening techniques, new types
of grass, fondue recipes, but lately the fluorescent hum of the
lights makes me feel stoned and dumb.

"Really?" Billy steps closer to look at what I've been writing.
I am always surprised at his height, that people younger than me
might be taller than me, though it's something I've understood
rationally for years.

I take the pad and turn it upside down on top of the cart of books. "What did Alyssa assign you to do this morning?" I feel my shoulders dropping in a conscious effort to appear taller, older, more responsible.

Billy shrugs. Then he swipes his hair out of his eyes and looks at me in a way that makes me certain of his desire, the hidden treasure of my naked self. I stare back. And slowly, I let myself smile, just at the corners of the lips, just the barest mirror of his post-adolescent lust. At this, Billy blushes and looks away.

"She said I should do the cart you're doing."

"All right." I take my notepad and use the cart as a barrier between myself and Billy as I squeeze past. When I am a few feet away I turn to face him. "Billy?" I say his name like it has meaning, like an invitation. I watch his eyes gauging me, trying to understand, to guess at what I might say next.

He moves toward me, hesitant. There are maybe three feet between us. Books on the civil war. The reconstruction. I can smell his soap. Or maybe it's body spray. A musky maleness.

His eyes are brown. Big wet ponds spoiled by movement. His lips open partly but he doesn't speak.

"Never mind." I can feel the heart in my chest like a seedling. "I'm sorry." I shrug my shoulders and turn away, willing him to watch me leave. But without turning back to look, without sacrificing everything, I cannot be sure if he is watching.

*

There are stages of recovery in betrayal. At first, when Jason told me about Erin, at night in the kitchen, the frogs of late August bellowing through the windows sealed tight to facilitate the air-conditioning, I felt pain, fresh and undisguised. This woman with inflated breasts, my double.

How it was that the person you understood in nearly their complete self could become so immediately unfamiliar, and yet wrapped in the same old skin and hair and odor. The pants stiff with creases made by my hand's gentle back and forth with the iron. The dark hair trimmed slightly too short from a recent trip to the salon. It is unreal to see the face that gives you comfort slice your innards, the lips dumb and moving, wet spit forming globules like dew on a blade of grass. Apologies spilling out like fertilizer. The words nonsense. Disbelief.

I couldn't even think of what to say back, like some confused child clinging to the counter, hands limp, onion stinging my eyes. "It's the onion," I had said. Or maybe I had only thought it.

Late that night, Jason asleep in our bed, exhausted and drugged with his relief, I went out to the garden with the intention of hurting my tomatoes. It was a melodramatic wish, but it was all I could think of to do at the time to get even. Self-destruction is one form of remedy, is one form of violence against those who claim to love you.

But the flashlight showed my tomatoes were too good, too innocent. Instead, I sat in the dirt in my shorts and my camisole, and I put my hands in the dirt. I rubbed the dirt all over my arms and then on my face. I made streaks with my fingers, and I imagined my pores clogged and beautiful. My mother would always say that knowledge is embedded in the world around us. That there's always something to be understood by someone willing to see it.

I was in the garden maybe an hour before I came inside and washed my face and hands and arms in our bathroom sink. I was careful to wash away all traces of dirt from the pale porcelain. May there never be a time when you are not in control.

"Soph?"

Jason's call sounds quiet from the dining room, its worry a

flash forward to this present moment, this strawberry afternoon. He's looking for me, anxious to see my face and confirm that I'm still his wife. It's been eleven months now since the revelation of his infidelity, and things are almost entirely back to normal, except that this isn't the normal we once understood.

"I'm in here." My voice is too bright, too happy, and I think about responding again but dropping my pitch. I'm in the living room, a room I never used to spend time in, but lately I've found a cool patch of rug by the nonworking fireplace that offers a good view of the garden. I sit here after work and think until I've lost all sense of time and language. Then, something brings me back.

Jason comes in the room looking flushed from the outdoors. His head looks meatier to me than normal, but I wonder if this is a result of the sunburn he received from helping me in the garden the past weekend. I never thought Jason was beautiful until I fell in love with him and then there was nothing he could do to dispel the kindness my gaze gave to his body. The gentle movement of his lips in sleep, the melancholy child I imagined trapped in his irises. The way his eyebrows arched when he laughed, or how it felt to be scooped up in arms so much stronger than my own, or the way he'd draw doodles of elements all over my notebooks in an attempt to teach me about the structures of the things I loved to grow. What does it say about me that I love him still. To hurt someone you love is human. To endure in harsh conditions, to hunker down, to root.

"What're you doing in here?" Jason comes over to where I sit cross-legged on the floor and stands beside me, so I can lean into his legs. I don't answer him because I don't have anything reasonable to say.

"How was work?" I ask. Erin no longer works at the company, but it's difficult not to feel like I'm insinuating something dark when I ask these simple questions.

"Work was okay. Maybe some promising results coming. How was your day?" Jason takes my outstretched hand and pulls me up so I'm standing near him. I smell the way his light sweat has offset the scent of fresh laundry.

"It was fine." I try to think of something else to add, a detail, but all I can remember is the sterile coldness of the circulation desk. The bodies of patrons moving around asking questions and the hope that I was making sense in my responses. Then I see Billy, his thin lips. "Alyssa's off next week for vacation, so I'll have to stay a couple hours later on Wednesday." It's true. It's something I can offer as fact.

Jason nods. "You feel like going out for dinner? Something light like sushi?" He takes my hands in his and squeezes my fingers, rocks me back and forth as if we're dancing. I keep my feet planted, and I feel like a little girl standing on her father's shoes, dancing. In the past, he might have grabbed me and thrown me down on the couch, pulled up my skirt and put his mouth between my legs until I begged him to fuck me, but, as I said, the old normal is gone. Our sex now, on the rare occasion I allow it, is shy and curious and incomplete. Even when I do my best to remember the innocence of our initial love, I am haunted. I can no longer tell if it's because of the affair or because I am meant to be different from the affair. Lately, I wonder if I'm the stranger in our house. If I'm the one who cheated. If I'm the one with whom he had the affair.

"Sushi sounds perfect."

*

Three months after Jason and Erin ended things, when I'd forgiven Jason and we'd stopped only talking about my hurt and his pain and his confusion and self-hate and my fear of intimacy and my coldness and my complacency, we decided that if we were going to make things work, we'd have to move forward whatever it was that that took.

It was Jason's idea that I should sleep with someone outside the marriage. He said it first late at night, wine-drunk during an episode of *House of Cards.* He said it was the only way he'd feel normal, to know that I was as at fault as he was. To know that imperfection was something we had in common. The logic was broken, and I told him so, but he continued the appeal the following day. And then about once every few weeks in the months since. This is his practical solution, and yet he has forgotten the control.

I'd like to know the pain you felt, Sophia. I'd like to have an inkling of how badly I've made you feel, sweetheart. I want to know that you're with me because you forgive me, and you love me and not because of any other reason, Soph. These are his words. See how they shine and blister.

First, I see these words blue and earnest, then red and filthy. I imagine them in different colors like the variations of zinnias from my mother's garden. Anything that can be said aloud, can take shape and so exist in the world however awfully or grossly. Anything that can be put into words can live, fester, dig into the soul and rot. What grows in the garden is innocent. What grows in the mind is human.

Jason does not want to know the details of any future transgression but only that it has taken place. What does it even mean to love another person? Sometimes I am not sure.

Erin and Jason had sex fourteen times over the course of their five-month affair. Jason never told her he loved her, but he did, through text message, affirm that she was hot and not undeserving of kindness.

Billy is not unattractive. He is twenty years old. He has dark brown hair that's longer on top and shaved on the sides. He's skinny in a way that makes me realize the difference between his boy-ness and the man-ness of Jason. There is the occasional patch of acne on his chin, and the pocked scars of prior outbreaks on his cheeks. I am not sure that he understands that I'm a person, but I am unsure whether or not it matters, given the circumstances.

I have not decided what I will do, if I will trust in Jason's healing insight or if I will simply lie and make myself trust again, believe again, that we can ever fully understand another person.

The way it started with Erin was casual. A client lunch, some wine, an empty lab, white lab coats, a blowjob, an experiment on mice, tumors attached to the backs, the fronts, breasts exposed and nipples dark and lovely.

I became a librarian because it was a structure I understood. Here are the books and here are the numbers. Water daily and plant on the fourth, seventh, and ninth days of the lunar calendar. Put your tongue inside the mouth of the person you love. Prepare and eat salads. Prepare and season the tuna steak. See how the watermelon grows inside the belly of she who swallows the seed. Books on nuclear war proliferate.

The first time I made Billy laugh, I had asked him to find the book I'd intentionally misshelved. It was a book on *The Dick Van Dyke Show* and I had placed it by the self-help books on thinking outside the box. I appreciated the deep sound of his laugh, as if it came from a newly discovered voice inside his young body. I told him I wanted to call him Billy after Billy Budd though I've never read the book. He said it was one of his favorites. I wonder if he's lying. I can only assume it does not matter.

*

"What do you want to be when you grow up?"

"Is that a real question?"

"I guess so."

"Then I guess I don't know. A sea captain? A financial planner? An architect?"

"The answer was librarian."

Again, Billy laughs, and the sound is loud and sweet. We are in the stacks. Alyssa, the head librarian, is on vacation and I am now the second in command instead of the third in command. The skirt I've worn is slightly shorter than normal. It hits just above the knee as opposed to at the knee. It's pale blue in color and lacks a pattern. My bare calves make me human.

I was sitting on the floor, supposedly reshelving, when Billy found me and now he sits on the floor as well. We face each other our legs stretched toward the opposite shelves. I feel the slightest warmth in my neck and a gentle note of panic that we could be discovered, and I could be made to feel shame for my lack of diligence. I was once the most diligent of the librarians. I was once the most hard-headed and prim.

"What do you do when you're not here?" Billy smiles at me then drops his eyes to my knees. He is awkward in his flirtation.

I shrug my shoulders. "I read books. Or I used to."

"What kind of books?"

I uncross and recross my legs at the ankles. My skin looks tan, somewhat red in the library's yellow light. "I like to garden."

"So you read gardening books?" Billy wants to connect. His mouth hangs open waiting for my answer.

"Of course." Then I smile and lean forward to stretch, touching my toes then rubbing my hand slowly up the length of my leg to pull up my skirt just the slightest bit.

"Gardening makes you tan, huh?" Billy's eyes are where I

have led them. See how the skirt does not reveal paleness but more color.

"That it does." I rest my hand on my exposed thigh long enough so Billy begins to move his own hand toward my leg, and then I laugh once, awkwardly, and pull my legs together to stand. "Better get back to work."

In the background, Billy nods and I smooth down my skirt with my hands. I give him a small smile and then head back toward the circulation desk to relieve Megan.

I had planned to grow a new kind of lettuce this year, but I realize now that the seeds were not purchased. Frisée. The curly fronds so delicious with a bit of heat, a bit of goat cheese. Maybe it's not too late. I can check the almanac, I can purchase what's necessary. I can ask Jason for his help this weekend. His hands so good at digging into the earth, at prying loose what does not belong.

With Erin, was there pursuit or was it accidental? Letters side by side, elbows accidently graze and the lab coat loses its sterility, the books disordered. Against my will, between my legs, a wetness forms.

*

All throughout my childhood, my mother kept a butterfly garden. To attract the butterflies, she planted particular flowers—lavender, lilac, fleabane—and she would let me help her plant the seedlings.

My father fed the birds and the squirrels alike. He kept a feeder filled through all the seasons, even though my mother was against the idea. He liked to watch them, their colors and their antic movements like frames spliced together in an old cartoon.

Sometimes my father would sit on the stone bench he gave my
mother for her birthday one year, and he would pretend to watch
the birds. He was instead watching her, now I am sure of it.

In the early years of our marriage, I would lie on Jason, my
back against his chest, and I would pretend that he was an island
of safety in the otherwise dangerous sea of our bedsheets. He
would hold my wrists and move my arms through the air like
flying fish. Then slowly, I would rotate my body so our faces
touched. We would breathe the same air until one of us laughed
and pushed the other to upset the delicate balance of our bodies
perched like seashells.

Sometimes at work, I'll pull out a book and try to read it
upside down. To see if sense can be made of the words as they
appear backwards and wrong. I am not sure that anything means
anything. Sometimes I am embarrassed that it took Jason's phi-
landering to make me see the world for what it is. How lovely and
how unexpected. How mean and how bleak.

When I was twelve, my mother went to her sister's house for
a long weekend. I remember at the time how strange it seemed
to me that she should want to leave us for any amount of time.
That she could want to be away from her family, her flowers, the
insects she'd drawn to our garden. And what was the draw of her
sister's house, their oft described antipathy, her sterile twin beds.

I am not sure I would remember the weekend at all, but that
the second night she was gone my father got very drunk. I'd gone
to my bedroom to read sometime after dinner and fallen asleep. I
awoke around midnight, confused and startled, and when I went
downstairs to get some milk, I saw my father in the living room.
He sat by the reading lamp, the one that leaned forward like a
nightshade, and he was crying, a book sloppily set on his lap. It
was a silent cry, and I didn't interrupt him. When my mother
came home, I told her about my vision. Her husband, red-faced

and gripping a glass of whiskey, the frail, wet book. My mother shrugged. She wouldn't say what it meant.

The first time Jason and I had a serious fight over our domestic responsibilities, I tried to push him, and he grabbed me and took me in his arms, and though I struggled and begged him to put me down, he would not let me go. We had before been quietly cruel to one another, but I could not excuse his taking something that I loved and using it to hurt me. Sober, later, I told him never to lift me in his arms again.

After my father died, my mother told me that she'd once had an affair. It had only lasted two weeks, one weekend, and she said it was the most selfish thing she'd ever done. "It's the only thing I regret, Sophia." Her mouth a thin red line. I nodded, smiling and put my hand on hers.

\*

Early Saturday morning, I wake Jason with breakfast in bed. Coffee, coffee cake, and a halved banana. Afterwards, we make love in our new gentle and bargaining way. Each touch fraught with feeling. Each stroke wet with remorse and promise. An attempt to make the other feel at ease, wanted, known.

"So, you'll help me in the garden?" I ask the question brightly, half-naked, post-coitally.

Jason nods at me and smiles, reaches for my arm to pull me back into bed, but I slip away, knowing that he will follow.

According to the farmer's almanac, we have just missed the last good day for planting lettuces, but I am in the mood for a gamble. I place the new straw hat which Jason purchased for me on my head, and I step barefoot outside to the garden and its stifling late July heat.

I begin to dig with my trowel, finding an empty patch in the planter which houses the kale, slightly shaded at certain times of day by the pecan tree which grows at the far back of the lot. A few moments later, Jason is beside me in sneakers and shorts, his skin smelling of suntan lotion self-applied.

We work quietly together for some minutes. I point to places where he might unearth soil, neighboring weeds which might be plucked from the earth. Sweat drips slowly down the backs of my legs, along my spine. I wait to speak. The heart, it wobbles.

"So. It's happened, you know." The words slip out so quietly, so without performance.

Jason is on his knees combing through the neighboring planter for signs of weeds. I am not sure he has heard me, so I open my mouth to speak again.

"I mean, what you wanted to happen." In my mind, I wonder if I should have practiced the line ahead of time. If I sound convincing, too happy, too contrite. "So. It's okay."

Jason squints at my face, his ball cap suddenly unbecoming on his squarely built face. "That hat looks good on you." He pretends not to understand.

Blushing, I touch the straw hat. In the heat, I can smell its straw odor, its fragrant heat. I touch my lips not thinking, thinking of the pressure of his mouth earlier in the day. The morning. What I want from him. An irrecoverable past.

Then Jason's hand is on my arm, his dirt-tinged fingers slowly moving the hairs of my forearm up and down. "Thank you. I mean. I know it's not easy."

I nod and feel suddenly the heat of moisture behind my eyes. The tension of all our months of absence. "I need you," I say.

Jason nods. He pulls me toward him, he kisses my neck. He pushes me down into the earth and his body on top of me follows.

\*

My favorite part of being a librarian has always been the feeling of existing in a space where my being, my voice, are an intrusion. The silence of the stacks. The quietude of so many minds accruing meaning all at the same time, all wordless, all sucking in and absorbing letters, words, feelings, self-worth, nothingness.

When I was a child, I decided it was my aim to read every book, every picture book, that the local library held. For hours, at the small round tables accompanied by my father on summer weekends, I would sit and read and read and take home only what I couldn't finish in my allotted hours. Then, when I was eight, I found one book that I didn't want to stop reading, and my plan was put on hiatus. Permanent hiatus it turns out. What's funny is that I can't remember the book anymore. It was about ghosts, I think, but it gave me such a feeling inside that I couldn't contain it or describe it. Its words ended my language. Its images lost me the ability to speak.

It's the first week in August when I ask Billy to stay late and help me close the library. The closing librarian on Thursdays is Sheila, and she's on vacation for the week, so I have been given her duties. On Thursdays, we stay open an hour later than normal, till 8:00 p.m. Billy and I divide the library at closing time, sweeping the stacks, the reading room, the children's area, the bathrooms, and the computers for stray, lingering patrons. When the last guest has left, I lock the front doors and we turn off the lights in each section. Billy and I work quietly and efficiently. We do not speak. Then, when all that is left is to move the cash drawer to the office's lockbox, I ask Billy for a suggestion of what to read.

"Find me something historical maybe?" I have told him that I'm leaving on vacation the following week, which is true. Jason and I have rented a beach house. A bungalow on the gulf.

I follow Billy to the stacks and as he reaches for a book, I put my hand on his back. My fingers are light, tentative. This touch is all that he has needed.

"Sophia."

I am embarrassed to hear him say my name in this way, but then he has me in his arms, he guides me to the floor and his tongue is in my mouth.

Our clothing comes off piece by piece until we're naked. His hands are young and gentle. Without the overhead fluorescents, my mind feels sober. I am no longer dumb.

In the garden, everything has been organized according to what it needs. The sweet potatoes like a certain amount of moisture. The zucchinis need structure. The tomatoes need support.

"Oh, Billy." Oh, sweet Billy of the seas.

See how I have always been able to intuit what is needed. I trim the vine. I add the mulch. I pluck and tend and water but never too much, too often. You have to let it grow. You have to let the seed take root.

My lips graze his smooth and hollow chest, its hairlessness so unfamiliar, so unhappy. There is no grace in our discarded clothes, your thin T-shirt, its lack of collar, of care.

In bloom, the blues and the yellows, the reds and the pinks, the spit and the sweat, they riot beyond our reach. See, Jason, how violence grows like mulberry, like kudzu, like desire—like something we cannot or will not control.

But, please. Please remember, Jason. What comes after rot is always something living.

# Acknowledgments

Thank you to the following journals where these stories appear: "Our Daughters Whose Blood" in *Sou'wester*, "First Date" in *Witness*, "Harold, Protector of the Children" in *Southwest Review*, "Gardening" in *Colorado Review*, and "The Pleasures of Television" in *Shenandoah*. Thank you also to the editors Greg Brownderville, Morgan Davis, Joe Milan Jr., Geoff Schmidt, and Steven Schwartz.

Thank you to my agent, Sorche Fairbank, for her expert guidance throughout this process.

Thank you to Clancy Tripp and the staff at *The Journal*, and to Nick White for selecting my manuscript. Thank you to everyone at Mad Creek Books for your help, care, and patience through this process.

Thank you to my teachers at UNT in whose workshops these stories were produced. Scott Blackwood, keeper of the appetites, Ian McGuire, who taught me the value of register, Miroslav Penkov, who challenged my impulse to overwrite, and John Tait, who helped me consider my audience in the work these stories are attempting. Thank you also to my peers in workshop for their generosity, support, and advice.

Thank you also to my fiction professors at Vanderbilt who gave me the foundation I needed to take my work where it needed to go. To Tony Earley, who saved my metaphors and instilled in me the value of the thing and the other thing, to Lorraine Lopez, whose guidance on the sentence level was vital, and to Nancy Reisman for raising the questions that mattered. Thank you to my cohort and workshop mates for your friendship, intelligence, and keen advice.

Thank you also to the other teachers who have been so meaningful in my education along the way: Chris Bagg, Kate Daniels, Peter Guralnick, Christopher Lloyd, Kara Mahoney-Lopez, Ifeoma Nwankwo, and Jill Talbot.

Thank you to Blake and Michael, and all my former students at KSR for letting me be a part of your lives. Thank you also to my students at Vanderbilt, JCTC, Ivy Tech, and UNT for your excitement, patience, and brilliance. And thank you to the teens at Denton County CTC whose energy and words were both challenging and inspiring.

To my dear friends who offered notes on these stories over the years and to those who helped form me and support me as a writer: Amanda Abel, Chad Abushanab, Luke Allen, Matt Baker, Claire Burgess, Iqra Cheema, Lee Connell, Melissa Cundieff, Jenny Dowling, Sara Henry, Barbara Honegger, Susanna Kwan, Claire Jimenez, Marysa Larowe, Alyssa MacLeod, Colleen Mayo, Siobhan McBride, Leslie Pietrzyk, Scott Ray, Jim Redmond, Kate Ritchie, Jill Schepmann, Morgan Inigo Smith, Nat Sobel, Janet Thielke, Annie Welch, Jenna Williams, and Josh Zimmerer.

Thank you to all the Bernards, Dowlings, Honeggers, and Schroens in my life. Thank you to Ellie for being an excellent hound.

To Robert for his supreme patience, love, and support.

Thank you to my father, Peter, and my stepmother, Susie, tireless first readers of each of these stories. And to my mother, Betty, the first writer I knew, whose capacity for empathy enabled me to write these stories.

# THE JOURNAL NON/FICTION PRIZE
(formerly The Ohio State University Prize in Short Fiction)

*Our Sister Who Will Not Die: Stories*
REBECCA BERNARD

*The Age of Discovery and Other Stories*
BECKY HAGENSTON

*Sign Here If You Exist and Other Essays*
JILL SISSON QUINN

*When: Stories*
KATHERINE ZLABEK

*Out of Step: A Memoir*
ANTHONY MOLL

*Brief Interviews with the Romantic Past*
KATHRYN NUERNBERGER

*Landfall: A Ring of Stories*
JULIE HENSLEY

*Hibernate*
ELIZABETH ESLAMI

*The Deer in the Mirror*
CARY HOLLADAY

*How*
GEOFF WYSS

*Little America*
DIANE SIMMONS

*The Book of Right and Wrong*
MATT DEBENHAM

*The Departure Lounge: Stories and a Novella*
PAUL EGGERS

*True Kin*
RIC JAHNA

*Owner's Manual*
MORGAN MCDERMOTT

*Mexico Is Missing: And Other Stories*
J. DAVID STEVENS